MW01611045

RESCUING CARA (SPECIAL FORCES: OPERATION ALPHA)

MORGAN THOMPSON SECURITY, BOOK 3

DANIELLE PAYS

This book is a work of fiction. Names, characters, places, and incidents are products of the author's imagination or used fictitiously. Any resemblance to actual events or locales or persons living or dead is entirely coincidental.

© 2022 ACES PRESS, LLC. ALL RIGHTS RESERVED

No part of this work may be used, stored, reproduced or transmitted without written permission from the publisher except for brief quotations for review purposes as permitted by law.
This book is licensed for your personal enjoyment only. This book may not be re-sold or given away to other people. If you would like to share this book with another person, please purchase an additional copy for each recipient. If you're reading this book and did not purchase it, or it was not purchased for your use only, please purchase your own copy.

* * *

Cover Photography: Furious Fotog/Golden Czermak
Cover Designer: Maria @ Steamy Designs
Editing: Wallflower Edits
Proofreading: ReGina Raham

Dear Readers,

Welcome to the Special Forces: Operation Alpha Fan-Fiction world!

If you are new to this amazing world, in a nutshell the author wrote a story using one or more of my characters in it. Sometimes that character has a major role in the story, and other times they are only mentioned briefly. This is perfectly legal and allowable because they are going through Aces Press to publish the story.

This book is entirely the work of the author who wrote it. While I might have assisted with brainstorming and other ideas about which of my characters to use, I didn't have any part in the process or writing or editing the story.

I'm proud and excited that so many authors loved my characters enough that they wanted to write them into their own story. Thank you for supporting them, and me!

READ ON!
    Xoxo
    Susan Stoker

CAST OF CHARACTERS

Morgan Thompson Security
Owners
Josh "Cowboy" Morgan (Shaw Seymour)
Poseidon "Stormy" Thompson

Employees
Cody "PP" Anthony (Lucy Gardiner)
Donny "Maverick" Reis (Sarina McIntyre)
Dax "Rover" Adams (Connie Stevens)
Grayson "Peaches" Walsh (Cara Harding)
Ford "CT" Mora
Reed "Fox" Davenport
Lance "Trax" McClure
Aaron "Trip" Anderson

Reed Hawthorne Security Employees
Lars "Thunder" Guthrie (Madison Wilkes)
Paxton "Lightning" Beck

CIA
Cara Harding – Special Agent
Canton – Special Agent

Pat Anderson – Cara's boss
Whitlock – Deputy Director

FBI

Carter – Special Agent in Charge of Seattle's Field Office

CHAPTER ONE

Cara Harding

WATCH MAX ACRILE from a distance but don't let him see you. That was my assignment. Well, the assignment I fucked up because Max is now following me through the streets of a mountain town in Chile.

To lose him, I pick up my pace and turn down an alley. The sound of footsteps behind me also picks up. I don't dare look back. Ahead is a field of tall grass. The sound of footsteps grows closer.

I run into the grass and toss my binoculars and phone away from me. Without those, I can claim to be a tourist or a hiker. Hopefully, the photos have already uploaded to the cloud and my boss, Anderson, has them.

"Stop!" a man shouts.

I stop. As a CIA agent, I'm trained in hand-to-hand combat, and I can get out of this if needed. Hopefully, this won't get physical.

"Come here," he demands.

I don't turn around.

"Were you photographing me?" His thick Brazilian accent gives away he's the man I've been watching.

I still don't turn around, hoping to avoid showing my full face. But I do respond. "No. I'm just visiting the city."

"An American?"

"Yes."

"Well, let me buy you a drink to welcome you to our fine town."

Something is wrong. He's being too nice. There's a rustle in the grass. I turn quickly to the sound, but it's too late. Something pricks my neck.

I turn, and Max is right there, smiling.

I'm lightheaded. I sense I'm falling, but I don't feel the ground.

* * *

My eyes flutter open. The room is dark.

"She's awake," a woman says.

I try but can't move my arms.

Max steps to my side. "Your hands are tied down for now."

I stop pulling and try to assess my situation. There are two people in the room—Max and a woman. Based on what I can see, which isn't much due to the dim lighting, it appears to be a hotel room.

"What's your name?" he asks.

"Erica," I say. If he went through my backpack, he found the fake identification.

"Why were you in Chile, Erica?"

"Sightseeing."

He arches a brow. "Odd location for sightseeing. Are you traveling alone?"

"My boyfriend is supposed to meet me tomorrow," I lie.

"Where?"

I swallow. "At the café." I remember the café across the street from the hotel.

"Well, I'm afraid you won't make that date, Erica. You're my girl now."

I frown, acting like I don't understand. Sadly, I do, and I need to find a way to get out of this situation. But then what he said registers. "Wait. You said I *was* in Chile like it was past tense."

He laughs. "Yes, you were. We're in Brazil now. Beautiful country. You'll enjoy it."

Brazil? How the hell did they get me here? I close my eyes. Of course, Max has a private plane and the ability to pay off whoever he wants.

The woman steps into view. "Sir, isn't she too old?"

"Perhaps, but she's American. A lot of my clients request an American."

The woman smiles. "Very well then."

Max steps away. "Get her ready. I want her at the event tomorrow night."

Tomorrow night? I have no knowledge of any event planned. Of course, I wasn't aware he was flying girls to Brazil, either. Damn, how is he communicating with the men? That is one thing we haven't been able to figure out.

"Erica, I'll see you tomorrow night. Do what Trudy asks, and everything will go smoothly."

He leaves, and Trudy stares at me. "We have a lot of work ahead of us. First, you must sleep."

"Wait," I say before the woman can leave. "What's tomorrow night?"

The woman unzips a satchel she's holding and pulls out a hypodermic needle.

"What's that?" I ask.

She sighs. "Tomorrow night is a very important night. We have a large number of clients coming in from all over the world. They will be expecting company. The kind of company you can provide."

How can this woman be so calm about all of this?

"You're going to make me a prostitute?"

The woman frowns. "No! There's no exchange of money

3

for sex. We provide women as a courtesy for all the clients offer to us."

"What do they offer?"

She holds up the needle. "That's none of your business. Now while you're sleeping, I'll prep you."

"Prep?"

The woman stares at me. "Yes, *prep*. You'll thank me tomorrow that you were able to sleep through it."

Before I can ask what she means, the needle pricks my arm. I attempt to fight the sleep trying to take over. Tomorrow night. I have twenty-four hours to get out of this mess. I blink, but my lids are heavy. I must stay awake. But despite my effort, the room goes black.

* * *

I STARE at the dress hanging over the back of the chair. The other girls in the room have already changed.

Harper leans over. "Hurry. If they see you aren't dressed, they'll punish you," she whispers.

She never makes eye contact. None of them ever do.

Punish. This mansion is huge, and I don't doubt there are rooms here used for that purpose. My eyes move to the clock. We were told to be ready for the party by seven. I don't have much time.

The last thing I want is to draw attention to myself, so I put on the dress. I stare at my full cup of tea. They gave us all tea to relax for the night. Based on how fast some of the girls gulped it down, it wasn't just tea. Now those girls appear to have zoned out. But not Harper.

"Did you drink yours?" I nod to my cup.

She glances around, wide eyes before she gives me a quick shake of the head. "I poured it under the bed."

We are all waiting in a bedroom. Under the bed, that's brilliant. No one would think to check there. I hold my cup, and I pretend to bend down and scratch my ankle. When no one is watching, I dump it out under the bed as well.

"Where are they taking us?" I ask Harper.

I only met her an hour ago when I was thrown into this room with the other girls. She was the only one willing to talk.

She closes her eyes. "To the men."

Shit. I wish I had my gun, but when I woke up yesterday, it was gone. So was the knife I keep strapped to my ankle.

I wasn't surprised Max confronted me when he discovered me watching him. What I hadn't expected was being poked with a needle while standing in an open field. Nor did I expect to wake up to find a woman named Trudy explaining she had to prep me for this party.

That was before they drugged me again. I shiver, realizing what Trudy had done to me while I was asleep. From the neck down, there is no hair anywhere on my body. Unfortunately, there is some skin that is red and inflamed, but I can't think about that now. I must stay focused.

When I get the chance, I'll make sure Max suffers for that and for everything he's done to these girls.

I take in the room as we wait. The furniture is old but appears expensive. The room is rather large for a bedroom, but from what I saw of the house when we walked in, I'm not surprised.

The door opens. "It's showtime!" Max directs us out of the room and down a set of stairs.

Including myself, there are eight girls. And I do mean *girls*. I'm clearly the oldest here at the ripe old age of thirty-one. I try not to glance around too much because if I appear too aware, he'll know I didn't drink the tea.

Max gathers us at the bottom of the stairs. "Girls, tonight there will be a very important man at this party. It is imperative that you all do your best."

He turns back around. Like anyone in here has a choice.

Before bringing me to the bedroom to change, Max made sure to fill me in on what happened to the last girl who tried to ask for help during one of these outings. He showed me a photo of a girl, beaten and lying in a shallow grave.

Let's just say if that is what he's showing the others, I get why they don't try to escape.

He leads us through several rooms into a very large sitting room. The walls are decorated with art that, based on my limited knowledge, is worth millions. The opulence of the décor is a bit over the top. Whoever owns this place likes to show off his wealth.

Without looking up, I memorize the layout as best I can. If I can escape, I can make my way toward the US Embassy. Last night, Max mentioned we were now in Brazil. On the drive over, I recognized a town we drove through. I worked on a past assignment nearby and, fortunately, am familiar with the area.

A helicopter flying over causes a few of the girls to glance up. Maybe they aren't as drugged as I first suspected.

"I notice you, girls, looking up. This very important man has constant security, including from the sky."

Well shit. That would make running through the countryside a lot harder to pull off.

"Now, all of you, form a line," Max instructs.

He walks slowly to the head of the line inspecting us. When he reaches me, he smiles.

"Erica, I'm glad to see you falling in line. You're my girl now, and I want you to remember what I told you last night. All right?"

I don't make eye contact but simply nod.

"Good. Now follow me." He goes to the front of the line, and we follow him into yet another room. This one is darker, with lights down the center of the room as if a dining table were once there.

"Stop here," Max instructs.

Men are standing several feet from us on either side of the room.

"Now, girls, please do a quarter turn to your right."

We all turn. I glance up and see the men all wearing suits. Most have graying hair.

"Another quarter turn to your right."

We all turn.

"One more quarter turn to your right."

We all turn again.

"Men, make your selection."

The men walk up to our group, and several are standing next to the blonde beside me. She can't be more than fifteen.

No man has walked up to me. Maybe I won't have to fight off anyone.

The three men next to me can't seem to come to an agreement on who should win the blonde. Poor girl. I really hope I can save them all soon.

"Gentlemen, why don't one of you take Sasha?" Max says as he puts his arms around my shoulders—I guess that's my name tonight. "She's new."

The men's eyes roamed over my body.

"She's a little old for my taste," an older, very overweight man says.

Thank God, but damn, now I really feel bad for this girl.

"I'll take Sasha," a man with a Russian accent says from behind me.

Shit. Guess I get to make a scene after all. When I turn my eyes up to the man walking toward me, I blink several times. He looks just like Peaches from Morgan Thompson Security, except he's clean-shaven and apparently Russian. I must be hallucinating from the drugs they gave me yesterday because there's no way he could know where I am. While I did miss my check-in with the agency this morning, there couldn't have been time to figure out where I was, fly in Peaches from Seattle, and plan this mission.

"And who are you?" Max asks. "I don't recognize you. How did you get in here?"

The Peaches lookalike says something in Russian. It can't be him. I would know if he spoke Russian. Or would I? Before I can mull it over too deeply, he speaks in English again.

"I'm sorry. My English isn't very good. I received an invitation."

Max narrows his eyes. "You did?"

The man nods. "Yes, by that man over there." He points toward the corner of the room.

Max and the other men turn to see what he's pointing at. He winks at me, and I realize it is Peaches.

"Who?" Max asks.

Peaches grabs my hand. "Let's go," he says as he pulls me with him toward the door. It really is him. I'm not dreaming.

"What about the other girls?" I ask as we are running as fast as we can.

"Later," he says.

We manage to get out the front door before anyone catches up to us. There's a Porsche parked at the bottom of the stairs.

"Get in the car!"

I jump into the passenger seat, and he's tearing out of there before I get the door closed.

"This was your plan?" I ask.

He turns around a corner fast, squealing the wheels. "I landed twenty minutes ago. I wasn't given much information and didn't have time to make a plan."

"How could you get here so fast?"

He frowns. "What do you mean?"

"I only missed one check-in this morning."

He glances at me, then back to the road. "You missed your check-in yesterday."

Yesterday? I lost a day?

Peaches rounds the last corner of the driveway, and the gate ahead closes. Armed guards stand in front of it and aim their guns at us. Peaches lays on the brakes and cranks the wheel until we are facing the opposite way. Then he slams on the gas.

"I don't suppose you know another way out of here?" he asks.

"No, that's the way we came in."

The driveway is taking us deeper into the property. Suddenly, the road ends, and we are in a grassy field. The car slows and finally stops.

"Fuck!" he yells. "We're stuck in the mud. Let's go."

We both get out of the car, and my heels sink into the

mud, so I run on my toes, but there is nowhere to go. Several flood lights come on.

"Stop!" a man shouts.

We turn to find a group of guys with guns swarming us.

"Okay, get ready for plan B," Peaches says.

I stare at him. "What the hell is plan B?"

He grins. "I'll tell you once I figure it out. For now, we better do as they say."

Shit. These men won't hesitate to shoot Peaches. I count the men around us. Five. We need a distraction. Between the two of us, we should be able to take them down.

Max walks up. "Who the hell are you?"

Peaches smiles and turns on his Russian accent again. "A business associate of the count's. You said select a girl. Why are men pointing guns at us now?"

Max crosses his arms. "It appears the count forgot to fill you in on the rules. You cannot leave the premises."

Peaches tilts his head. "No? What about privacy?"

Max blows out a breath. "Follow me."

Peaches doesn't move. "Where are we going?"

Max turns back to him. "To verify the count knows you."

I hope he comes up with a plan B really soon because once the count confirms he has no idea who Peaches is, I don't think they'll hesitate to kill him.

CHAPTER TWO

Grayson "Peaches" Walsh

WELL FUCK. I hadn't intended to get captured, but then, I wasn't lying when I said I hadn't had time to form a real plan.

As soon as I overheard Cara's boss on the speakerphone with Stormy stating she missed her check-in and was missing, I knew I had to go wherever she was. I volunteered. Somehow, she went missing in Chile, but en route, the pilot was informed to change course and land in Brazil. It turns out another agent had been watching a target's place in Brazil and called in that Cara was there and not of her own free will. Anderson explained she'd been watching Max Acrile and what exactly he does.

By the time I got off the plane, a car was waiting to bring me here. Unfortunately, I had no information before arriving other than it appeared there was a party of some sort in progress.

I was able to get past the guards and their easy questions. But when I walked in, I watched as Max had the girls move into the large room in a line.

Then I saw Cara standing there with all those girls and the men leering at them. It was all I could do not to get sick. I know exactly what is going on here, and I had to get Cara out. And she's right; we need to save the other girls. One step at a time. Right now, I need to focus on the two of us.

We are led back into the house, but instead of going back to the dark room, we walk a straight path to the back.

"Wait here," Max says.

The room is dark except for several candles lit on many tables. As I take in the space with its large couches and pillows everywhere, I realize what this room is intended for, and I'm nauseated.

Cara and I stand there while Max walks out the back door toward a helipad. A helicopter lands, and a man, I can only presume by his outfit, is the count, steps out. Apparently, he wants to make it clear who's in charge here.

The count frowns as Max points toward us. He shakes his head and walks away from Max toward another entrance to the house.

I think my cover is blown. Max walks toward the house and yells, "Bring them out."

My hand goes toward the side of my pants, where I have a knife hidden. If they think they are going to kill us on the patio, they have another thing coming. On our way out, I pretend to trip so I can grab my knife and move it up into my shirt sleeve. While I'm at it, I accidentally knock over a table of candles which immediately causes one of the couches to catch ablaze.

"Dammit! I'll take care of this," one of the men says.

The rest of us continue out onto the patio. We stop as we reach Max.

"You have one last chance. Who the fuck are you?" he asks me.

Now, I could go a couple of ways here. I suspect playing the jealous boyfriend will get me killed, so I go the other way.

With my accent still intact, I answer. "Russ Kralik. I believe you know my cousin. I'm sorry for running out of here and lying about the count, but the man in the navy pinstripe suit was taking photographs. And I can't be seen here."

My accent is near perfect despite not using it for some time.

"No one takes photos," Max says.

I stand taller. "I saw him taking photos with his phone up some of the girls' skirts. I cannot risk being seen, especially here. I'm sorry if I caused you any alarm."

Max squints as he stares at me. Something tells me he isn't buying this. And why would he? I've dealt him one bullshit story after the next.

"And why her? Why not someone younger?"

I laugh. "I like my women older."

I glance at Cara, who is glaring at me now.

Max nods. "I don't buy your bullshit for a minute." He turns to one of the men. "Take these two to the chopper."

Two men come up and roughly grab me.

"What are you doing? Do you have any idea who I am?" I yell.

The men are undeterred.

Another man grabs Cara. I notice she's not trying to fight back, so I don't, either. She's had time to assess the situation better than I have.

The men shove us inside the helicopter. The pilot doesn't turn around.

"Wait here," one man tells the other.

The other man stands, aiming a gun at us.

"What the hell is your plan now?" Cara hisses. "And for the record, I'm not that much older."

I grin. No, she isn't. How do I know this? Because I've had a crush on this woman for the last year. I've taken a lot of teasing from the guys at Morgan Thompson Security on the matter, too. They're all waiting for me to ask her out.

Well, I already did. Sort of. I asked her to stop and see my band play. She hasn't taken me up on it yet. Yeah, that isn't exactly a date. But I have no idea what this woman thinks of me, and I need to tread carefully since we often work together.

I keep my eyes trained on Max. Then I lean toward Cara. "Max is telling them to fly us to a canyon and kill us."

"How the hell do you know that?"

I turn to her and grin. "I read lips."

She stares at me for a beat, trying to decide if I'm bullshitting her or not.

"You ever jump out of a helicopter?" I ask.

Her eyes widen. "No. I've jumped out of a plane, though."

"I see one parachute behind us. We might need to make a fast exit."

She turns in her seat and spots it before glancing back at me. "With one parachute?"

I grin. "You'll have to hold on tight."

Her eyes narrow. "No, you'll have to hold on tight."

Before we can argue further, the man who had spoken with Max gets into the front seat and doesn't even acknowledge us. The other man holding the gun backs away while keeping the gun trained on me.

They don't give us protective ear coverings. It's fucking loud. We both buckle in as the chopper starts to lift off. Slowly, I lean a little and replace my knife into my leg pocket. The fact I wasn't patted down has me curious.

Below us is mostly dark, which is good. If we jump over a city, we could be found easier.

The two men up front are carrying on an animated conversation. I can't hear what they are saying, but they look over at each other often and laugh. While they are distracted, I reach back, grab the parachute, and slowly pull it to me. I lean forward and place it on my back. Despite all my movement, neither man upfront has noticed.

Cara pinches my side. I turn to her, and she points to the parachute and then to herself.

"Sorry," I mouth to her.

Once the pack is securely on, I unbuckle my seat belt. Fortunately, the sides of the chopper are open. Cara unbuckles her seat belt, too. I take her hand, and before she can object, I stand the best I can in the small space. I've got her facing me in a bear hug. She wraps her legs around my hips.

"What the hell?" the man up front yells.

I jump.

I ignore the yells from the men and focus on where we are going.

Once we clear the chopper, I pull the rip cord. We're over pastureland, but there is what appears to be a forest to my right. I aim the best I can, and we come down near the edge of the trees. My feet hit the ground first, but I'm still going too fast. I roll onto my side and back, making sure not to hurt Cara. When we finally come to a stop, she's on the ground next to me.

"You all right?"

She nods.

"We need to collect this parachute fast. They might be able to see it from above." The white fabric against the dark grass definitely stands out.

We ball it up, and I carry it as we dive into the woods as the chopper flies lower. The moon is nearly full, and enough light falls between the trees that we can sort of see where we're going. Unfortunately, if they choose to land and chase us, they'll be able to see well, too.

"Why are you carrying that?" she asks.

"Because I'm not sure how long we'll be out here, and we might need protection from the insects if we try to sleep."

She points straight ahead. "If we walk this way, we'll hit the edge of a town by morning."

"You sure about that?"

She turns and gives me a smile. "Pretty sure. I had an assignment in this area once before. But don't you have a compass on you?"

I sigh. "Normally, I would, but I thought for sure I'd get patted down before I got inside."

She fights a grin. "And you think a compass would have blown your cover?" Her voice trembles.

"You're cold." Of course, she's cold. All she has on is a thin dress that barely covers anything. "Here." I stop and drop the parachute and remove my jacket. "Wear this."

"But you'll get cold."

"I'll be fine. I'm not wearing a thin dress."

"Thank you," she says as she puts it on. "You shaved your beard. I didn't think it was really you at first."

I reach up and run my hand over my chin. "I shaved on the plane. Thought it might help me blend in better. Now I can't wait for it to grow back."

She tilts her head. "Why's that? It's nice seeing your strong jawline and full lips."

Wow. I blink a few times. Did Cara just compliment me?

Her eyes widen. "I'm sorry. I shouldn't have said that."

I grin. "I'm glad you did. Feel free to compliment me anytime." I wink.

We walk for several hours. I don't know how she's managing in those shoes. They must be uncomfortable as fuck.

"Are your feet okay?" I ask.

"Yeah, thankfully, they gave me wedges to wear. If these had been stilettos, I wouldn't be doing so well."

I don't know the different names for the heels, but as long as she says she's good, we'll keep going.

The moonlight reflects off the water as we approach a bog. The trees to our left and right are thickening up, but from what I can see, this bog extends quite a distance in both directions.

"We're going to have to go through it."

She nods.

I step in, hoping this is only knee-deep. When I hit the middle, I sink to my waist and hope like hell there are no critters floating in here that see us as a meal.

"The water is cold," she says.

"Yeah, and the temperature is still dropping. We might have to warm up with this parachute," I say as I hold it above my head to keep it dry.

As we step out of the water, I feel something on my calf. "Fuck, something is inside my pants."

I drop the parachute on dry land and yank my pant leg up. I can't really bend to see.

"Can you check it out?"

She bends down and pulls something off my leg.

"That better not have been a fucking leech." I can't stand the damn things.

"Don't worry, it wasn't."

She pulls my pants back down my leg before wiping her hands on her dress.

"Well, what was it?"

She shrugs. "Just a spider."

Motherfucker. I hate those, too.

"Come on, we need to keep moving," she says.

Fortunately, we warm up as we walk fast through the woods. We continue until daybreak. As the sun comes up, we get a better idea of our surroundings.

"Let's take five." Cara drops to the ground.

"I'll be right back."

I climb up a tree as far as I can and look around. All I see are more trees. I climb higher. In every direction, trees.

"Uh, Cara."

"Do you see the town?"

"No." I climb back down the tree and sit down on the ground next to her. "All I can see in all directions is forest."

She frowns. "No, that's not right. We should be able to see the coast by now. There are a number of towns along there." She glances up toward the sun and stares a moment. "Oh, no."

I don't like the sound of this "oh no."

"Peaches, we had to have walked north. In any other direction, we should have crossed a road by now." She drops her head to her knees.

"If we keep going this way, where will we end up?"

She lifts her head. "Wait, this means we're probably close to Sao Paulo. There's a US Consulate there, and I have a friend we can trust."

"Why weren't we headed there to start with?"

She points at her feet. "I wasn't sure I could walk that far.

17

I figured if we hit a coastal town, we could find a way to make a call."

"But if I were Max, I'd be all over those towns, waiting for us to show up."

"You know who Max is?"

I nod. "I was briefed. Very quickly, so I didn't get a lot of details."

She glances away. "If I'm right, we have a day or more of walking ahead of us. We should get as close as we can until it gets dark. Then get some sleep while we're still deep in the forest."

Her lack of eye contact concerns me. Maybe I didn't get to her in time.

"Hey."

She turns to me.

"Did Max hurt you? I mean, did he…" Shit, I have no idea how to ask this.

Her eyes meet mine. "No."

I nod and stand up. "I agree with your plan. Hopefully, we can get some sleep tonight and come out of the woods at daybreak tomorrow."

She stands and wipes off her dress. "I don't suppose you have a granola bar or something on you."

I laugh. "I'll be honest, food wasn't my first thought when preparing last night."

"What was?"

I turn to her. "You. Getting you out safely."

She holds my stare for a beat. "Thank you. If it weren't for you…"

"You would have had to beat a few asses." I pull her in for a hug. I've never hugged this woman outside of the parachute situation, but I have a strong need to now. I breathe a sigh of relief when she squeezes me back. Holding her, I realize she fits perfectly in my arms, and I don't want to let her go. But as her grip loosens, I do the same.

We walk another couple hours before I spot what I was hoping to find.

"Ah ha!" I say.

"What?"

I point up. "Bananas." I climb the tree and use my knife to cut a bunch down. They're a bit green, but a couple of them are ripe enough to eat.

"Thank you," Cara says after we've eaten. "I was getting a bit lightheaded."

I watch her. "You're dehydrated. We need to find a source of water."

She smiles. "We might be in luck. Unless the forecast changed, it might rain this afternoon."

"You know the forecast?"

She sighs. "Well, I did for Chile, where I was watching Max before he found me. It was supposed to rain there last night. I'm not sure how well the forecast translates to Brazil."

"I'm afraid to be the bearer of bad news, but August is the dry month here. I wouldn't count on rain."

She stares at me. "It will rain. Think positive thoughts. Now come on, we need to get going."

I chuckle as we each grab a couple of bananas for the road, and I toss the rest of the bunch into the bushes. I doubt Max and his men are trekking through the forest, but no point in leaving a trail if they are.

"Can I ask you a personal question?" I ask as we walk.

"Sure. No guarantee I'll answer it." She turns back to grin at me.

I've never heard her talk about anything personal so that doesn't surprise me. She's always very professional when we all work together.

"Why the CIA?"

She doesn't answer at first, and I think she won't. "My dad. He was an agent. After I graduated college, I was recruited. Now my turn. I have a question for you."

I smile. "Shoot."

"What's your real name? Don't get me wrong, I like the name Peaches and the reason you got the name."

I can feel my cheeks heating at that comment. My damn teammate, Rover, told Cara I got my call sign because of my butt. It's true, but damn, he said it right in front of me, then

19

spun me around to show her the evidence. It wouldn't have been so bad, except I wasn't wearing good jeans that day.

I clear my throat. "It's Grayson."

She turns and takes a few steps backward. "Gray. I like that."

I stop close to her. I like the way my name sounds on her lips. "No one has called me that in years."

She cocks her head. "What about your family?"

I stare out through the forest. "That's a topic for another day." If ever. I've had a lot of ups and downs with my brother. Most of which I don't want to think about. Not now. We need to stay focused.

"Okay." She turns and continues walking.

"What do you do for fun?" I ask, hoping to get our conversation back.

She shrugs. "I don't really have much spare time. I guess when I can, I enjoy a crossword or two."

I can't help it, but I laugh.

She turns, and her hands go to her hips. "What?" The pointed look she's giving me makes me laugh harder. "Gray, you better tell me right now why you're laughing at me."

Her use of my name wipes away the laugh. "I expected you to say some sport or hobby. You do crosswords for fun? Really?"

She crosses her arms. "Really. What do you do?"

"I play guitar, have a vegetable garden, and enjoy going to comedy clubs."

Her lip curls up, and she laughs. "That sounds more like a dating profile."

I shrug. "Did it impress you?"

A twig breaks behind us. I hold my finger to my mouth. We both squat and assess our surroundings. Leaves rustle closer. A squirrel runs across the path.

She sighs. "Sounded bigger than a squirrel."

"I agree."

We continue walking for another hour in silence. A raindrop hits me. Then another. Cara turns and smiles at me. The rain quickly picks up, and we each snag a large leaf from a tree and make our way to a small clearing. Holding up the leaf, we collect the rainwater and let it run down the leaf and into our mouths.

The storm passes before I get my fill.

"Well, back to walking. Hopefully, we'll dry off before the sun sets," she says.

Unfortunately, with this humidity, we won't. Maybe the parachute can keep us warm.

CHAPTER THREE

Cara

As the sun begins to set, Gray finds a spot between two trees for us to sleep. After setting up the parachute, which he somehow managed to keep mostly dry during the rainstorm, he calls for me.

"Ready?"

I step closer and stare at this man. I can't say I've ever seen him without a beard. It's a shame he wears one because he has a strong jaw that I could imagine kissing my way down. I swallow and glance at what he has set up, hoping he can't read my thoughts. I've been fantasizing about this guy for longer than I care to admit.

"You want to lie down first?" he asks.

"Is that all it usually takes to get a woman in bed?" I slap my hand to my mouth.

His expression grows serious. "Uh. Um."

Why did I say that? I never cross the line of unprofessionalism. "I'm sorry. That was very inappropriate." I sit on the parachute.

He sits next to me. "No, it's fine. I just wasn't expecting it. We should get to know each other better."

I take a moment, staring into his deep-blue eyes because what I want him to mean and what he really means aren't the same thing. Sleeping this close to him isn't going to be easy.

"Is that all right?"

I smile. "Yes." My heart is pounding hard. I've been on dangerous missions, jumped out of planes—and now helicopters—and had all sorts of people trying to kill me, but this man makes me more nervous than any of that.

"Good. As for your question, no. I mean, not that I have tried recently."

Well, that's interesting. "Why not?"

He meets my gaze. "Getting someone into bed isn't what I want."

"Oh." His answer surprises me.

"Shit, no. I mean, I love sex. I don't want you to think I don't. Not that you should think about that. Or maybe you should." He lies on his back and covers his face with his hands. "Fuck."

I laugh. "You okay?"

He laughs, too. "Yeah. All I'm trying to say is I want more than just sex. Does that make sense?"

"It does."

"Here, let's cover ourselves, too."

I lie down next to him, and he pulls the rest of the parachute over us.

The sun has set, and it's growing dark quickly. The temperature is dropping as well. Normally it wouldn't be too cold to sleep, but I'm still damp from the rainstorm. I shiver, then try to wrap the parachute tighter around me.

"What's wrong?"

"I'm too cold to sleep."

"Come here," he says.

"Why?"

He laughs. "I'm cold, too. I haven't been able to dry out. If we share body heat, we might get warm enough to fall asleep."

I chuckle. "Why is everything you're saying sound like a line?"

He blows out a breath. "It's not a line. We really do need to get some sleep."

He's right, and I've slept in crazier circumstances, so getting close to him really shouldn't be an issue. Yet, I'm not moving closer. When he senses my hesitation, he puts his hand on my hip. I'm more turned on by that simple touch than I care to admit. But it also justifies my hesitation. As much as I enjoy his touch, I can't let myself get distracted. One wrong move and we could be killed.

"Cara, I promise I won't bite."

Finally, I scoot over and snuggle up to him. I'm immediately rewarded with his warmth. He holds me tight until I stop shivering.

"I'm older and all, but unfortunately, I'm not having any hot flashes yet, so I appreciate the warmth."

He laughs. "Oh shit. I forgot I said that. You know I was kidding, right?"

I don't respond. What can I say? He just admitted he was kidding about liking older women. I have no idea how many years I have on him. It shouldn't matter, but the last thing some guys want is a woman in her thirties. They assume we all are rushing to have children. News flash, we're not.

"Cara?"

"Hmm."

He pulls me tighter against him but doesn't say anymore. Sleep soon pulls me under.

The sound of birds chirping wake me. When I open my eyes, I'm surprised it's daylight.

I sit up. Gray rubs his eyes.

I stretch my arms over my head. "How did we sleep this long?"

He stands up. "We were exhausted. Plus, sharing body heat really helped."

I stand up and help him fold the parachute.

"I can't remember the last time I slept that soundly," I say.

He grins. "Good to know. I'll have to arrange to jump out of the sky and run through a forest with you again then."

I chuckle. "We better get moving in case they're tracking us."

As we walk, I steal glances at him.

"What?" he asks.

"Why the military? You were in the Navy. A SEAL, right?"

"Yes, ma'am."

I groan. "I'm not a ma'am."

He puts an arm over my shoulders. "You need to stop focusing on thinking you're older. I don't see you that way. Besides, I'm only two years younger than you."

I stop walking. "No."

He turns to me with a grin. "It's true."

Then he takes the lead.

"How do you know how old I am?"

He glances back at me. "Cara, I know a lot of things about you. You fascinate me."

His words cause my stomach to flutter. It isn't every day I have a hot, sexy man telling me I fascinate him.

"How?"

He continues walking as he speaks. "How could you not? You're a badass, Cara. You're smart, beautiful, and different from any other woman I've known."

I'm walking behind him, grinning like a fool. Despite all my training, I just can't wipe the smile off my face.

He stops. "You hear that?"

I listen. "A car?"

"I think so."

We pick up our pace, and soon, we spot a road in the distance. And several buildings just beyond that.

"We're almost there," I say.

We manage to make our way into the city undetected. Most businesses won't open for another half hour or so, including the embassy. About a block north is a park I lead us to.

"We can wait here," I say.

He smiles. "You knew this park was here."

I cock my head. "I told you. I had an assignment in this area before."

He nods. "You mentioned you have a contact at the US Consulate Office."

"Robert Benson. At least he was in charge when I was here last year. I haven't heard about any changes."

Gray walks the perimeter of the park, then returns to join me under the shade of a tree. "There are two men in a car parked across the street from the embassy. I couldn't get a good look without them seeing me, but I think one of the men is Max."

"Shit. He's supposed to be searching the beach towns for us."

If we can't go to the embassy, that leaves one option I'd rather not use, but I don't think we have any choice.

"Then it's time for plan B. But first, I need to know who is with Max. Any chance it's a woman?" I stand up, and he does, too.

"I'm pretty sure it was a man."

More people are out on the street now as the town is close to opening. I step away from the direction Max is parked and around a large building until I am behind the embassy. We walk up the side of it.

"At the corner of the building, if you look across the street and a little to your left, you'll see him," he says.

Once I'm at the corner, I slowly peer around. There is a car parked across the way, but it's empty. I turn a little more and spot Max walking to the embassy. Then I spot the other man. I turn back, grab Gray's arm, and yank us back behind the building.

"What?" he asks. "You look like you've seen a ghost."

"I have."

He frowns.

"The man with him is Ivan Kralik." I rub the back of my neck. "It can't be. He's dead. His brother-in-law killed him right after I was in Spain." I lean against the building.

If that video the agency obtained wasn't of Ivan being killed, then who was it? We never found Doug, the man I hunted for earlier this year, only to discover he was also a

CIA agent working deep undercover. So deep only the top levels were aware of who he was.

The video showed a burning car. A team analyzed the video and confirmed there was a body in the car. I need to get this information to Anderson.

"Huh. Why would Max bring a dead guy with him here?" Gray asks.

"That's a good question. But for now, we need to get out of here and ask questions later. This way."

We make our way through the city, and I try to stay off the main roads as much as possible. My mind is whirling, trying to piece together how Ivan can be alive and why he would be here.

After about an hour, Gray stops. "Where are we going?"

I turn around to face him. "A friend's place. He can help us."

He stares at me. "You trust him?"

"I do. It's not much farther."

He nods. "Okay."

We continue walking until we reach the edge of the familiar house. A house I didn't think I'd ever return to. As we enter the yard, I spot Hannah.

"Miss Cara! You're back!" She runs up and hugs me.

"Just for a little bit. Where's your daddy?"

"He's in his shop." Hannah takes my hand and leads us there.

When we step in, my memories of the last time I was here come back to me. Hannah and her dad, Sven, were rescued and brought here.

"Cara?" Sven smiles as he sees me. "It's been too long." He gives me a hug then his eyes move to Gray.

"This is my friend—"

"Peaches." He holds out his hand.

Sven shakes his hand. "Nice to meet you."

"Sven, I really hate to ask, but can we stay here until nightfall?"

Sven frowns. "Are you okay?"

"We will be," I say.

He nods. "Yes, of course, you can stay here as long as you need."

I turn to Hannah. "Hannah, you cannot tell anyone we're here. Understand?"

She nods. Despite only being eight, she's wiser than most kids.

"Do you, by chance, have a phone I could use?" Gray asks.

"Oh, yes." Sven pulls his cell phone from his pocket and hands it to him.

"Thank you. I'll just be a moment."

He moves to the other end of the shop to make his call, leaving Sven and me alone.

"Cara, what's going on?"

Sven motions for me to sit on a bench. I do, and he sits next to me.

"I was working undercover, and something went wrong. Peaches tried to save me. I was headed to the embassy but saw the man after us entering. We're not safe here."

Sven nods. "I'll drive you to the border tonight."

"Actually, if you can drive us to an airfield, we can get a flight tonight," Gray says as he steps up to us.

"I can do that. There's an airport nearby."

I walk to the window. "No, they'll expect us to go to the airport."

"Is there a large field we could use?" Gray asks.

I turn to him and smile. "Can they send a chopper? There's a hospital with a helipad outside the main city they would never expect us to use."

He nods. "I can make that happen."

I give him the name of the hospital, and he arranges for the flight. Sven agrees to drive us there at nightfall. Gray steps outside for air, he claims. But he's likely checking the perimeter and taking in all our exit options.

"Thank you, Sven. I really appreciate this."

Sven touches my cheek. "Anything for you."

Gray coughs from the door. "Sorry, didn't mean to interrupt."

Sven smiles. "No interruption. If you two would like to

rest, you can use the main house. There is a bedroom, first door on the left." He points to the door separating the shop area from the house.

"Thank you," Gray says as he walks past us into the house.

I follow him. The guest room has a double bed and not much else.

"I'm going to rest for now if you'd like some time with Sven," he says as he lies on the mattress. There's something in his tone.

"No, I don't need time. I'm good."

He avoids my eyes and stares at the ceiling.

"Sven was someone I was assigned to protect, not a boyfriend." I don't know why I felt the need to tell him that, but I did.

He rolls onto his side and stares at me. "Why don't you get some rest, too? We'll hear anyone coming. The walkway is covered in gravel."

"Okay." I still feel uneasy after what I blurted out. I'm always professional at my job. Even when I work with my good friend, Thunder, I don't blur the lines. But being around Gray, I'm struggling. I've worked with him before, but now, it's different.

I lie next to him and close my eyes. Our arms are touching, and part of me wishes I could get closer to him. It's totally inappropriate since we are in danger, and I shouldn't be thinking like that. No, I need to keep those thoughts to myself. Once we are back in the States, I can...

What can I do? I'm out of the country more than in it for work. There's a reason why I don't date. It isn't realistic. Of course, one of the main reasons is that I can't tell anyone what I do. But Gray knows. Dammit. I need to get out of my head.

"You'll never relax if you're thinking that much," he says.

"How do you do that?" I open my eyes and turn to him.

He's still on his side and close. So close. His blue eyes seem darker than before. He smiles, and I'd give anything for him to gaze into my eyes like that always.

"Your hands."

I frown. "What?"

"When you're thinking too hard, you clasp your thumbs."

I hold up my hands, and sure enough, my fists are wrapped around my thumbs. "I never have a tell."

He grabs my hand and gives it a squeeze. "You're comfortable with me. I like that."

I turn my gaze back to his. His eyes move to my lips. My heart rate picks up. I feel like I'm back in high school and about to be kissed. He moves closer, and I lick my lips.

"We should get some rest. It could be a long night," he says as he gives my hand one last squeeze before letting go. Then he turns around so his back is to me, leaving me wondering if I misread the entire situation.

CHAPTER FOUR

Grayson

SVEN DROVE us to the hospital. We weren't followed, which is good. Cara and I walk to the front door, only to find it is locked. I turn around and stare out. The lot is empty.

"We should find the emergency entrance. Maybe we can get in there," I say.

"It won't be open. This hospital shut down a few years ago. Can I have your knife?"

I hand it to her, and she slides it between the doors. I'm unclear what she does next, but the door opens. She hands back the knife and walks inside. I follow. "And how did you know it was still closed?"

She glances back over her shoulder with a grin. "It's one of our escape routes. Just in case."

"Our?"

"The agency. We'll have to take the stairs."

Just inside the stairwell, she bends down and turns on a flashlight. That's when I notice a box with several more in it.

"Always have to be prepared," she says.

We climb up the stairs until we hit the last door to the roof. Before she can burst through the door, I grab her arm.

"Does anyone at the US Embassy know about this place?" I ask.

She cocks her head. "Do you think someone there would sell us out?"

I shrug. "Wouldn't be the first time I've seen something like that."

Stepping back from the door, she stares at me. "It was Robert Benson who originally told Sven and me about this place. I can't believe he would betray us, though."

Yeah, just what I thought. If the head of the embassy here knows about it, odds are Max knows about it, too. I didn't have much time to do research before coming here, but I did read what was given to me about that man. And there was nothing in his profile that would give him a need or reason to deal with anyone at the embassy.

"Then tell me why Max felt comfortable walking into the embassy when it opened this morning."

"I don't know."

The sound of a chopper nears. I check the time. "It's them," I say.

I step in front of Cara and open the door. Unfortunately, neither of us has a gun if we are ambushed on the roof.

As we step out, my eyes are everywhere. There is a large, white-painted area for the helipad. Behind the building is a road with a full view of the rooftop. It's where a sniper would likely hide. I squat down, pulling her with me to keep us out of sight of the roadway.

The helicopter comes into view, and I hold Cara's arm. We will run for it. But then I spot headlights heading directly toward the hospital from the roadway. Maybe there's no sniper, after all.

Instead of landing, a ladder is thrown down from the chopper's open door. A man waves us to run to it.

"We need to go now!" Cara yells and pulls away from my grasp.

She glances back at me, and I follow. We both run as fast as we can. Cara jumps on the ladder first and climbs up several rungs. The moment I jump on, the helicopter begins to ascend and turns toward the road.

"Fuck, no!" I shout, but it's useless; the pilot can't hear me.

Flashes of light come from a car.

"They're shooting at us," Cara yells.

Yes, and we're sitting ducks on this ladder. She picks up speed, climbing into the chopper. I follow.

I glance back one last time before I'm inside, and two men are aiming their guns at us. The chopper continues to ascend and finally turns again and flies out of range of the bullets.

"Holy shit, that was too close," I say, leaning back in the open seat. I turn to Cara, and she isn't saying anything, just staring at me with wide eyes.

"What's wrong? Are you hit?" I ask.

I glance down, and her hand is on her leg. She pulls it back, and there's a lot of blood.

"I got shot."

Shit.

The man who waved us on says something into his headset, nods, then turns to me. "We're fifteen minutes from medical."

I press down on her leg, adding pressure.

"Is it the artery?" she asks.

I glance at where we are holding her leg. "No, it's lower."

She nods. "I'm lightheaded."

"You're in shock," I say. "Just rest. We'll have you healed up in no time."

Those fifteen minutes were the longest of my life. Cara closed her eyes and passed out. I kept my hand on her leg and hoped like hell she wasn't going to bleed out.

* * *

Now I'm stuck in the waiting room of a hospital. I can't even tell you what country or city I'm in. Fortunately, the nurses speak English, although all they tell me is to sit and wait for a doctor.

I shouldn't complain because the place is nice. I contacted Thunder, who alerted Cara's boss to the fact she'd been shot.

I keep pacing around the empty waiting room. I need to call Stormy and find out more about Max and this Ivan Kralik that Cara mentioned.

"Peaches?"

I stop.

An unfamiliar voice comes from behind me. "I'm agent Canton. I work with Anderson. He told me what happened and asked that I check on Harding and make sure she gets home."

Home. I want that, too. She needs to be all right.

"I want to thank you for saving her."

"Well, don't thank me yet. I have no idea how she's doing?"

Canton smiles. "She's doing well. That's one of the things I wanted to talk to you about. The doctor said he got the bullet out, and she will be all right. After some rest and healing, of course, which will likely be impossible for Cara."

How the hell did he get all that information? I'll have to ask Cara about that later.

"Now that she's in the clear, I've arranged a plane to fly her out tonight. We'll fly you back to Seattle as well."

I'm surprised since Cara just got out of surgery. "Tonight? Can't it wait until the morning, at least?"

"No. We recently discovered that our contact here has likely been paid off by Max. I'm certain others have as well, and it won't take long for word to get back to Max where Cara is located."

"Is this contact Robert Benson?"

"It is."

I sigh. "I don't know all about this Max guy, but whoever he's working for or helping, there's a lot of money there." I think back to all the armed guards outside the mansion. Although their security wasn't that great since I managed to walk in with a group of men without question.

Canton nods but doesn't say more. The CIA never likes to

give any more information than they have to. And often-times, they still don't give us enough.

"Do you have a phone I could use?" I ask.

Canton reaches into his jacket pocket and hands me his.

"I'll be quick. Thank you." I step away and dial the office number for Morgan Thompson Security. That is protocol for calling in after hours. It's usually forwarded to Stormy's phone, so I'm surprised when my coworker, Fox, answers.

"Hello?" he sounds half asleep.

"Fox?"

"Who's this?" He's suddenly more alert.

"Peaches."

"New phone?"

I turn back, and Canton is watching me. "Borrowed. I need to talk to Stormy."

Fox yawns. "He's on a red-eye to New York. He has calls forwarding to me. Are you heading home?"

"Soon, yeah." I need to tell someone. "Cara was shot."

Rustling comes through the phone. "What? Is she all right?"

"The doctors say she'll pull through, but for a while, I wasn't sure." I can't help the quiver in my voice.

"Shit, man. I'm sorry. But hey, this is Cara. If anyone can pull through, she will. She's tough."

We're both silent for a moment.

"Does she know yet?" he asks.

I rack my brain, but I'm not sure what he's referring to. "Know what?"

The man groans. "You know. How you feel about her."

Yeah, all the guys at the office know how I feel about her. Fox likes to bring it up, and I don't know why. He has his own crush he's doing jack shit about.

"Does Julia know about your feelings yet?" I counter.

Julia McNamara is a detective we often work with, and Fox has had a thing for her for as long as I can remember.

He sighs. "Touché. You know what? Life's too short for our bullshit. I'll make you a deal."

"A deal?" I lean against the wall.

"Yeah, the first one of us to take the woman we want on a date wins. The loser has to clean the other's car for a month."

Interesting. After this trip, I'd say I'm already ahead of Fox. "Deal, but I want my van cleaned weekly for three months."

Fox laughs. "Fine. Deal. And just to be fair, if there is any question as to what defines a date, we'll let Maverick decide."

I scratch my forehead. "Why Maverick?"

"Why not? He's found someone and clearly knows what he's doing."

"Okay, deal. But you better order supplies now because my van needs some special TLC."

He laughs. "Not worried. But you should be. I like to take my truck through the mud, and it cakes on real good."

A nurse walks into the waiting area wearing scrubs.

"Hey, I gotta go."

"Good luck. And tell Cara we are all rooting for her."

"Will do." I end the call and stand up straight.

"Are you Grayson?" she asks.

"Yes."

"Cara wants to see you. Follow me."

I give the phone back to Canton before I follow the nurse down a hall and into a room. I'm expecting a lot of things when I walk in but Cara sitting up in bed, typing on a phone is not one of them.

"You look good for someone who just got shot," I say as I approach her.

She sets down her phone and smiles at me, and I can't help but grin back. To see her up and alert is the best outcome. I really did think I might lose her.

"Hey, it takes more than one bullet to knock me out." Her smile fades as she pats the bed next to her, and I sit. "Thank you," she says as her eyes meet mine. "If you hadn't arrived when you did to rescue me from Max, I don't want to even think about what would have happened."

I take her hand and give it a squeeze. I don't want to think about that, either.

"I have good news." Cara smiles. "Since no one heard

38

from you or me after you barged into the mansion, a team went in and raided the place. The girls were still there, and they are now somewhere safe."

"A team?" I ask.

She nods but doesn't say anything more.

"But Max wasn't there?"

"No, his whereabouts are unknown." She leans her head on my shoulder, and inside, I'm giving myself a fist pump. "Gray?"

"Yeah?"

"Is that offer to see your band still open?"

I chuckle because this is the last thing I'd thought she'd bring up. "Yes, why do you think I was the one to come to save you? I need more people in the audience."

She laughs as she turns her gaze to mine. Her lips are so close. I lean forward just an inch, and her eyes fall to my lips. Hell, life is short, and I want to kiss this woman.

"Thank you, Doctor," Canton says from just outside the door.

His voice causes Cara to pull away and sit upright. I immediately miss the warmth of her hand.

Canton walks into the room. "Ready?" he asks Cara.

"Yes."

He grabs a pair of crutches leaning against the end of the bed and hands them to her. That's when I notice she's wearing scrubs.

She turns to me. "Do you have a way home?"

"He does. He's flying home with us," Canton says.

She uses the crutches to stand up.

"Good." She smiles. "Maybe we can continue our conversation."

"I'm afraid I need you to sit with me, Harding," Canton says.

That snaps my attention to his.

The man is arching a brow at me. "Anderson wants me to go over everything that happened in case we missed any detail."

Cara frowns but nods. "Understood."

"Let's go. There's a car ready to take us to the plane."

She swiftly moves to the door. Something tells me this isn't her first time on crutches.

"Wait, shouldn't you be in a wheelchair?" I ask.

Cara stops and turns to me. "Nah, I got this. You know how it is." She winks before she takes off down the hall.

Canton falls in line next to her, forcing me to follow them. Fortunately, we aren't too far from the exit because it's taking all my strength not to pick Cara up and carry her. She was just shot and had surgery. Walking farther than down the hall is crazy, even for her. But I don't do that because it would piss her off. Cara is strong and doesn't like to show weakness. I get it. But it doesn't mean I like it.

Once we get to the car, Canton opens the door for her, and she slips into the back.

"Peaches, can you ride up front?" he asks.

"Sure."

What the hell else can I say? The man probably saw how I looked at her and thinks he's protecting her. At least, I hope that's all it is.

We make it to the plane, and not surprisingly, I'm told to sit in the rear while Cara sits with him up front. I lean my head back and close my eyes.

"Hey," someone says as they jostle my arm. "You awake?"

I open my eyes to find Cara sitting next to me. I glance around and spot Canton's head leaning to the side in his seat.

"You broke free," I say.

She grins. "He fell asleep, and I was hoping to talk to you before we land."

"Yeah? What about?" I sit up straighter.

She takes my hand in hers. "Thank you again for saving me."

I grin. "You're welcome, but you don't need to keep thanking me." I can't help running my thumb across the back of her hand.

She shivers. She feels this, too. This small touch is turning me on.

Her eyes meet mine, and she licks her lips. If only we

were in a more private place, I'd bend down and kiss her. Instead, I intertwine my fingers in hers.

"You know, if you want to get together before your leg heals, we could do something other than have you watch my band."

"Harding?"

Both our heads turn to the front to see Canton awake and staring at us. She gives my hand a squeeze.

"Guess I better go." She makes her way back up to the front seat.

"Did you read that case file from Anderson? He wants you to read it before we land," Canton says.

"I did. That was three hours ago."

He nods. "Good."

I haven't seen her interact with the man before, so I can't say if this is normal, but he seems very controlling for a coworker. Maybe he outranks her in some way.

I fall back asleep and don't wake again until we land. Before I can even think of what to say to Cara, Canton has them both out the door and in a car.

I step off the plane to find a sedan waiting for me. I give the driver my address. Once I'm home, I power up my phone and text Cara.

Me: *If you need me to sweep in and save you again, just let me know. I'll clear my calendar.*

She responds right away.

Cara: *I will. Text me your band schedule. I really do want to come see you play.*

Me: *I will.*

I've never known another woman like her. She's tough yet can be tender. She's smart and resourceful. And she's sexy as hell. Yeah, I'm in trouble when it comes to Cara Harding.

CHAPTER FIVE

Cara

"WHAT THE HELL are you doing here? You were shot. Go home, rest," my boss, Anderson, says as he spots me stepping off the elevator.

"I heard Deputy Director Whitlock would be here today, and I need to speak to him in person."

Anderson's brows shoot up. "Shouldn't you be talking to me?"

Usually, I would talk to my direct superior, but this is about Kralik, and I always reported to Whitlock on that matter.

"Harding?" The man in question steps out from one of the offices. "You're looking good for someone who was shot. Back to work already?"

"No," Anderson says at the same time I say, "Yes."

"Deputy Director Whitlock, I'd like to speak to you. It's regarding a prior assignment."

The man nods and motions for me to enter the office he just exited. It's a spare office that's empty. There is only one chair in the room. "Please sit down," he motions to the chair.

Because I'm tired of standing on these crutches, I take him up on it.

"If this is about Alex Kralik, I'm afraid I don't have any more information to share," Whitlock says.

I cut right to the chase and tell him something I kept out of my report. "I saw Ivan Kralik in Brazil. He's alive."

Whitlock laughs. "Wow. You would say anything to get back in the field, wouldn't you? We confirmed he was killed by Alex."

I shake my head. "You're wrong."

Whitlock's smile drops. No one tells this man he's wrong. He didn't get to be Deputy Director of the CIA by being nice. "What did you say?"

"I said your intel is wrong. I saw him. And so did Peaches, if you want to ask him. He isn't familiar with the man, but I'm sure he could point him out of some photographs."

Whitlock paces the room. "Why would Alex go to so much trouble to convince us he killed his brother?"

I don't answer. This is how Whitlock processes. He talks to himself. And I learned the hard way it's best to not interrupt him.

He turns and paces back toward me. "It turned our attention to Alex. But we lost contact with our agent who was assigned to him. We spent our time trying to find him. While that left Ivan free…" Whitlock stops pacing and stares at me. "Where exactly did you see him?"

"He was with Max Acrile, and they were heading toward the US Consulate's Office in Brazil."

Whitlock lets out a sigh. "Is this why you haven't filed your official report from your last assignment yet?"

"It is. I wanted to tell you in person. On the flight back from Brazil, Canton mentioned you'd be in Seattle today."

"I appreciate that." He leans against the wall, keeping his eyes trained on me. "Are you sure it was him?"

"I spent three years tracking that man down. I've never been more sure of anything. He still has the scar on his right cheek."

He sighs. "Okay, tell me everything."

"Peaches and I were trying to get to the US Embassy. Max was waiting in a car across from the entrance, so we made our way to the side of the building. We peered to the front, and I spotted Max walking from the car with Ivan."

He pushes off the wall and walks toward the door. "We have no idea where Ivan has been." He spins around to face me. "Did Ivan see you?"

"No."

"Good."

He stares at the wall, likely going over all the evidence we had that suggested Ivan was dead. I already did the same thing.

"I'll get an analyst to see if we can track where he is now. Thank you for telling me about this."

He continues to the door and opens it. This is his way of ending a meeting.

"Do you have enough evidence against Alex Kralik yet?" I ask, even though I know he won't share that with me.

"Yes, but he's disappeared without a trace."

I'm surprised by his admission.

"The agent working on that case turned in a report that included evidence. He informed me in a call he had more evidence. But now that he's presumed dead, I fear whatever else he had is lost."

That agent would be Doug Patterson. A man I was chasing as a suspect because I wasn't told he was an agent until it was too late. He was working deep undercover, aligning himself with Alex Kralik. From what I've heard, it worked. Until his partner double-crossed him.

"You must go home and rest and heal, Harding."

He extends his hand to help me up. I don't need it, but I accept it as the olive branch it is. Keeping me in the dark about Doug Patterson really did piss me off.

"Thank you." I grab the crutches and slowly make my way out of the room.

On my way to the elevator, Anderson stops me.

"Harding, how long did the doctor say before you're good for work?"

I force myself not to laugh. Right here is the difference between Anderson and Whitlock. Anderson would send me out tomorrow if I thought I could go. But Whitlock insists we wait the time the doctor orders or longer if we aren't ready.

"Two weeks for desk work and four more for field work."

Anderson smiles as he stares at his phone. "I'll see you in here next week. I have plenty of paperwork that needs to get done."

I force a smile. "Great." I love my job, but I can't stand the paperwork that goes with it. And now I'll get to help with someone else's paperwork. Oh, joy.

"Safe travels home," Anderson says, then spins and walks back to his office.

I hobble into the elevator, trying not to grumble. As much as I hate desk duty, at least I'll get to be back in the office, which is better than sitting around my apartment, twiddling my thumbs.

By the time I make it home, I'm exhausted. I take some ibuprofen and lie down on my bed. As I stare at the ceiling, I really wish I had a television. I never bothered to get one because I'm rarely here. But now that I am, I'm going out of my mind with boredom. I close my eyes and hope for sleep until the medicine kicks in.

I jerk awake and sit up. The room is now dark. I reach for my phone on the nightstand. Wow, I slept for a few hours. And I feel better. Good. I scroll and discover four missed messages. The first one is a text from Thunder. The moment I open it, I roll my eyes. I scroll and scroll. Shit, Thunder, why the hell do you have to write a book each time? I'm too tired to read it right now. He's always got some story to tell me. While they are entertaining, I need to be in the right mood.

My eye catches on a text from Peaches.

Peaches: *Hey, I just wanted to check in and see how you are doing.*

I stare at it as my stomach flutters. It's been years since I've felt an attraction like this to anyone.

Me: *I'm doing better. Thanks for checking. Did you make it home safely?*

I send it, then cringe. Shit. Of course, he made it home. It's been a week. If he hadn't, I would have heard about it by now. I vow not to send another text to him without thinking it through first.

I stare at my phone. Nothing. Great. He's probably wondering what the hell. I change his name in my phone. Another message pops up.

Gray: *Can I call you?*

Suddenly, my palms grow sweaty. I'm nervous. Why the hell am I nervous? It's just a phone call.

Me: *Yes.*

I set my phone down and stare at it. He didn't ask to do it right now. Fuck. I can't sit here, wondering when and if he will call. I grab my phone to ask him when it rings.

Oh. Now.

"Hello?" I answer.

"Hello." His voice is deep and warms me. "How's your leg?"

I shrug. Then roll my eyes at myself. "It's healing slowly."

"That's good. I hope you don't mind, but I wanted to hear your voice. You know, make sure you were good."

I smile. "I don't mind. How have you been? Did they send you out again?"

He laughs. "No. I'm still doing the paperwork for our assignment. Every time Stormy walks by my office, he shakes his head."

I laugh, too. Stormy is part owner of the company he works for, Morgan Thompson Security, or MTS, as the guys call it.

"I've been doing paperwork longer than we were out on assignment. That isn't right," he says.

"I go back to the office next week and will be on desk duty for two weeks. I'll be able to sympathize soon."

Something creaks in the background.

"What's that sound?" I ask.

"I just sat on my bed."

An image of Grayson lying on his bed, shirtless, fills my mind.

"Cara?"

"What?"

"You all right? I asked you a question, but I don't think you heard me."

No, I was too busy fantasizing. "What was the question?"

"Shit. Sorry. Stormy's calling. I have to take it. He said I'd likely be going on an assignment soon."

"Oh, okay. Good luck on your assignment."

"Take care." He ends the call.

I roll onto my back and smile at the ceiling. He just wanted to check-in.

Since Caleb, I've told myself I couldn't date because I can't share with anyone what I do for a living. But Gray not only knows, but he also gets why I can't share where I'm going or how long I'll be gone. His job is similar.

My smile falls. Caleb, my ex, and Thunder's brother. He was my first love. I thought we'd spend forever together. Even when he was having trouble, I foolishly thought I could help him through it. After he died, I swore I'd never let myself get close to anyone again. It was too painful. But somehow, Thunder wormed his way in. The truth is, I don't think either of us could have gotten through it without the other. He's the brother I never had.

But something about Gray is different. The comfort I felt with him when sleeping in the woods or running from the men shooting at us makes me want to try again with him.

CHAPTER SIX

Grayson

I LAUGH as I reread the last text from Cara. Since we're both stuck in our offices doing desk duty, we've been exchanging a lot of messages. I want to ask her out for a date, but her responses have been so matter of fact that I'm concerned I read her wrong while in Brazil.

But that's her personality. She's direct.

My phone buzzes, and I check it to find a string of messages from my bandmates. Johnny, our singer, says Duke wants us to play at his bar for a couple of nights. I grin. Cara did say she wanted to see me perform. Maybe I can take her for a drink after.

I text back that I'm in and wait for confirmation from the other guys. Once confirmed, I call Cara. I should probably text her, but I want to hear her voice.

"Gray?"

Damn, I can get used to hearing my name on her lips. Her voice is like silk. I lean back in my chair and grab my fidget spinner off my desk. "I hope I'm not bothering you."

"No, not at all," she says, then yawns.

"Shit, I woke you, didn't I?" I check the time, and it's just before noon.

"No, I'm at work. Just doing more paperwork and trying to stay awake. I'm on my third cup of coffee already."

I laugh. "Third cup, huh? Guess you've got a good tolerance." I wince at my own comment. I clear my throat. "Anyway, the reason I'm calling is to see if you want to see my band play Friday night?"

"Oh, uh."

Shit. Maybe she only said that to be nice.

"If you don't want to, that's fine. I just mentioned I would tell you when we're performing again."

"No, no, I want to. Sorry, I hesitated because, well, it depends on where it is. I'm still on crutches."

I drop my spinner on my desk. Fuck, why didn't I think of that?

"You know what? I could pick you up and get you there with no issues."

She laughs. "No issues?"

"I'll carry you if I have to."

She laughs harder. "Okay, I'll go. Send me the details."

"Harding!" a man's voice yells.

"Gotta go!" She ends the call, and I sit there, smiling like a fool.

I'm not sure if it's a date or not, but it's my chance, and I'm going to take it.

Then I notice CT standing on the other side of my desk, grinning at me. "Any chance you were talking to Harding?"

I shrug and try to act casual but don't pull it off.

"I'm happy for you," he says. "It's about time you get the woman you've been pining for."

I cross my arms. "What about you? Shouldn't you get the same, too?"

His smile drops. "I told you to drop it."

I give him a curt nod, but I don't drop it. "You should talk to Rover about this. I bet he'd be more open than you think."

CT grinds his teeth. "Trust me, he wouldn't."

"CT? You ready to go?" Rover yells from down the hall.

"I better go," he says. "Don't screw up this thing with Cara."

I nod. I don't plan to. As CT leaves, he plasters a smile back on his face, but it doesn't reach his eyes. He's a great guy who's in love with a woman he views as off-limits. Sometimes you don't have a say in who you love, but you do have a say in whether you let that chance at love slip by.

"Got a minute?" Stormy asks, standing in my doorway.

"Of course."

He walks in and closes the door behind him. "I was going over your report so far, and I have some questions."

I sit up straighter. "Okay."

"You and agent Harding were forced to spend a good deal of time together alone, isn't that correct?"

I shift uncomfortably, not sure where this is going. "You could say that, yes."

Stormy leans back and looks me in the eye. "It's no secret around here that you have a crush on her."

My brows shoot up, and my face warms. I'm blushing like a high school kid caught by his dad.

Stormy raises his hand. "I don't care who you like. What concerns me is how close you two become and what effect that might have on future assignments."

With no idea how to answer, I reach for the coffee on my desk and drink it down to buy me a minute to think. "We grew closer, but nothing romantic happened if that's what you're asking."

He nods. "If it does, you'll let me know, right? The last thing I need is to send a fighting couple into the field."

His words wash over me, and instead of nodding and agreeing, I grow angry.

"If we were to date, and I don't know what the future holds, you know we are both professionals. We would never let any feelings jeopardize an assignment."

Stormy stands. "Not on purpose, no. But sometimes, emotions can cloud your judgment. Just keep me apprised. Got it?"

I nod, and he leaves. Leaning back, I'm feeling anger at his doubts about us but respect that he is aware enough of what is going on with his team to ensure its safety. I rub my hands over my face and try to finish what I'm doing, but I'm struggling to concentrate.

My phone rings and again plays a song about Peaches. I have to laugh. It never happens when I'm on assignment, and that's why it has to be one of these guys.

But my smile fades when I see it's my brother calling. Against my better judgment, I answer. "Jasper, how are you doing today?"

"Fucking bad, bro," he slurs. He's drunk. Again. "I need some money." That's all he ever wants.

"How much and what for?"

"A hundred bucks for the water bill."

Reaching for the stress ball on my desk, I squeeze it tight. Normally I can keep my emotions in check, but my brother brings out the worst in me. Friends have told me I shouldn't keep giving him money. But they don't understand; I owe my life to him.

"Fine. I'll drop it off on my way home."

"Thanks, brother!" He hangs up before I can change my mind.

I reach into my desk and pull out the yellow notepad. Every time my phone has a peach song ring tone, I check off who is in the office and who is gone.

Trax had been in the office every time until today. He's out on assignment, so it can't be him. I cross his name off the list. Dammit! I've crossed every name off except for Stormy and Cowboy, the other co-owner of MTS. But they're my bosses. They wouldn't spend their time fucking with me. Would they?

At one point, I thought everyone here was in on it, but I questioned Cody and Maverick, and neither one gave any indication they were lying.

I'll figure it out. Just not today. I put the notepad back in my drawer and turn to my computer, forcing myself to focus.

* * *

Since I asked Cara to watch my band play, I started sending her dumb jokes to keep the conversation going. She's gotten into it and sent some back.

But tonight, I'm hoping we have time to talk after my set. I send her a text, asking for her address so I can pick her up. The guys are cool with me dropping off them and the equipment and then going to get her.

Cara: *Actually, I don't need a ride. I'm going with a friend. I'll see you tonight!*

I stare at my phone. A friend? Like a friend-friend or a date? I have no idea. And this could be a problem for my plan.

Me: *Will you have time to talk after the show?*

At least she'll know I want some time with her.

Cara: *Yes.*

Good. Okay, instead of focusing on the change, I get ready for the gig.

We are playing our second song when I spot Cara entering the bar. Her friend is a woman who holds the door for her and helps her to a seat. The place isn't too crowded, so she manages.

She spots me on stage, and I smile. She smiles back.

For the rest of our set, I try like hell not to stare at her the whole time, but it's hard. Her dark, wavy hair is down, and she's wearing more makeup than usual. With her tight jeans and low-cut shirt, she's gorgeous.

Our set ends, and I join them at their table.

"Peaches, this is Vega. She works with me. Vega, this is Peaches."

Interesting, she used my nickname. I hold out my hand, and Vega takes me in before shaking it. Her hair is long and black. And her clothes are all black as well.

"Good to meet you," I say.

She simply nods. A phone on the table vibrates. Vega answers it and steps away.

Cara leans close to me, and I smell her shampoo and get a glimpse of her cleavage. She's smiling and places a hand on my shoulder. Just like in the jungle, her touch lights me up.

"You're very good. I'm glad I got to see you tonight."

I take her hand in mine. "Me too."

Vega returns but doesn't sit. "I'm sorry, Cara, but we have to go."

Cara turns her attention to her friend. "What?"

"Anderson called and said he needs to see us both. We have to go."

Cara stands up.

"Both?" I ask. As far as I understand, Cara is still on desk duty, and I can't imagine any paperwork this urgent.

"Yes. It was a good show. Nice meeting you." She turns to Cara. "I'll bring the car to the door." She leaves.

"Let me walk you out," I say to Cara.

"Okay."

Once outside, I turn to her. "I'm sorry you have to go. I was hoping to get a chance to talk." I move some hair off her face. I want to kiss this woman.

She's staring at my lips, and I think she wants the same. "Yeah, I wanted that, too."

I step closer, and she doesn't back up. Her hands go around my neck. I bend down, and our lips are almost touching when a loud horn causes us to both jump back.

"Dammit!" Cara yells.

A car pulls up, and the window goes down. "Let's go," Vega says.

Cara sighs, then points at me. "I want to see you again, but next time, I don't want it to be around any of my coworkers."

"Sounds like a plan."

She gets into the car, and I watch until the taillights fade away. Next time I'll make sure we're alone because I'm getting that kiss.

CHAPTER SEVEN

Grayson

I HAD every intention of asking Cara out on a date the next day, but I got called away on an assignment. An assignment that I just returned from last night. For a month, I was out of touch with her. No funny jokes, no checking in, nothing. She understood the reason, but I worry I lost any ground I had gained.

I glance up and find CT waving his arms from the other side of my desk. I pop the earbuds out of my ears. "What's up?"

"Stormy wants us in his office. You didn't hear him yell?"

I point to the earbuds. "No, I was listening to music."

"Peaches, CT!" Stormy hollers from the hallway.

I laugh. Why the man can't send an email or text for the meeting still baffles me. I asked him once if that's how they used to do it in the olden days. He didn't appreciate that joke.

We all tease Stormy that he's older than he is because his hair is graying prematurely. One time he even dyed it all back to brown, but that didn't look too natural.

I shuffle into Stormy's office behind CT and am surprised when I spot Cara. Next to her are Thunder and Lightning from New York. Fox is shaking Thunder's hand. CT and I grab a couple of seats at the large conference table in Stormy's office. Stormy has been stretched thin lately since he recently bought interest in another security company based in New York. That's where Thunder and Lightning work. We've been getting to know the men in New York slowly, and so far, I have to say they are all great guys.

Despite Stormy's now-busy schedule, the other owner of MTS, Cowboy, still leaves most of the day-to-day operations to Stormy so he can run his ranch.

"Almost seven weeks ago, Peaches and Harding were on an assignment in Brazil," Stormy starts.

CT lifts his hand up. "Wait." He turns to me. "You didn't mention you were with Cara."

"It was an assignment, so it was confidential." Hopefully, he leaves it at that. I glance at Stormy to continue, but he doesn't.

"Confidential, huh?" CT grins, and I can tell this isn't the last I'll hear about this.

Sadly, the man knows I have a thing for Cara. Everyone here does. I don't hide it very well. But dammit, I don't need anyone bringing it up now with her in the room. Or Thunder, who is like her older brother. Her big, protective, older brother.

Speaking of Thunder, I think he's glaring at me, but I refuse to glance over at him to confirm. I focus on Stormy instead.

"Anyway," Stormy cuts in finally, "Agent Harding spotted a man named Ivan Kralik. He's wanted for arms dealing. He's sold US secrets and weapons to foreign governments and terrorist organizations."

Fox crosses his arms. "How did he get his hands on secrets? And what kind of secrets?"

I hide my smile. Leave it to Fox to ask direct questions. We never get the answers, but he always tries.

Stormy frowns. "I can't say. But Harding worked with Thunder and Lightning on the matter, and they all believed this man was dead until Harding spotted him in Brazil."

Stormy stands and walks to his desk. He picks up some papers and returns to the table with them, handing them out before he sits down.

"What's the plan?" I ask. "Are we all going to Brazil?"

Cara stands up and walks to the whiteboard hanging near the window. I'm happy to see her leg has healed. She said it had in her text last night, but I wondered if she was downplaying it.

That wasn't the only thing that bothered me about her message. It was friendly but not flirty. A lot can change in a month, and I'd be lying if I said I wasn't worried about finding out if something changed with her.

Damn, she's beautiful. Her hair is pulled back into a ponytail that moves over her shoulders whenever she glances back at us.

Fuck. I really can't stop thinking about this woman. Over this past month, in my downtime, I went back and forth about whether it would be smart to pursue her. What if something went wrong? I have to work with her from time to time.

"Peaches? Did you catch that?" CT asks.

"Sorry. What was that?" Like right there. I'm always focused. I need to stay focused on this meeting. I turn my attention to Cara, and she's smiling at me.

"We're going to Costa Rica."

"Who?" I ask.

"The six of us."

I glance around the table. I've worked with CT and Fox before but not as much with Thunder and Lightning.

Cara turns back to the board and draws a blob that resembles Costa Rica. "Since my return from Brazil, a couple of agents from my office have been gathering intel. One agent also tracked Ivan Kralik." She draws an X on the coast. "Ivan owns a boat and is staying at Les Escondida Marina on the Pacific Ocean side of Costa Rica here." She circles the X. "He's had the boat moored there for the past couple of months."

"Is he still selling secrets or weapons?" Fox asks.

Cara turns to face us. "We don't have any evidence that he has. It's hard to believe he would give up such a lucrative business. And there was something else that came up in the intel that I think indicates he's working on a large deal."

"What's that?" Thunder asks.

"There's another man on the CIA's watch list who will not only be in Costa Rica, but he's also throwing an elaborate party. Oscar Reyes is not known for parties, but he's invited dignitaries and quite a few of the top names in the business world."

I glance around as several of the guys are frowning. So, I ask what we're all likely thinking. "Why does having a party raise suspicions?"

Cara smiles at me. "Because Reyes transferred a large sum of money to an unknown account yesterday, and the party is in two days. We believe the party is a cover to hide the fact a large deal is going down."

Lightning crosses his arms. "Please tell me you have more than that? I mean, no offense, but how do you know the money wasn't for catering or fireworks or whatever the rich do at these parties?"

She walks back to the table. "Reyes was seen on Ivan's boat yesterday. And this man is suspected to be one of the contributors of weapons to one of the deadliest gangs in El Salvador."

I nod. "Sounds like we're going to the party."

"CT and Lightning will be. The rest of us will have eyes on Ivan. This party might be a cover. We need to follow him and catch him in the act."

"Is the Costa Rican government supporting this assignment?" CT asks.

Cara sits down at the table and clasps her hands. "They do not know about any of this. We don't know who we can trust down there."

Stormy clears his throat, and we all turn to him. "It's believed Ivan is still selling US weapons. Once you detain him and verify this, he'll need to be brought back to the States."

"And if the weapons aren't from the US?" Lightning asks.

"They will be," Cara says. "It's Ivan's specialty."

"Are you sure you don't need more of us to attend the party?" Fox asks. "Because I have a tux and can be ready to go."

"Sorry, Fox, but no," Stormy says. "Now stop interrupting Agent Harding, and you'll know what you're supposed to do."

All eyes turn to Cara. "Thank you, Stormy. Now, the six of us will go to Costa Rica undercover. We'll be staying aboard a yacht at the same marina."

"My parents have a boat there," CT says casually. "Quite a few Americans do, actually."

Of course, they do. CT's parents are loaded, and while I don't know his entire story, I'm under the impression they weren't around too much, leaving CT alone in a mansion for much of his youth.

"A boat?" I quirk an eyebrow. "How big?"

CT shrugs. "Maybe seventy feet or so."

I rub my temple. "That's not a boat; that's a yacht."

CT shrugs. Okay, his parents aren't just loaded; they're insanely wealthy. You wouldn't know it because CT tries to play it down. But a seventy-foot boat in Costa Rica. Damn. You gotta have respect for him, though. Instead of sipping tropical drinks and hanging out on their yacht, he chose to go into the service and continues to work.

"Huh, well, that could change things," Cara says.

Fox crosses his arms. "How so?"

"Well, the plan was for Thunder and me to be a couple who owned a yacht, and the rest of you were to be our crew."

I clench my fists. Thunder is going to be her pretend boyfriend. That's bullshit.

"I got a better plan," CT says.

I glance around, and it appears like everyone is willing to hear him out.

"We go hang out on my yacht. You can be my friends from college."

Cara nods. "That's one option. We have already chartered the yacht in question."

CT holds up his hands. "I got it! I'll be on my yacht with Fox, Thunder, and Lightning, having a guy's trip. You and Peaches will be a newlywed couple on the chartered yacht."

CT winks at me.

What the fuck did he just do? If he were sitting closer, I'd kick him.

"Why should Peaches be her husband?" Thunder asks. "I know her better, so it's logical it's me."

CT nods. "True, but I thought you two were like brother and sister."

Thunder shrugs. "So?"

CT leans forward. "Are you ready to act like newlyweds with your hands and lips all over each other?"

Thunder's eyes widen, and Cara's cheeks flush.

"Uh, that wouldn't be such a good idea." Cara laughs.

"Yeah. Madison would kick my ass," Thunder says.

"It's settled. Peaches will be your husband."

"CT has a point," Stormy says.

I turn in astonishment to my boss.

CT grins. "If you want to sell this newlywed idea, you will have to act like newlyweds."

Cara stares at me. "Is that something you could do?" she asks.

I'm still surprised how it went from being a couple to newlyweds based only on CT's suggestion. "I think I can manage." I wink at her, which makes her cheeks flush even more.

How the hell is this happening? It's one thing to be on an assignment with Cara, but to pretend to be newlyweds? I'm sweating. This meeting needs to end so I can get some air.

But memories of us cuddling together when we were on the run come back to me. She fit perfectly in my arms. Maybe this is what we need.

I shut my eyes. No. No, if we are meant to date, we can date. How the hell can I stay focused under these circumstances?

I open my eyes. Because you are a trained fucking SEAL, that's how.

Fox leans over to me. "You feeling all right?"

"Yeah," I huff out.

Stormy stands up. "Well, it's decided. Anderson said we could work out the details, and I believe we have. You all leave in an hour, so go home and grab your bags."

I guess I better get my head wrapped around this idea fast.

"Peaches? You have a minute?" Cara asks.

Everyone has left the room except Stormy, who is at his desk, and Cara, who is standing next to me.

"Sure, we can go to my office."

She follows me, then sits in one of the chairs, and I close the door. She's holding her thumbs, and I can't say I've ever seen her this uncomfortable. I have to give her an out.

"I'm sorry about all that. If us acting like newlyweds makes you too uncomfortable, I understand, and we can talk to Stormy about it."

She smiles. "Actually, of all the guys here, you're my first pick for being my fake husband."

That smile. It lights up her brown eyes, and I'm a goner.

"Me too." I realize what I just said. "I mean, I'd be happy to be cooped up with you on a boat."

Shit, that wasn't any better.

She laughs. "I'm glad that's settled."

"You called me Peaches. Why?"

"I figured we'd keep things professional in the office."

"Of course. You're right."

"Okay. I'll see you in an hour."

Before she opens the door, I stop her. I want more inter-action from her even though I don't know what to say right now.

"How's your leg?" I blurt out.

She smirks. "It's still good. Thank you."

She leaves, and I scratch my chin, wondering if this is a good idea. But I don't have much time to think because CT walks in and sits in the chair Cara just vacated.

He's grinning. "You're welcome."

"You think I should be thanking you?" I want to punch that smile right off his face.

CT rolls his eyes. "Yeah, at the rate you two are going, you might get to kiss her when you're ninety. Trust me, I did you a favor."

"A favor? I have to sleep on the same boat, possibly the same room with her, while pretending to be newlyweds. Do you have any idea how hard that will be?"

CT laughs as he gets up. "Oh, it will be hard. All the time."

I'm about to chew him out, but my phone rings. Well, not actually a ring. No, it plays a song about peaches in a can.

I stand up and yell. "Who the hell is fucking with my phone?"

I hear giggles. Actual giggles come from down the hall.

"Bastards."

I miss the call, but that's fine. I have to figure out how I'm going to deal with being Cara's fake husband.

CHAPTER EIGHT

Cara

I MAY HAVE KEPT my cool in Stormy's office this morning and as I got into my car and drove out of sight. But then I freaked out. I had originally planned for Thunder to pretend to be my newlywed husband because I'm comfortable around him. We can talk and laugh. Why the hell had I not thought about anything physical? Ivan is a suspicious man by nature. Anything that seems off would catch his attention.

But Gray? The chemistry is there, but I can't say I'm comfortable. No, I'm nervous as hell. The man sent me funny and flirty texts until he left on his last assignment. I wanted to start them up again last night, but I'm sad to say I have no idea how to flirt. I try to type up witty responses but end up deleting them and sending something safe in reply.

The idea of him kissing me, even if it's for show, is both exhilarating and scary at the same time. My phone buzzes. It's him, and I smile.

Grayson: *Ready for the show?* (Kiss emoticon)

Now I have butterflies in my stomach.

Me: *I'm nervous.*

Grayson: *About the assignment?*

About being your wife. But I don't say that. Instead, I keep it simple.

Me: *Yes.*

I pocket my cell, grab my bag, and head to the plane.

CT is standing outside, talking on his phone. I step inside, and Thunder and Lightning are already onboard, bickering about something.

"If I hear you bring up cats one more time, I swear I'll end our friendship," Lightning says as he turns away from Thunder.

I suppress my laugh. There's an ongoing joke about Lightning liking cats after an unfortunate incident at a furry conference on our last assignment together.

"Good morning, everyone," Fox says as he steps onto the plane.

"You are certainly in a good mood," I say.

Fox takes a seat near the back. "I am. I've always wanted to go to Costa Rica. Can't wait."

I check the time. We're supposed to take off in five minutes. No missed messages from Gray. As I worry he's cutting it close, he enters the plane and tosses his bag into the cubby above our heads.

"I hope you don't mind, but I thought we should talk before we are in our roles."

I nod. "Yes, of course."

He takes the seat next to me and puts on his seatbelt. "I had this great idea, but now that I'm about to share it, I think maybe it's terrible." He's staring straight ahead and has a fidget spinner in his hand.

"What is the idea?"

He sighs. "Well, now I think it's stupid."

I angle in my seat to stare at him. "Now I have to know what it is."

He chuckles. "Okay, but don't say I didn't warn you."

The captain interrupts to announce we are ready for takeoff. Once we are speeding down the runway, he continues.

"I thought we should have a thing. Any couple I see that's

in a honeymoon phase does something. Like they rub noses or something they consider cute."

I smile. "You want to rub our noses together?"

He licks his lips, and it draws my attention to his beard. It's grown back. As much as I like his strong jaw, I have to say there's something sexy about a man with a well-kept beard.

"No, not that. I was thinking when I hug you, I could play you like a guitar."

My eyes immediately go to his hands. And his long fingers. Fingers I noticed that night in the bar when he was playing the guitar. The way they moved so fast and so purposefully, I couldn't help but wonder what he could do to me with those. The thought of it now has me heating up.

"You want to play me like a guitar?" I ask, still envisioning his hands in places that are not my back.

He leans back. "Hearing you say it, it really is stupid. Sorry I brought it up."

I take his hand in mine. "Now wait, I like the idea, maybe not the guitar part, but the idea."

I think about it for a minute. "Why can't we touch noses? It's subtle, and there's no chance it will end up with you tickling me and me screaming."

His brow shoots up, and he turns to me. "First, you're ticklish? I thought that was against the CIA rules."

I laugh. "I can fight it, but yeah, if I'm relaxed, I'm a little ticklish."

He grins. "Good to know. Second, why would you scream?"

I tilt my head to the side. "Doesn't everyone scream when tickled?"

His eyes light up. "You're a screamer, huh?"

Now, as a trained agent, I should be able to handle any question and remain calm. But my cheeks warm and I can't hide my reaction.

"Maybe," I say, staring at him. Hell, that was an opportunity to flirt. Why didn't I take it? Yeah, because flirting is not a skill in my wheelhouse.

His eyes move to where I'm holding his hand, and he

intertwines our fingers. "How about we ask each other questions to get to know each other better? You know, in case it's important that we know each other's favorite color or food."

I blow out a breath of relief at his change of topic. "Red and eggs."

He frowns. "Eggs are your favorite food? Out of everything in the entire world?"

I nod. "They are usually easy to get, and they provide nourishment that can hold you over. So yes, eggs."

He laughs and then fires off about twenty questions, asking me my favorite soup, favorite animal, and even favorite day of the week until I yawn.

"I'm sorry. It's not you. I just didn't sleep well last night," I explain.

He smiles. "Go ahead and get some rest. I think we can fake this newlywed thing just fine. We'll hold hands and maybe snuggle together in a chaise on deck. We can pretend it's a parachute wrapped around us."

I laugh. "That night was surprisingly comfortable."

"It was."

I yawn again.

"Let's try to get some sleep," he says.

I lean back and close my eyes. It isn't lost on me that he's still holding my hand. I simply try to enjoy being near him in the safety of this plane. After a few deep breaths, I fall asleep.

"Cara," Gray says.

I open my eyes. I'm leaning on his shoulder, and I quickly sit up. "I'm sorry." I wipe my mouth, hoping I didn't drool.

"Why are you sorry? I enjoyed having you close," he says quietly.

"You guys ready?" CT asks from the aisle where he's grinning.

CT and the other guys exit the plane first. It turns out CT's parents' boat is in a slip that is two away from Ivan Kralik's. Unfortunately, we still don't know where our rental boat is located, but knowing CT and the guys can have eyes on Ivan is good enough for me right now.

By the time we get to the marina, it's dark. We are guided

to our boat by a man who appears half asleep. Well, boat isn't accurate. It's a freaking yacht that is way too big for two people. We walk on deck. Fortunately, the lights are on inside. And wow. It's nice. I'm surprised the agency sprang for this, considering all I've been hearing about for the last year are cutbacks and budget reductions.

"Check this out," Gray says.

I follow his voice. He's in the kitchen. On the counter is a bucket with a bottle of champagne in it. The ice has melted. Presumably, since we didn't make it here till late.

"There's a note. *Congratulations on your new marriage. We hope you have the best honeymoon, Paradise Rentals.* Shall we crack it open?"

I shrug. "Sure, why not. Any chance there's food here?" I begin opening cupboards in search of anything.

"If not, I packed some protein bars."

I search everywhere and come up empty.

"Here's another note," he says.

I walk over to where he's standing next to the kitchen table.

"Someone is bringing groceries in the morning when they come to do a daily service."

Gray pops the champagne and pours us each a glass. Then he fishes in his bag and pulls out a protein bar for me. I pull out a map of the marina and discover we are in the slip next to Ivan's.

"Well, I guess we will be able to keep a better watch than the guys," Gray says.

We go back on the deck and take in the clear night and stars.

"To us," he says.

I turn my attention to him. He's holding up his glass. I clink it with mine, and we each take a drink. He catches me off guard by setting down our drinks and pulling me into his arms.

"Dance with me. I think Ivan is watching," he whispers.

I place one hand on his shoulder and am about to grab his hand when he chuckles and pulls me tight against him.

"We're supposed to be newlyweds, not cousins dancing."

Now, if it isn't obvious, I don't really have a lot of experience with men. I was with Caleb for a few years, but other than that, I really haven't dated much. And I can't say I've ever slow danced with a guy.

"You all right?" he whispers into my ear.

His breath on my neck, along with his arms around me, has me more turned on than I've ever been. I manage to nod in response.

After our dance, he steps back. "Let's go check out the rest of the cabin," he says, taking my hand.

Once we are back in the kitchen, he turns to me.

"I'm sorry. I didn't mean to make you uncomfortable."

I take a great interest in the floor. "It wasn't that. I just don't really know how to slow dance."

He pulls me to him again. "It's easy. All you do is get really close to me and sway." He moves us side to side. "You never danced with a guy before?"

I shrug. "I've danced with a cousin but not a date or anything."

He whistles. "I just don't see how that's possible. I imagine all the guys in your school had a crush on you."

I snort. "Hardly."

He cocks his head. "I suspect you just didn't notice."

My cheeks tingle at his compliment. "No, I wasn't popular. I was more into books than people. And after I joined the agency, I haven't had too much of a social life. I've only had one real relationship, and we didn't dance."

Without warning, he dips me, and I hold on to his shoulders tightly. "Well, you're in luck because, in our relationship, we dance. You'll be a pro before you know it."

When he pulls me back upright, our mouths are mere inches from each other. He stares at my lips, and for a moment, I think he's going to kiss me. But instead, he steps back and scratches his head.

"We should check out the rest of the boat."

"Good evening!" a voice booms from outside.

We step onto the deck and spot a tall man wearing a white button-down and white pants.

"You must be Mr. and Mrs. Timmons."

Gray steps forward. "Yes, we are."

It's at this moment that I realize I have no idea what his last name is. That strikes me odd. At the agency, we all go by our last names.

"I'm your attendant while you stay here. You can call me Haynes. As you know, the boat must remain docked during your stay per your agreement. If you need anything at all, you can contact me. Here is my card, and I work out of the marina's office building up there." He points up the dock. "Let me give you a quick tour."

Must remain docked? What if Ivan goes somewhere? I guess CT will have to be on call for that purpose.

"Why does it have to remain docked?" I ask.

Haynes turns to me, frowning. "A ship this size requires a captain, and that option was specifically declined in your reservation. Do you not remember making the reservation?"

Gray pulls me into his arms. "Actually, my parents made the reservation as a wedding gift, so we aren't fully aware of all the details."

Haynes's smile returns. "Of course. That makes sense. It was requested there be no captain or crew onboard during your stay."

"That's fine," I say. "But can we do the tour tomorrow? I'm afraid we're very tired."

Haynes gives a tight smile. "Yes, of course." He begins to walk toward the deck but turns back. "You can call me at any time. Otherwise, I'll see you at seven when I deliver the groceries."

"Perfect," Gray says.

We wander down the hallway. "Two bedrooms. Shall we each pick one?" Gray asks.

"Uh. I'm afraid we will have to stay in the same one. We don't know if Haynes will tell anyone the newlyweds aren't sharing a bed and if Ivan found out..."

He frowns. "How would Haynes know if we didn't share a room?"

"Well, I wouldn't put it past him to check in on us or if we sleep too late. Plus, if he's buying our groceries, I guarantee you someone is coming on board to make the beds."

"You're right." He smiles. "Let's go find the largest room."

He takes off deeper inside. I follow him into what must be the master bedroom. It's large and has its own bathroom attached. The bed is, fortunately, a king, which means we will have plenty of room.

We get ready for bed and slip under the covers.

"You good?" he asks.

I nod, and he turns off his lamp.

Suddenly in the dark with him near me, I'm not so tired.

"Gray?"

"Yeah?"

"What's your real last name?"

He laughs. "Walsh"

"Grayson Walsh. I like that." I turn on my side to face him. "Thank you again for saving me that night."

He's silent for a moment, and I wonder if he fell asleep.

"When I heard you were captured, I insisted on going. But nothing prepared me for actually seeing you. When I walked in, before you saw me, your eyes were vacant."

I swallow. "I didn't think anyone would be coming to save me in time. I figured I had to save myself."

"You could have kicked all their asses."

I laugh. "Yeah, but that would have given away the mission."

"You mean like my trying to rescue you and failing did?"

"That might have clued them in."

I like this, joking around with him. Before all this, he barely spoke a few words to me. I thought it was because he just didn't talk much, but now I see he just has to get comfortable with me.

"I really enjoyed our texts over the last month or so."

His words cause my stomach to flutter. "Me too."

"This isn't a come-on, but I really enjoyed cuddling with you in the forest, too."

Now my body is tingling all over at the memory. "Me too."

"If you get cold, I'm here for you."

"I'll keep that in mind," I say, now wishing I had turned the air conditioning on high.

"Good night, Cara."

"Good night, Grayson."

CHAPTER NINE

Grayson

DESPITE BEING TIRED, I, unfortunately, didn't sleep well. And it was due to the fact Cara was sleeping next to me in some sort of skimpy pajama short set. When she first came to bed wearing that, I wasn't sure what to think. But somehow, I managed to drift off after lying awake for several hours.

Well, until seven this morning when Haynes came into the bedroom to wake us. Yes, he walked right in. He had questions about what we wanted for breakfast.

Apparently, in addition to delivering groceries, he thought he'd be kind to make us breakfast. I was too tired to argue, but I'll have a talk with him later.

We can't have a stranger walking into our bedroom. I mean, if we really were newlyweds, I would have had her bent over the dresser, or the lounge chair, or up against the wall. Fuck. My imagination ran wild all night. This was all I could think about.

But I need to stay focused. Even though this appears to be an easy assignment, we are dealing with dangerous men. And if they figure out who we really are, they won't take it well that we are set up next door.

DANIELLE PAYS

That's right, we verified Ivan is in the slip next to us when we saw him this morning. Yes, I told Cara I saw him last night. I saw a shadow, and it could have been him. But really, I was just dying to hold her.

After the rude awakening at seven, I went for a run. First, I needed to blow off some steam. But second, and more importantly, I wanted to learn the lay of the land, or in this case, the marina.

On my way back, I spotted Ivan eating at the marina's restaurant with another man I did not recognize. While changing out the song on my phone, I snapped a photo. It's not great, but hopefully, it's good enough for Trip to identify the other man. Trip doesn't work in Seattle, but he's our go-to for finding anyone through security cameras and the use of credit cards, and he is the best at reverse image searching. That's why I'm certain he'll figure out who this guy is.

As I walk the dock back to our boat, I take in as much information as I can. Most of the boats appear to be unoccupied. I step onto our deck and spot Cara sitting in a lounge chair, reading something on her phone.

"Hey, I'm going to shower before breakfast."

She smiles. "Sounds good."

I go inside to our bedroom and lock the door. I'm actually surprised the door has a lock, but I am happy to find it.

I shower and put on a T-shirt and shorts, then join Cara on the deck. Haynes made us an omelet that is fantastic, and the view is stunning. To think some people live like this all the time. Hell, I want to live like this. Well, the view part. I could take or leave the large boat.

Cara stares at the yacht next to us.

"He's at the restaurant having breakfast with another man," I say before taking a sip of my orange juice.

Cara turns to me. "Any idea who the other man is?"

I grab my cell and pull up the photo I took. "I sent this to Trip. Hoping I hear from him soon."

Cara takes the phone from my hand and stares at it. "I don't recognize him. Did they know you snapped their photo?"

74

I arch a brow at her. "Of course not. I was switching songs as I jogged."

She smiles. "Where did you go?"

"Around the restaurant and through the small town. I finished by walking the docks. No one was really out yet."

We finish our breakfast.

"You know, we need to talk to Haynes about just waltzing into the bedroom," I say.

She nods. "Yes, I was thinking that, too. What if we were discussing things?"

I lean back and stretch my arms over my head. "I'll let him know how much you love morning sex and not to barge in on us again."

She reaches over and slaps my stomach, which causes me to laugh. But when I glance at her, all I see is the heat in her eyes. For a moment, a crazy thought enters my mind. What if I lean over and kiss her? But before I can think too hard about it, she stands up.

"We need to get ready."

"Ready for what?"

She leans in close enough I can smell her lotion. Coconuts. Maybe it's sunscreen. Whatever it is, it's intoxicating.

"Apparently, Ivan left his boat to have breakfast, and neither one of us knew that until you literally ran past him. We can't have him out of our sight again. Let's be ready to head out if we need to."

I nod and lean back. "I'm ready."

She rolls her eyes. "I'm going to change shoes. I'll be right back."

I glance down and notice she's wearing flip-flops. I chuckle because, knowing Cara, she could still outrun most guys in those things.

While she's inside, I check my messages.

CT: *Have fun last night?*

I roll my eyes and reply.

Me: *Asshole.*

There's a missed message from Cara earlier this morning.

I read through it. It states Ivan goes to a local market every morning and walks on the beach every afternoon. The message was sent to all of us down here. But I'm left wondering what else Cara knows about Ivan that she isn't telling me.

When she reappears, it's hard to stay mad at her. Her long hair is flowing in the wind instead of pulled back like it usually is. And on her feet are sneakers.

"What's wrong?" she asks as she sits next to me. "You get a line right here," she touches the spot between my eyebrows, "when you're in deep thought."

I grab her hand and bring it to my lips, kissing it gently. Her eyes widen as she watches me. Yes, the reaction I was hoping for.

"I'm sorry. I guess I'm a little on edge today," I tell her.

She continues to stare at her hand that I'm still holding, but instead of calling me out on it, she goes in an unexpected direction. "Don't worry. We'll work off that tension." The moment the words fall from her lips, she turns away.

I grin. "Oh, we will, will we?"

She shakes her head. "I meant with all the walking and sightseeing we'd be doing today."

I continue to grin, enjoying the moment. Her cheeks are flushed. She shifts uncomfortably in her seat.

"We need to focus on why we're here," she says. And she's right.

I need to keep my mind focused. I release her hand. "You're right. I'm sorry."

Her brows knit together, and she sighs. "I'm sorry. I'm not good at mixing professional with personal. When I'm on the job, my mind stays in that place."

I nod. I truly understand that. We have to stay focused to stay alive.

"But," she continues, "in our case, part of the job is getting personal." She stands, and I stand, too. Then she kisses my cheek. "Maybe we'll keep it PG up on deck."

I wrap my arms around her. "And below deck?" Shit. I wince. I did it again. "Sorry."

She laughs. "No, it's fine. I like this side of you."

Out of the corner of my eye, I notice someone coming down the dock. I glance up and spot Ivan moving toward his boat with a phone to his ear. He's speaking a language I'm not familiar with.

Cara stiffens in my arms as she leans in. "He's meeting someone at three this afternoon on the beach."

I stare at her, and she shrugs.

"How many languages do you speak?" I ask her quietly.

"Four or five, depending on how fluent you mean."

I lean down and whisper into her ear. "I'm going to share that information with the guys. I'll be right back." I touch our noses, and she laughs.

"Well, that's not going to work if you find it funny."

She drops her smile. "Sorry, you're right."

I smile at her. We're both struggling to walk this professional and personal line. Maybe she should have partnered with Thunder. At least we'd all be focused. Although, who am I kidding? I'd probably be a jealous mess.

I go inside and send a text to the guys about what Cara heard. Then I relax in a lounger next to Cara on the deck, playing a game on my phone.

Ivan exits his boat and wanders up the pier. Cara turns to me, but before she can speak, a text from Fox comes in.

Fox: *We got this. We'll let you know where he goes.*

I show Cara the text. "Guess we wait."

"Okay, we wait."

A little while later, another text vibrates my phone.

Fox: *He's at the local market.*

I show Cara this message, too, and we head out.

As we approach the market, I spot Thunder, Lightning, CT, and Fox standing outside, talking with a vendor. Once they spot us, they end their conversation and stroll toward the beach.

Ivan is near the front of the store at a flower stand. Cara wraps her arm around mine as she leads us in his direction. "I'd love some fresh flowers. Why don't you buy me some, honey."

There's humor in her gaze. "Of course, babe. What would you like?"

She points to one of the bins of flowers, and I grab the bouquet.

"Young love. Such a precious thing." Ivan smiles at us. "I was in love once. I miss her terribly. Enjoy each other while you can."

"We will. Thank you," I say as I lead us away from the stand.

"Why did you pull us out of there? He was talking to us."

Once we are farther away, I turn to her. "And he'll talk to us more once he discovers this lovely couple is in the boat next to him. We can't push too fast."

She gives me a fake smile as we pay for our items and leave. Once we cross the street, she spins to face me.

"Too fast? We're supposed to collect as much intel as possible in a couple of days. At this rate, we'd need months." She throws her hands into the air.

I step into her space and pull her into my chest. "We're deep in love, not arguing on the street. And yes, I'm aware of our time limitations. But if we do anything to tip him off, we won't gain *any* intel. I'm already wondering if showing up at the beach this afternoon is too much."

She bites her lip. "What are you suggesting?"

I shrug. "Maybe the guys should be on the beach without us."

She stares off in the distance. "Well, that would give us the option of going to wherever the guys follow him to next if he doesn't come back to his boat." She sighs. "But I really want to hear what he's discussing. What if it's a language they don't know?"

I reach out and put my hands on her shoulders. "They aren't going to be able to get close enough to hear his conversation. Short of sneaking a wire onto Ivan somehow, the best we can do is get photos of the man for Trip to search."

"Have you heard back on the breakfast guy yet?"

I shake my head. "I hope he finds something soon. With

the party tomorrow night and possibly two unknown men involved, I'm nervous about our plan."

A plan that Cara worked out with Thunder and Lightning. CT and Fox agreed with it, and so did I, although with more hesitation than the rest. They all believe it will work. But I've seen enough in my life to know things don't always go according to plan. If they did, my brother would be in a very different place.

Wow, where the hell did that come from? My brother left a voicemail before I left, and I still haven't called him back. He knows what I do and why I can't call, but that won't stop him from making me feel like shit about it.

"Are you all right?"

I glance down to see concern in her eyes.

"Your body tensed."

I kiss her forehead in case Ivan is still around and because I want to. "I'm fine. We need to tell the guys we won't be joining them at the beach."

She pulls out her phone. "Got it." She types up a message, then smiles at me. "Let's go back to the boat."

We head to the boat in silence. I study her. She's staring at the ground, something she never does. When we reach the boat, she heads inside. I need some time alone to get my head on straight. Anytime I think about my brother, it knocks me off kilter.

To my surprise, there's a guitar sitting on the deck with a note.

Thought this might help you woo the girl. CT

I laugh. "What an asshole." But the truth is I appreciate the thought. Playing relaxes me, and right now, it's exactly what I need.

I strum a few familiar songs while the ocean breeze blows, cooling me off.

During the entire last song, my phone is buzzing in my pocket. I finally give up and check it.

I have messages from Trip and CT.

Trip: *Got an ID. Justin Bace. It's his son-in-law.*

Ivan has kids?

CT: *At the beach. He's meeting this guy.*

A photo comes in. It's the same guy from the restaurant this morning.

Cara: *That's the guy from this morning.*

Me: *Yes, it is. Trip just came through. The guy is Ivan's son-in-law, Justin Bace.*

Cara: *What the hell is he doing here? Ivan's daughter has refused to talk to her father for years.*

Thunder: *Maybe he's trying to mend the relationship.*

Fox: *Okay, but why meet at the beach and not on Ivan's boat?*

CT: *Maybe the guy gets seasick.*

Cara: *Maybe. Until we know for certain, we should find out where this guy is staying and what he really wants.*

CT: *I'll follow him.*

Cara steps out on the deck, holding her phone. "Why can't any of this be easy? Too many loose ends." Then she spots the guitar. "Where did you get that?"

"Gift from CT."

"Interesting."

I lean back. "He wants me to use it to woo you."

She grins. "You think that will work?"

I meet her gaze. "I hope so."

CHAPTER TEN

Grayson

I wake up with my arms around a sleeping Cara. I smile, not wanting to move. But today is the big day. I didn't sleep as well as I needed to because something has been eating at me. I'm not sure what it is, so I slowly untangle myself from Cara. It's a miracle she didn't wake.

Five minutes later, I'm up on the deck, tying my shoelaces. One thing I do love about this place is the view. I jog along the shoreline, enjoying the morning breeze off the ocean. Most people aren't up yet. I take advantage of the quiet to go over our plan. The party is tonight, and we are certain this is when Ivan will make the exchange for the weapon. The problem is we don't know exactly where the deal will go down. And we need to capture him in the act of selling the firearm.

If he can pull it off at the party, he'll have a whole house full of people as alibis should he need it. But how the hell will he get the weapon there without detection?

Fuck, it would help if we had some idea what this weapon was or, at the very least, the size of it.

My gut says a man like Ivan would never make a deal like

this at a party. The man and his brother, Alex, have never been caught dealing, only suspected. They also aren't known for attending parties, especially parties for wealthy diplomats.

Everything about this feels wrong. I stop jogging and pull my phone from my pocket. I call Fox.

"Hello?" he answers.

"It's me. I've been thinking about tonight."

"Me too. It doesn't feel right."

"Agreed."

Fox sighs. "Guys like this operate in secrecy, not out in the middle of a large party."

"Cara did say this could be his alibi."

"I think that's more likely. We'll have to make sure we never lose eyes on him tonight," Fox says.

A loud motor cuts off his last words.

"What's that?" I ask.

"I'm not sure. Let me go up on deck." The patter of his feet on the deck comes through the phone. "Oh shit."

"What?"

"Ivan's boat just pulled away."

I turn around and begin jogging back to the marina. "I'm out on a run. Can one of you guys stay with him?"

"Unfortunately, not. Thunder and CT are out on the dinghy, scoping out the house where the party will be held tonight."

"Call them," I shout, then shove my phone into my pocket.

Something feels wrong. These aren't boats you just take out on a whim. No, this was planned.

By the time I make it back to our yacht, sweat is pouring down my back. "Cara!" I call out, but there is no reply.

The empty slip beside us is a reminder that we were caught off guard. Why the hell don't we have a dinghy?

I race inside the cabin. "Cara?"

No answer. I sprint back up to the deck. A flash of light catches my eye, and I race to it. Her phone is under the lounge chair. She wouldn't go anywhere without it. I grab it as I scan the deck. One of her flip-flops is upside down over by the far bench. Shit.

I run down the dock to CT's boat and jump onboard. "Cara's gone. Her phone and one flip-flop were on the deck.

"You think Ivan took her?" Fox asks.

"You got any other theories?"

CT and Thunder pull up in the dinghy. I yell down at them. "Ivan has Cara."

Thunder jumps up onto the deck and points to the empty slip. "Where the hell is he?"

"We don't know. He pulled out of here at least twenty minutes ago," Fox says.

"Why the hell didn't you radio us?" Thunder asks.

Fox tosses his hands in the air. "I tried."

Lightning comes out from the cabin rubbing his eyes. "What's going on?"

"Ivan sailed away with Cara."

Lightning darts to the side of the deck, seeing the empty slip. "Ah fuck. How'd he make us?"

"No idea. Let's go!" I yell, trying to get into the dinghy.

"Where?" CT asks. "Once you're out of this bay, we have no idea which way they turned."

We scan the horizon. There are many boats around, but none that we can say for certain are Ivan's.

"Shit! Why would he take her?" I ask.

Thunder gives Lightning a knowing look.

"What?" I'm in Thunder's face, but at this point, I don't care.

Thunder rubs his temples. "The only reason he would take her is if he made her. Where the hell were you?"

Now he's in my space.

"I went out for a run to clear my head."

Thunder narrows his eyes. "Did you go out yesterday too?"

"Yeah."

"Same time?"

"Shit. He was on to us the entire time?"

"Appears that way. Hell, this is Cara. She always carries a

knife at her ankle. If it gets too crazy, she can take care of herself."

I fall onto the bench on deck. "She was having coffee on the deck. Would she have the knife if she was simply relaxing?"

Thunder sits farther down the bench. "Cara doesn't relax. But whether she's armed or not, we need a plan."

Lightning holds up his phone. "Already on it. I asked Trip to see if he can find if any plan was filed for Ivan's yacht or if he can find it at all."

I jump up because I can't sit still. Ivan wouldn't file any plan. No, he grabbed Cara and is doing God knows what. "We're wasting time. We need to get in that dinghy and start searching."

Fox comes up to me. "And if we find his boat, then what? He'd see us coming."

"Yes, but at least we'd know where she is. What if he throws her over? We could at least save her."

Visions of Cara being tossed overboard go through my mind. I imagine her tied up in the cabin, being tortured, and who knows what else.

"Stop."

I glance up, and Lightning has his hands on my shoulders.

"I can see you visualizing all sorts of things. We all know you two have feelings for each other, so I need you to put those aside and remain objective, all right?"

I nod. He's right, but damn, it's hard to stop the images floating in my head.

"Now, they've only been gone twenty minutes. Ivan is likely trying to get as much distance from us as he can, which means she's probably locked in a bedroom. Throwing her into the ocean wouldn't benefit Ivan."

I back away from Lightning. "How would you know? Do you have any idea why he took her?"

He doesn't respond.

"No, you don't. I know you're trying to make me feel better, but unless we know something for a fact, I don't want to hear it."

"Peaches is right," Thunder says. "We need to focus on the facts."

Lightning holds up his phone. "Trip says no sailing plans were filed."

"Fuck!" I yell. Even though I knew there wouldn't be, I'm still frustrated. *Where the hell are you, Cara?* I stare out into the ocean.

"Everyone, inside the cabin. We need to talk privately," CT says.

We all shuffle inside. It's definitely nicer than the one we're staying on, and that's saying something.

"Everyone sit," CT demands.

"This better be fast," I say as I reluctantly sit.

CT places his phone in the middle. It rings.

"It's Stormy."

"Stormy, we're all here."

"Good. CT filled me in briefly on what happened. I got Harding's boss, Anderson, on the line as well."

"Hey, guys," Anderson says. "What do we know?"

We fill him in, which really isn't anything CT hadn't already told Stormy.

"Stay put," Anderson says. "I have a special team I'm calling in. They'll be coming out of San Diego, so they might not make it there until tomorrow."

"Tomorrow? That's too late," I say.

Fuck, this is her boss. Why isn't he rushing this?

"I'll do the best I can," Anderson says. "We'll be in touch."

There's a click indicating he left the line.

"I agree with Anderson. I'll find out who this team is he's bringing in and let you know. In the meantime, I'll make sure this is Trip's top priority. I'll update you as soon as I know something."

He ends the call before we can complain.

I jump up. "I'm not going to sit here and do nothing."

Lightning stands, too. "I agree."

CT nods. "Why don't you two take the dinghy out and see if you can find anything? If you do find Ivan, call us immediately. Got it?"

"Got it." Lightning says.

"Where did you say her phone is?" Thunder asks.

I pull it out of my pocket. "It was on the deck. I grabbed it."

Thunder takes it from me. "I'll see if I can get anything off of it." He heads out of the cabin.

Lightning and I hop in the dinghy and take off.

An hour later, we've passed many boats, but none of them are Ivan's. He must be moving fast.

"You really like her, don't you?" Lightning asks.

I shift uncomfortably. I'm unclear how close Cara is to Lightning.

"She likes you, too."

I stare at him. "She said that?"

He shrugs. "Not to me but to Thunder. She hasn't really dated much since Caleb."

"Caleb?"

Lightning frowns. "She hasn't told you about him yet?"

I frown. "No."

"She will. He was Thunder's brother. That's why they're so close."

I don't miss his use of past tense. Instead of asking him about it, I'll wait until Cara is ready to tell me.

"But I think you two would be good together," he continues.

I clench my fists. "We need to find her first."

Lightning grins. "Never underestimate Cara. She's more capable than any SEAL I've known."

We pass the last vessel we can see.

"We should head back and see if the guys have anything," Lightning says.

I'm about to protest when he holds up his hand.

"If we keep going, we'll run out of fuel."

I stare at the engine and know he's right, so I nod and try to keep myself calm when I'm feeling anything but calm.

I sure as hell hope the guys have some news. Because I'm not sure what Ivan wants with her, but I don't think he'll just let her walk away freely.

CHAPTER ELEVEN

Cara

HOW THE HELL did Ivan figure out who I am? I mean, he must have since I'm locked in a bedroom on his boat going who knows where. Dammit! I'm angry at myself for being in that situation. I'm always on guard, but I laid back on the lounger in the sun and let the lull of the waves relax me. Hell, I never go anywhere without my knife strapped to my ankle. But the damn weather here is too hot to wear long pants.

When the first man put his hand over my mouth, I pulled him down and slammed him into the deck. But a second guy knew what he was doing. My hands and feet were bound before I could defend myself. He carried me to Ivan's boat. It was so early that no one was out to see what was happening.

And now here I am, no weapons, hell, hardly any clothes, and one flip flop, waiting for whatever terror Ivan has planned. I can't believe I thought I could relax. This is a job, and I need to be on at all times. They're probably taking me out to the middle of the ocean to dump me. That means I don't have much time to figure out how to get the hell out of here.

It's a small bedroom, but there is a dresser and night-stand. I go through each and find nothing. I sit on the bed. My gaze returns to the dresser. There's a mirror on top, and I stare at myself. Wait, a mirror.

The music is playing loudly from somewhere else on the boat, so they won't even hear it. I grab the blanket folded at the foot of the bed and wrap it around my fist. I punch the mirror, and it cracks. One more hit and a piece falls down. Perfect. I put the blanket back on the bed and stand near the door, waiting for someone to enter.

The music shuts off. Then the engine powers down. This is it. I wait, but no one comes for me. There's laughter outside. I open the window as far as I can. It only opens half-way, which isn't enough for me to squeeze through.

"When are you expecting him?" Ivan asks from the deck.

I strain to see out the window, but no one is in view.

"Maybe an hour or two. He travels on his own time, so it's hard to say," a man with a Costa Rican accent says.

"Well, I guess in the meantime, I should enjoy the party," Ivan says.

"Yes, of course. Let me get you past security."

Ivan comes into view, walking with a man I don't recognize. They're walking on a dock that leads to the back of an enormous house. A large balcony juts off the top floor, and several people are standing around, holding what appear to be flutes of champagne. Wait, the party is tonight. What is this? A celebration in the morning?

Several women near the edge start cheering, and that's when I realize they are piss drunk. Maybe things started early. I could figure that out if I could get out of this room and up to the house.

I strain to open the window to hear better, but it doesn't budge. The man who took me appears outside, staring at me. He places his hand on his gun.

I step back. I'm being watched. Well, if he thinks I'm going to sit here and wait for Ivan to return, he has another thing coming.

I scan the room again. Nothing in here I can throw at the

window. Oh, wait. I pull a drawer out of the dresser and throw it against the window. It cracks. I do it again. Another crack. Footsteps run down the hall in my direction. I grab the broken piece of mirror and position myself next to the door. It flies open, and without hesitation, I stab the man who tries to enter. He doubles over, and I jump over him. My hand hurts like hell. I spare a glance as I make my way through the cabin. Shit, the cut on my hand is deep. I grab a kitchen towel, wrapping my palm as I walk from the cabin. Apparently, Ivan didn't have any other men on board. I hop onto the dock and run to the house.

"Hold on there," a man says as he grabs me around the waist just inside the door. "What is your name? Are you on the list?"

The list? "No, I was kidnapped on that boat. I need to call for help."

The man stares over my head at the yacht. "Wait here." He pulls his cell phone out of his pocket and speaks in Spanish. He thinks I don't know what he's saying, but I do. And if he thinks I'm waiting here for Ivan to return to retrieve me, he's wrong.

While he's distracted, I run out the door and around the side of the house. I'm almost clear of the house when someone steps in front of me. I bounce back.

Ivan. Shit.

"Erica, where do you think you're going?" he asks.

Erica? That's the name I used when tracking Max. Speaking of Max, he steps up.

"Erica! I'm so happy to see you again. Ivan mentioned you were staying next to him. I asked that he bring you here today."

His words are sinking in. Ivan doesn't know I'm CIA? He thinks I'm the girl who escaped Max.

"You married your hero, did you?" Max asks.

Gray. What the hell game are these two playing?

"I need to get back. I'll leave you two," Ivan says, then steps away.

Max grabs my arm. Hard. Too hard. "Erica, it's time we

leave. And don't worry, I'll make sure someone takes care of your husband."

He yanks me toward the front of the house where cars are parked, but I dig in my heels. Max leans down and whispers, "If you make a scene, I'll order your hero to be killed."

Shit, they caught me off guard. Could they have Gray, too? I willingly go with him as he leads me to a car. My hand is throbbing from the cut as Max pushes me into the back seat. He gets in behind me.

"To the house," he tells the driver.

The car pulls away, and I scan everything around me. Unfortunately, I don't see anything that will help me get out of this situation.

"That's a nasty cut you have," Max says. "I'll make sure Trudy takes care of it for you."

Trudy. I guess she travels with him. That was another person I never wanted to see again. But I do have one advantage; they don't seem to suspect I'm nothing more than a woman caught in the wrong place at the wrong time.

"Tell me, Erica, was your hero the boyfriend you were supposed to meet at the cafe in Chile?"

I nod.

"Huh. I've been very curious about one thing."

I turn to stare at him. He's watching me closely.

"How did he find you? I flew you to another country, and we were in the home of a friend."

A friend the CIA had under observation. But I keep my mouth shut. When I don't respond, he continues.

"I pondered on that for quite a while. You see, we take care to make sure we aren't followed. And I think I finally figured it out." He grabs my wrists, his tight grip causing my cut hand to throb even more. "You have some sort of tracking device in you, don't you? Is it in your wrists?"

I frown. A tracking device inside me? Is this guy watching too many sci-fi movies?

"Is it?" he asks again.

"No. I don't have any tracking device."

He pulls a knife out of his pocket and opens it. "Are you sure? Because if I dig around in there and find one, I'm going to get very angry, Erica." He presses the knife to my wrist.

"No, there's no tracking device!" I shout.

He nods. "Well, tell me how this boyfriend of yours found you."

I think back to the day I woke up and was told I was in Chile. My backpack was there, out of reach, but it was there.

"It was sewn into my backpack." *Please believe that.*

Max folds the blade and returns it to his pocket. "Thank you for telling me. I suspected as much. Now what I need to know is why a woman simply traveling with her boyfriend would have a tracker in her backpack?"

I take a breath, trying to remain calm. Then I turn to him. "There is a tracker in all of my luggage. The airlines have lost my bag a few times, and I didn't want it to happen again."

That's actually true and something I do. Thunder laughed when he found out, calling it a bit excessive. This from the man who never checks luggage.

Max cocks his head. "That's actually a brilliant idea." He glances out the window. "We're almost there. We're going to my house. Trudy will fix you up. Tomorrow we will fly back to Brazil. And at the next party, I want you to smile more. Got it?"

Max is staring at me, waiting for my answer. Is this man for real? I stare at him with anything but a smile.

I don't see it coming. His hand smacks me across the face. Damn, that stings.

"Erica, when I say smile, you smile. Understand?"

I nod.

"Good, now show me you're happy to be here."

I turn my gaze to his and give him a fake smile. The driver stares ahead, not paying us any attention. Clearly, he isn't here to help me.

I need to find a way out of this situation and fast. But with my hurt hand, I don't think I can overpower Max to get his knife. No, I need to wait for another opportunity. And I have to hope like hell he doesn't drug me again. Because if I end up back in Brazil, I don't think Gray can save me a second time.

CHAPTER TWELVE

Grayson

"You're going to wear a hole in my damn floor. Can you sit still?" CT grumbles.

I stop pacing. "Cara is out there, possibly being tortured or worse." I ball my fists and try not to let my mind wander to the worse part. "No, I can't sit still."

"Well, where's your damn fidget spinner?" CT asks. "You're driving me crazy."

My phone vibrates on the kitchen table, and all eyes are on it.

"Trip, I'm turning it on speakerphone. Please tell me you have something."

"I do. I called all my contacts down there, and Ivan's boat has been spotted. It's at a dock of a private home."

He gives us the address, and I thank him. I'm about to hop in the dinghy when CT gets a call from Stormy.

"Hey, I just spoke to Anderson. Apparently, there's a team of SEALS already in Costa Rica, and they are headed your way."

"How soon?" I ask.

"They'll be there in under ten."

I growl out of frustration.

"Peaches, you are to wait for them, understand?" Stormy demands.

I want to scream. She could be killed in ten minutes. Now that we have the location, we need to get there.

Thunder walks to me. "Hey, I want to get her now as well, but we need a plan."

I sigh. "I don't like it, but I understand."

"Good. Now the guys who are coming—"

"Stormy, what the fuck sick joke is this?" Rover yells in the background. "Those chocolates of yours are full of maggots!"

CT scrunches his face in disgust. "Boss, you brought in maggot chocolates as a joke?"

"That might be a bit much," Fox adds.

Stormy sighs. "No, I didn't bring them in. They were in the kitchen when I got here. They're probably old. Just throw them out. And Rover, don't interrupt one of my calls again!"

"Who cares about the fucking chocolates," I mutter.

"Sorry, the men who are coming, you know them," Stormy explains.

"Hell, yeah, they know us," a familiar voice says.

We all turn to find Rocco grinning at us from just outside on the deck. Next to him stands Gumby, Bubba, and Phantom. Now I'm smiling from ear to ear. If anyone can help us extract Cara safely, it's these guys.

We all exchange quick greetings, then sit down and devise a plan.

"This house is an hour away by boat and forty-five minutes by car," Bubba explains as he holds up a map on his phone. "One team will go on this dinghy and the other in our SUV."

"I'm going in the car," I say. The sooner I get there, the better.

Bubba nods as the rest of the guys divide into teams.

Rocco, Phantom, Fox, and Lightning join me while Bubba, Gumby, Thunder, and CT take off in the dinghy. The men barely fit in the damn thing.

Fortunately, their vehicle is a large SUV, so we aren't crammed inside. Rocco drives as Fox navigates. The roads are winding and Rocco is taking them fast, so I'm holding on tightly. Lightning grabs his phone and puts it to his ear.

"Hello?" he says tentatively. His brows shoot up. "Shit. Are you sure?"

I don't know what's going on, but I don't like it.

He nods. "I'll let them know. Text me the address." He ends the call.

"That was Anderson, Cara's boss. Apparently, they finally tracked down Max Acrile, the man Cara was following on her last assignment. He's here in Costa Rica."

Well, shit, is everyone in fucking Costa Rica?

"He's renting a house. Anderson is texting the address. He thinks it's likely Cara is being taken there."

"Based on what?" I ask.

"Max has no business here. Anderson said he's known for holding grudges, and after Cara ran out on him, he's likely holding one against her. Anderson's been having someone track him, worried he'd go after Cara."

I run my hand over my face. "And how the hell would Ivan know who she is or to call Max?" I ask.

Lightning is fidgeting with his phone, then holds it up to me. "These posters are up in Brazil. Max must have taken her photo at some point."

It's a black and white photo of Cara with the words, "Missing Woman." And a number to call. "Apparently, Max offered a reward to anyone who returned her to him. Max must have shared the photo with Ivan."

I clench my fists. If Max has her, if he has touched her, I'll kill him myself.

"Max's rental is on the way to this other house. We should stop by. Just in case," Lightning says.

Rocco glances at us in the rearview mirror. "How far is this place?"

"Ten minutes," Lightning says.

"Let's check it out," I say.

Lightning directs us, and we find ourselves driving down a narrow dirt road.

"It's about another block up. We should park and walk," Lightning says.

Rocco pulls the SUV into a field of long grass, and we all get out.

"Phantom and Fox, you two go that way and come up from behind," he points through the grass field. "Peaches—"

"Max knows what I look like," I tell him.

Rocco blinks. "Well, I don't think he's going to welcome any of us into his home, so it really doesn't matter as long as he doesn't see you coming. Now Peaches, you and Lightning go around that way." He points to the other side of the road, meaning we'll need to walk through a few yards to get to the house.

"I'll make my way up the main road. If she's in there, we swarm and grab her. Got it?"

"That's the plan? Swarm? What if they start shooting?" I ask.

Rocco frowns at me. "Phantom will get her out. Trust me."

I don't really have a choice. We all go off in the directions Rocco ordered, and as I get close to the house, I see the windows are all closed. There's nothing to indicate anyone is here except the car parked out front.

"Shit, that hurts!" someone yells from inside.

"That's Cara," I tell Phantom.

"You sure?" he asks.

"Sit still!" a woman yells from inside.

"Let me sew up my own goddamn hand!"

I smile, loving that she's yelling at someone—that means she's all right. "Yes, that's her."

We move closer. I can see the other guys coming up from the other way. Rocco is counting his fingers. We go in on three. But when he gets to two, a car comes tearing down the dirt road. We all duck into the long grass.

The vehicle pulls up in front of the house, and a man gets out. I lift my head just enough to see it's Ivan.

"What the hell is Ivan doing here?" I whisper to Phantom like he has any more idea than I do.

A woman screams from inside the house. Ivan is halfway to the front door, and he stops. His hand goes inside his jacket, and he pulls out a gun.

"You bitch!" the other woman yells.

Then the front door opens, and Cara runs out. Her right hand is bleeding, and she's barefoot.

Ivan draws his gun. Max runs after Cara, and Ivan lowers his weapon. We begin to move closer.

Before any of us can save her, Max reaches out and grabs her hair. Her body jerks back, and she falls to the ground. Max falls, too.

I get to them first. "Let her go," I shout.

Max doesn't release his hold on her hair but turns his gaze to mine. He smiles. "Well, well. It's the hero. Or husband, from what I've heard."

Ivan is still holding his gun, but it's aimed at the ground. "Ah yes, the husband." Ivan looks around, but he doesn't spot a car or any sign of where I came from. The confusion in his eyes is evident. "How the hell did you find her?" he asks.

I don't respond.

"I was right, wasn't I, Erica? You have a tracker somewhere in your body. How else could you explain it?" Max asks.

"A tracker?" Ivan asks.

"It's the only explanation for how this guy keeps finding her. She told me she had a tracker in her bag, but now, she has almost no clothes, no bag. It must be under her skin. But why?" Max's eyes dart in every direction. Fortunately, the other guys haven't moved, and he has no idea he is surrounded. "You're trying to lead them here, aren't you?" Max asks.

"Lead who?" Ivan asks.

Max drags Cara toward the house. "She knows who."

I step forward.

"No," Max says, stopping me in my tracks. "Ivan, you take care of this man. I need to find the tracker."

Ivan is staring at Max. "Where is this tracker?"

Max narrows his eyes. "Not sure. Could be her wrists, her shoulder; I'll cut until I find it. No one pulls this shit on me and gets away with it." Max then yanks her by her hair back into the house.

I have to get in there. But Ivan aims his gun at me. "Not so fast, Romeo. Tell you what, you tell me how you found this place, and maybe I won't kill you." He grins like he's having a good time.

I need to keep Ivan focused on me so he doesn't see Rocco coming up behind him.

"Max rented this house in his own name. It wasn't hard to track. Once my wife went missing, I thought maybe he might have her." It's bullshit, and he knows it.

Cara's going missing at the same time his boat leaves was too strong a coincidence for anyone to ignore, but I don't care because Rocco is now behind Ivan.

Before the man can make another move, Rocco has managed to disarm him and has him on the ground. I run inside the house with Lightning and Fox. Cara is in a kitchen chair, her hands and feet bound. A woman is on the floor, surrounded by blood. She's either dead or very close.

"Good news, Erica, I found a razor," Max says as he rounds the corner. He's staring at what he's holding and doesn't see me until my fist connects with his face.

The punch knocks him back but not down. I hit him again, and this time, he goes to the floor, and the razor he's carrying flies back. The blade flips end over end, and I watch it. The reality of what this man was going to do hits me full force, and the rage builds. I jump on top of him and hit him repeatedly. I lost count of how many times, and I don't stop until someone pulls me off of him.

"Peaches, that's enough!" Lightning shouts.

I'm standing now. Fox has a solid grip around my chest. I turn to Lightning and see something I've never seen in his eyes. Fear. I turn my gaze back to Max. He's unconscious, and there's blood all over the floor and the wall.

Then I look at Cara. She's staring straight ahead. Her expression is vacant.

"Cara," I say. She doesn't look at me. "Cara!"

Slowly her gaze moves to mine. We hold gazes as she blinks a few times. Her eyes well with tears. I want to go to her, but Fox is still holding me tight.

She mouths, "Thank you."

"Let's go outside," Fox says as he pulls me through the house.

The air hits me, and suddenly, my right hand is throbbing. I glance down, and my knuckles are cut up.

"What the fuck was that?" Fox asks.

I continue to stare at my hand. I've never in my life lost it like that. All this time, I've been so careful, so deliberate because I suspected this was inside me. Fox is staring at me, waiting for an answer. He doesn't know about my past, and I sure as hell am not going to fill him in now.

"I saw the razor blade he was carrying. When I thought about what he was going to do with it, I could only focus on stopping him."

Fox leans against the house. "Shit, Peaches. You can't lose control, not on assignment."

"Yeah," I say quietly. Deep down, I wonder if Fox hadn't pulled me off, if I would have killed that man. Hell, maybe I did.

"But I get it."

I turn to him. "You do?"

"I do. But it can't happen again, understand?"

I nod. Does he really get it? Can anyone? When I close my eyes, I can still hear my mom's screams and my dad's angry voice. Jasper is yelling for him to stop.

The SUV drives up, pulling me from my thoughts. Rocco and Phantom get out.

"I talked to Gumby. They had already made it to Ivan's boat, and no one was on it. But they did find something I'm sure you will find interesting," Rocco says.

"What's that?" Fox asks.

Rocco smiles. "A weapon Ivan planned to sell at the party,

and quite a few US military files he should not be in possession of."

"We got him?" I ask. "We have the evidence?"

Rocco smiles. "We do. And Ivan has been secured in the back of the car."

I glance in the back window and see Ivan hogtied.

Cara walks out of the house, leaning on Lightning. I walk over to take her in my arms, but Lighting puts out his hand to stop me.

"We need to get her to the hospital. The cut on her hand is deep, and she's lost blood. I think she's in shock."

That's when I notice she's quite pale, and her eyes are vacant again. "Let's go," I shout.

We all pile into the car. Cara is between Lightning and me, but she's leaning on him. I won't lie; I'm a jealous motherfucker right now. But she's not fully aware of what's going on, and she needs any support she can get.

Phantom and Fox are up front with Rocco. Ivan is tied up nice and tight in the space behind us.

Rocco pulls up at the hospital, and Lightning carries her into the emergency room with all of us on his heels.

"She's lost blood. Please help," he says.

A nurse pulls up a gurney, and Cara is placed on it.

"Cara, I'm here for you."

She's staring at the ceiling, her eyes still vacant. Then they close.

"We need to go *now*!" the nurse yells.

They run Cara back through double doors. I race after her but am stopped by a man.

"Sorry, sir, you can't go back here." He sees my hand. "You should check in and get that examined."

"Not until I know she's all right." I stare through the doors and watch as they hook monitors and machines up to her.

Several doctors are shouting orders while I stand there, feeling helpless.

CHAPTER THIRTEEN

Grayson

AFTER SPENDING a couple of hours in the waiting room, I'm about to go crazy. Thunder, CT, Bubba, and Gumby finally arrive.

"What's going on?" Thunder asks as he walks up.

I jump up and walk to the nurse. "I need to know how my friend is doing."

The nurse looks to her right, and my gaze follows. A man in scrubs is coming my way.

"You are the friend to the American?"

"Yes."

The guys have all walked up behind me.

"You are all her friends?" the doctor asks.

"Yes," we all say in unison.

He ushers us away from the nurse's station to a vacant corner of the waiting room. "Your friend is going to be fine. The cut on her hand is very deep, but there should be no permanent damage. We were able to sew it up."

"What about the loss of blood? Is that why she passed out?" I ask.

He crosses his arms. "She did lose some blood, yes. But

she was also drugged, from what we can tell. She came to and stated a man named Max had injected her with something. We've sent her blood in for testing, but it could be some time before we get the results."

Thunder tenses beside me at his words.

"Can I see her?" I ask.

"Not yet. Because she was given something against her will and because we don't know how her hand was hurt, the police will need to interview her first. After they are done, they will let you know if you can see her."

Thunder steps forward. "How long until the police arrive?"

The doctor smiles. "I can't say. This isn't a high priority for them, I'm afraid. But we'll let you know."

He gives us one last smile, then turns and heads toward the nurse's station and through the double doors.

"Shit. The last thing we need is the local police involved," Thunder says.

"The police will say if I can see her?" I stare down at my bloody knuckles. "They will think I did this."

Thunder grabs my shoulders. "It doesn't matter what they think. What matters is that Cara will be fine. We just need to get her and leave before the police arrive."

Bubba crosses his arms. "And how do you plan to do that?"

Thunder sits in a chair. "I don't know."

Rocco pockets his phone as he approaches us. "Our plane's gone," he says.

"What plane?" I ask.

"We were scheduled to leave, then we got the call from our commander about this." He waves his hand toward us. "The plane couldn't wait. They'll try to get something scheduled for tomorrow."

"Why were you guys down here?" CT asks.

Bubba smiles. "You know we can't tell you that. Just be happy we happened to be in the country."

"Okay, let's break her out," Phantom says as he claps his hands together.

"How?" I ask.

Phantom grins. He points to Lightning. "You flirt with the nurse over there and distract her." He points to me. "You go in her room and carry her out here. When we see them, we all run like hell."

"That's a shit plan," Rocco says.

Phantom shrugs. "Got a better one?"

The double doors to the back fly open. Gumby is carrying Cara, who is grinning. Fox is right behind him.

They run past us, but Fox turns around. "Let's go!"

We all take off behind him. Several of the guys follow Rocco to the SUV, but I stay with Gumby, who takes Cara to a van. I climb in after him. Thunder gets in the driver's seat.

"Where did you get this thing?" I ask.

"Don't ask," Thunder says.

After Bubba and CT pile in, Thunder pulls out of the lot.

"What the hell were you thinking?" Thunder asks Gumby.

"While you all were bickering about how we were going to get this done, we got it done," Gumby says.

As Thunder drives, I turn my attention to Cara next to me. I stare at the bandage on her right hand. I meet her eyes to find she's smiling at me. "How are you feeling?"

"Not bad. I think they gave me something." She leans over and hugs my arm to her body. "I can't wait for our date Grayson."

"Grayson?" Gumby asks.

"Yeah, it's his real name. It's really cool, isn't it?" Cara slurs.

Gumby laughs. "You better watch out, Grayson; Cara was definitely given something."

Thunder takes a corner fast which causes Cara to lean more into me, and her hand falls on my thigh.

"Oh, so strong," she says as she squeezes. Then her left hand begins to move up, but I grab it and hold it still.

"How long till we get somewhere?" I ask.

Gumby laughs. "Take your time, Thunder."

I glare at him, and he winks back.

Thunder glances in the rearview mirror. "What's going on back there?"

"Nothing. Where are we going?" I ask.

"I know a place," CT offers. "Stay on this road for a few miles. I'll call the other guys and tell them to follow us."

CT places the call and explains he knows a house we can crash at for the night.

"Who's house is it?" Thunder asks. "Because I don't want any more surprises."

CT grins. "No worries there. My parents own it."

Thunder glances at CT, who is in the passenger seat. "They own a house here, too? Damn, they are loaded, aren't they?"

CT shrugs and turns his attention out the window. In the years I've known this man, he never talks about his parents' money. You wouldn't know he is wealthy himself except that he often picks up the tab whenever he can trick us into letting him.

We turn off the main road and wind down a long driveway shrouded in trees. I'm not sure what I'm expecting as we approach, but it sure as hell isn't what's in front of us. Despite it being dark out, it's apparent this is more than a house.

"Fuck, this is a mansion," I say.

Thunder parks and CT turns to us.

"It's big enough for all of us until we come up with a plan to get out of this country."

Cara has fallen asleep, leaning on my shoulder. I hate to wake her, but we need to get inside and figure out a plan.

CT jumps out first and uses the keypad to get us in. Once inside, I carry Cara to a couch. The couch is part of one great space that also includes a large kitchen and dining room.

"There should be some protein or granola bars in the pantry," CT says.

Fox rummages around. "Found them."

"My parents keep a few items on hand in case they arrive after the stores close."

As we all eat a bar, I can't help but notice how clean the place is. "CT, how often does someone clean this place?"

CT shrugs. "No idea. Why?"

"It's very clean for an unused house."

"My parents were here last month. They probably hired someone to clean it after they left. Anyway, there are plenty of bedrooms, and we can stay here tonight. But in the meantime, we should figure out how the hell we are getting out of here," he says.

Fox walks into the kitchen. "Got that covered. Stormy is going to arrange a plane to pick us all up. Once he has the coordinates, he'll call back."

Rocco sits in a chair at the table. "Our commander is supposed to be arranging a plane."

Fox nods. "Stormy is aware and will coordinate with Anderson and your commander. I doubt we can go to an established airport without getting picked up by the police."

"Not to mention, it will be risky for us to all drive together, especially with a man bound and gagged," Rocco says.

"Do you really think the police would be looking for us?" I ask.

Rocco shrugs. "We don't know, so we have to play it safe."

I glance around. "Where's Ivan?"

Rocco smiles. "Still in the car. I figured once we had a plan, we'd bring him in here and secure him."

"We should bring him in now," Lightning says. "If I had that much time in a car, I'd have figured out how to get out of it by now."

Lightning raises a brow at Thunder. I assume that's some kind of dig about what happened to Thunder earlier this year. He was locked in a trunk and wasn't able to get out. Fortunately, he eventually escaped the men who took him, but it took considerable effort on his part.

Thunder shakes his head and steps up to me while keeping his eyes on Cara. "She'll be all right. She's been through worse."

I tense. The man is trying to make me feel better, but

right now, all I can think about is Max walking toward her with that razor blade.

"I wish we knew what Max drugged her with. She's out of it," I say.

"A bit handsy is what he means," Gumby says before he shoves another bar into his mouth.

I glance up at Thunder. He's studying me, and I want to be very clear with him. "I stopped her. I would never do anything inappropriate."

He crosses his arms. "You care for her?"

I nod. "Very much."

"Don't hurt her. She's been through hell already, and I don't mean this trip."

I nod again. Hurting Cara is the last thing I want to do. But after what I did to Max, she might not want anything to do with me. Hell, maybe I should walk away from her for her safety, but I don't think I could do that at this point. Does that make me a selfish bastard? I turn around, and Fox is staring at me.

"You okay?" he mouths.

I nod. I'm not about to have a heart-to-heart here.

Phantom walks to the kitchen table and spreads out a map. "I found this in a drawer. When we talk to Stormy, we can coordinate where the plane will pick us up. We all agree an airport won't work."

Everyone nods or grunts in agreement as we hunch over the map, trying to find a good location.

After arguing for fifteen minutes, Bubba finally stands up tall. "I'm telling you this location is our best choice for a pickup."

Between the scene at Max's rental house and stealing Cara from the hospital, we all feel certain the local police will likely be searching for us. To avoid any unnecessary confrontation, we map out a way to get there, avoiding main roads. It's still a risk.

CT calls Stormy, who arranges for a private plane to fly us back to Texas tomorrow morning. From there, we will all go our separate ways.

"Do you really think the police will be on the road looking for us? I'll bet they are waiting at the marina for us to return," CT says.

"Why would you think that?"

He shrugs. "Gut feeling. And the fact I have five missed voicemails from my parents."

"What do they say?" Lightning asks.

CT stares at his phone. "I haven't checked. My parents never call me, so five missed calls tells me someone likely called them."

Lightning frowns. "Don't you think you should check them? Maybe it has to do with this house."

"Fine," CT says as he plays the messages. His eyes widen as he listens. Finally, he pockets his phone. "Apparently, we triggered some security cameras in front of the house when we arrived. The property manager called the police to check it out. My parents called to let me know so I wouldn't be surprised when they showed up."

"So much for a good night's sleep," Lightning says. "Let's get moving."

Thunder nudges me. "I'll get Cara."

CT fills a backpack with the remaining bars in the pantry, and we head out.

The moment we step outside, we hear the sirens. As we run to the cars, the lights from the police cars come through the trees.

"We're blocked in!" Rocco yells.

"Let's go!" CT says.

We all follow CT into the woods. Fortunately, between the moonlight and the trees not being too thick, we're able to see each other.

After walking for a short time, we come across a river that blocks our path. Thunder sets Cara down. Her eyes flutter shut as she continues to sleep.

"We're about a half mile from the house," CT says. "We're going to have to find another way to get to our extraction point."

"Hey, where's Phantom?" Fox asks, glancing around.

"He'll catch up. He's assessing the situation back at the house," Rocco says.

"Cara's going to be pissed we left Ivan back there," Thunder says.

"Hopefully, the police detain him," Lightning says.

Phantom comes up from the trail. "There are two uniformed policemen. Another man was with them I didn't recognize, but once they set Ivan free, the man hugged Ivan. That same man also slashed the tires on both vehicles."

Guess we can't count on the police for help.

"Any chance that man was Max?" Rocco asks.

Phantom shakes his head. "No, I saw Max at the house. It's not him."

"Okay, we need a plan. It won't be long before they figure out we had to have gone into these woods," Rocco says.

He's right. It was our only other escape route.

"Based on what I remember from the map, we follow this river north for many miles before we will need to head west," I say.

"Your memory?" Gumby asks. "Can we trust that?"

I nod. "Photographic memory. Trust me."

The guys don't seem convinced until CT steps forward.

"If Peaches says he's got this, he does. Let's go," CT says as he leads the way.

I bend down to pick up Cara.

"No, I got her. You make sure we're going the right way," Lightning says as he lifts her over his shoulder.

I nod. It's going to be a long night of walking, and we will each be taking turns carrying her until the drugs wear off. Although she's not going to be able to really keep up with us until we get shoes on her.

As we walk, I'm alone in my head with my thoughts. I really need to know if Max lived or died. I check my phone, and since the trees are just skirting a residential community, I have service.

"I'm going to check in with Trip," I tell the group as we all keep walking.

"Hot Dog Haven at your service," Trip answers as music plays in the background.

I laugh. He always answers with some random business name.

"Hey, glad you're up. It's Peaches. I have a favor to ask."

The music shuts off. "I'm a night owl. Did you find Cara?"

"We did. A man named Max was about to torture her. That's why I'm calling. Max got injured when we were freeing Cara. I don't know if he survived. Can you check local hospitals and see what you can find? His name is Max Acrile."

There's a pause.

"Is there a problem?" I ask.

Trip sighs. "Well, what are the odds he's using his real name?"

"Good. He was unconscious when we left him and not able to lie."

"Ah. Got it. I'll see what I can find and get back to you."

"Thanks."

I pocket my phone and find myself walking next to CT. "He'll let us know if he finds out anything," I say.

"How are you dealing with that?" CT asks.

I glance over at him. "With what?"

He continues to stare in front of him. "What happened with Max? Fox filled me in."

This isn't something I want to talk about right now. "I'll deal with it."

"Will you?" he asks.

"What the hell does that mean?"

CT is silent for a moment, and I think he's going to ignore my question. But finally, he speaks. "Honestly?"

"I wouldn't want anything else," I say.

He nods. "Remember that night you told me about your parents?"

I nod, really not wanting to talk about this.

"Well, you were right; your past fucked you up. Believe me, if anyone here gets that, I do. And I can see you struggling with what happened with Max. Yeah, you lost control, and now you're second-guessing yourself. And you're questioning if you're good enough for Cara."

Well shit. That hit a little too close to home.

"How the hell?" I ask.

He shrugs. "I'm good at reading people. But here's the thing you need to remember. You didn't hit Max because of what your father did; it was because you care for Cara. Any of us would have done the same thing if he was about to torture our woman."

I cock my head. "And do you have a woman?"

CT's been into one woman for years, and I really wish he'd move on or man up and do what needs to be done.

"Nah. But that doesn't change what I'm saying." He turns to me. "And I don't want to see you doubt for a moment that you are good enough. You are one of the nicest guys I know. And I also know you have had a thing for that woman for a long time. And from what I can see, she feels the same way. So don't get in your head and fuck it up."

I chuckle. "Yes, sir."

"I mean it. I'll beat your ass if you screw it up."

"Like you could." I love CT, but the man could not beat my ass.

Gunshots fire from behind us.

"We need to get away from the river," CT says. "They probably know we're following it."

We all turn and go deeper into the woods and hope they don't pick up our trail.

CHAPTER FOURTEEN

Cara

I WAKE to discover I'm bouncing as I'm carried over someone's shoulder. I begin to panic but spot Thunder walking behind this man.

"Nice to see you finally awake," he says. "I bet Lightning's getting tired of carrying you." Now he grins.

"Hey," I say to Lightning.

He stops and lowers me.

"How are you feeling?" Thunder asks as he comes up beside us.

"Hungover." I rub my head. "And whatever they gave me for pain has worn off," I say, holding up my bandaged hand.

Phantom joins our group. "Hey, you're upright. That's great. But we need to keep moving."

"Can you walk on your own?" Lightning asks.

I take a few steps. "Ouch. Where are my shoes?"

"I have some." CT hands her a pair of shoes. "They belong to my mom, so I hope they work."

They are sandals with straps, so as long as they aren't too small, I can make them work. I slip them on and adjust them. "They're fine. Let's go."

We catch up to the other guys walking ahead of us as I try to ignore my throbbing hand.

Lightning glances back over his shoulder at me. "Do you remember what happened?"

I nod. "Max caught me after I tried to escape Ivan's boat. And again when I tried to escape the house." I remember he had my hair and jerked me back into the house. It hurt like hell. And Ivan was outside with the guys. "Where's Ivan?"

"He was in custody," Thunder says. "There was enough evidence found on his boat that he would have gone away for a long time."

"Past tense? Is he dead?"

"No. The police set him free as we were fleeing the house we were at. But don't worry, we'll get him," Thunder says.

Oh, I'll get him. After all these years following that man, I won't let him get away

"Cara, do you remember Max giving you a drug?" Lightning asks.

The memory comes back as we walk in the darkness of the woods. Fortunately, the moon is bright, and I can see my way.

"He forced a pill down my throat. I tried to spit it up, but then he poured water into my mouth, and I ended up swallowing it."

I turn my gaze to the sky as I remember his words. "He said I wouldn't feel a thing, but I'd know what he was doing."

A tear falls down my cheek, and I let it. "What did he do? I don't remember much after that."

Thunder takes my good hand. "We got there in time, Cara."

I turn my gaze to his and can see he's being truthful. "Good. Where is he now?"

Thunder narrows his eyes. "You don't remember?"

I was tied to a chair. Max left the room, but Grayson burst in.

"Gray was there."

"Yes."

"Where is he?"

"Up front with Rocco, leading us," Thunder says.

"He hit Max. That's the last thing I remember."

The group collects in a clearing and stops walking, and Lightning turns around to face Thunder and me.

"Well, that's a shortened version. After we left, we called the cops to pick up Max. We don't know what happened to him yet," Lightning says.

I swallow at the thought Max and Ivan are free. "We need to find him."

"We will," Lightning says.

I glance around and take in the fact that we are in the middle of the woods. "Where are we walking to?"

"A plane to take us out of here."

"No, we can't leave."

Thunder laughs. "Yeah, we need to leave. This whole assignment has been one big clusterfuck."

I step into the middle of the group. "No!" That grabs the attention of the others. "We can't leave until Max and Ivan are in custody."

Thunder puts his hand on my shoulder. "Our assignment was to capture Ivan. We have enough evidence to put him away. In the meantime, we need to leave, and you need to heal."

I step back to the path to go the way we came from. "You all can leave, but I'm staying. My job is not done."

I make it two steps before Thunder grabs my arm. Lightning is beside him.

"Cara, your cover is blown."

I cross my arms. "No, it's not. They all think I'm Erica, the girl who got away from Max. I can use that."

"The cops are searching for us. For you," Lightning says. "You killed two people."

Two? I remember the man on Ivan's boat. Oh, Trudy. Shit. They're right. A lot of people saw me at that party. And with the cut on my hand, I won't be hard to find.

"That's why we took you out of the hospital. They were going to bring the cops in to talk to you, and we couldn't let that happen," Lightning explains.

"Fuck!" I yell.

Thunder pulls me to him. "We need to be quiet. There's a group following us. They fired shots, but we think we lost them. For now."

I turn to Gray. "If we leave, we'll lose track of where they are."

"No, we'll regroup and come back with a solid plan," Gray says, taking my hand. "Right now, we need to get out of danger."

They're right, but the idea of losing these men again makes me sick. I'm tired of being so close, yet not close enough.

"If Max harms one more girl because we left him here, I won't be able to live with it."

The guys exchange a look. Thunder and Lightning are trying to protect me from something. But Phantom will be honest. I turn to him.

"Phantom, what aren't they telling me?"

His eyes meet mine. "We don't know if Max is dead or alive." He continues when he sees my frown. "Peaches didn't just hit Max. He kept punching him until Fox pulled him off. If he hadn't, Peaches probably would have killed the guy."

My eyes go to Gray's right hand as he's standing in the moonlight. That's why his knuckles are all cut up.

"He was out of control, Cara," Fox says.

Grayson is avoiding my eyes. He walks away from the group, and CT follows.

"How well do you really know him? I mean, I thought you two together was a good idea, but now I'm not so sure," Lightning says.

Thunder is now facing us.

"Do you agree with him?" I ask my friend.

Thunder shoves his hands into his pockets and stares out. He opens his mouth but closes it again.

"Spit it out," I say.

Thunder turns his gaze to mine. "I'm concerned that maybe we don't know him as well as we thought we did."

"It sounds like he was protecting me," I grit out.

Thunder nods. "Lightning was there, so he can tell you, but it was more than that."

"It was. He was completely out of control," Lightning says.

I understand they are concerned, but they weren't there in Brazil when Gray found me in that room with all those girls. And all those men gawking at us like we were all for sale. And Max, the sheer delight on his face when he brought me into that house. He gets off on hurting women. So frankly, if Grayson didn't beat the guy senseless, I would have.

I catch up to Gray. He turns as I approach but avoids my eyes.

"Look at me," I say.

He slowly tilts his head until our eyes are locked.

"I know what happened with Max. I understand. These guys weren't in Brazil. If the roles were reversed, I would have done the same thing."

He frowns as he takes my left hand in his. "No, you wouldn't."

I open my mouth to protest, and he puts his fingers to my lips.

"There are some things you don't know about me. Some things I wish weren't true, but they are." He takes a deep breath and stares into my eyes. There is a sadness there, and I know what he's going to say.

"No." I pull back. "If you are about to launch into some sort of 'you are too violent for me' bullshit, save it. I'm a fucking CIA agent. I've seen it all. You are one of the good guys, Grayson."

His brow shoots up, and I've caught him off guard. Good.

I press my finger to his chest. "After the shit we went through in Brazil, I know you're a good man. And like I said, if you hadn't gotten to Max first, I would have. He's a monster who needs to be stopped."

I'm suddenly lightheaded, and I sway, but he catches me. "Thanks. I think I'm just hungry."

"I can help with that," CT says. He shucks off his backpack and pulls a protein bar from it, then hands it to me.

Before he gets back to the bag, a monkey gets inside and grabs a couple of protein bars.

"Hey, shoo!" CT says.

"You gotta watch out for those monkeys. They'll take anything they can," Lightning says.

CT glares at him. "Thanks for the advice." He roughly zips up the pack and slings it over his shoulder.

"Thanks," I say. "Why aren't we walking?"

"Rocco went to see if we lost the guys following us," Phantom says.

We wait quietly until Rocco makes his way back.

"They stayed with the river," he says.

"We need to find a new path," Gumby says.

"There's more," Rocco says. "They were talking to someone on a walkie-talkie who said there's a hurricane warning in effect."

"A hurricane?" Gumby says.

"Afraid so. Which means they will be moving inland, so we need to move farther in, too."

"Are you sure?" CT asks. "They don't get hurricanes here."

"Well, apparently, one is coming tonight," Rocco says. He turns to me. "Do you think you can walk for a while?"

I nod.

"If she can't, I already said I'd carry her," Thunder says.

I'd argue with him, but the truth is, whatever drug Max gave me is having lingering effects, and I might fall over from exhaustion.

"It's settled. Let's head out," Rocco says.

We end up at a clearing. "There are some houses on the other side of this field. Hopefully, one is vacant, and we can take shelter there," Bubba says.

As we walk across the field, the faint sounds of a helicopter grow louder.

"Run!" Rocco yells.

We all take off across the field as fast as we can. Before we make it into the trees, a light comes out of the sky, followed by the sound of a chopper growing louder.

I try to run, but I'm too weak. Gray picks me up and

tosses me over his shoulder. I glance up; the light is getting closer to us. Then gunshots erupt from the sky. Gray and I are in the back, and he picks up speed.

"Where's Phantom?" Gumby yells.

Phantom replies from our left. "I'm here!"

The gunshots draw closer. Bubba runs past, going the wrong way.

"We got this. Come on, Phantom."

Both men crouch and aim their guns as we keep running deeper into the trees. After many shots, the helicopter bursts into a ball of fire. I lower my head onto Gray's back as Phantom yells to everyone.

"We got them."

A loud crash of metal-on-metal sounds in the distance in what I presume is the chopper going down. That field will be loaded with police soon.

CT calls out from the front, "There's a road."

I tap Gray on his back. "Hey, can you let me down now?"

He stops and lowers me to my feet. I'm lightheaded.

"You sure?" he asks as I sway in his arms.

I grin. "Yeah, I was upside down for a while; I just need to get my bearings."

"You know, I'll carry you the whole way."

I glance up to see concern in his eyes. "I know."

I turn and begin walking, and he follows. We come to a road and pass several houses. No one needs to say a word. We all know the farther we can get not only from the crash but also around this hill away from the ocean side, the better.

Rocco and his team lead us down a new dirt road. A dark house sits hidden by the trees. The grass is long, and some vines have grown over the front door.

"This is a good sign it's vacant," Rocco says, pulling away the vines.

CT holds up his phone. "My phone's dead. Anyone else have any battery left?"

"I do," Fox says. "And service. I'm going to call Stormy and check in."

We all know if the hurricane threat is real, there will be no plane coming for us.

One of the guys gets the door open, and we all go inside. I follow them into the kitchen. The counters are covered in dust. No one has been here in quite a while.

My hand is throbbing, and I rub my wrist as if that will help.

"Hey, let's see if we can get you cleaned up and find something to replace that bandage," Gray says.

He leads me down a hallway. Fox and Bubba are standing in the first room with a large bed.

"If we take the covers off the mattress, we can lie down without choking on dust," Bubba calls out to the other guys.

The second door leads to a room with a bed as well, and Thunder and Lightning are in there checking it out.

The third door is a bathroom, but Gray leads me to the end of the hall to a larger bedroom. He closes the door and leads me across the space to an ensuite.

"How did you know this would be here?"

He turns and grins. "I didn't but hoped." He opens all the drawers and finds some gauze and tape. "It will have to do. Now we need to get you cleaned up."

I nod and hold out my hand.

He replaces the bandage and pulls me into his arms. "I was going out of my mind when you were missing, not knowing what Ivan would do to you."

"I'm all right," I say to reassure him.

"Fuck!" CT shouts from somewhere in the house.

We run down the hall and find him pulling on his hair in the kitchen.

"The hurricane warning is real. The wind is beginning to pick up out there. Because of that, no plane can land here until it passes."

Several of the guys let out a heavy sigh.

"Hey, we've all been through worse," I say. "Let's take shifts, and everyone try to get some sleep before the winds get too bad."

Rocco nods as he steps closer to all of us. "She's right. We have been through worse. And this house has good bones. It should withstand the storm."

"I'll take first watch," Bubba says.

"I'll sit with you," Phantom offers.

"We'll take the second watch," Thunder says, pointing at Lightning.

"Sounds good. We'll figure out if there is a third watch as the night goes on," Rocco says. "For now, get some rest."

Gray leads me down the hall back to the master bedroom.

I'm thankful we found this house and hope whoever is chasing us doesn't find it, too.

CHAPTER FIFTEEN

Grayson

I LIE next to Cara while she sleeps. Unfortunately, I woke up many times throughout the night. The sound of sirens continued for several hours after the crash. Likely related to the chopper going down. Between that and the winds whipping through the trees, I found myself staring at the ceiling most of the night.

Now the sun is coming up, I ease away from her and get up from the bed. Fortunately, she doesn't wake. She needs her rest to heal.

Rocco, Fox, and CT are staring at the map.

"I found a coffee pot and coffee if you want some," CT points to the counter. "It's a bit old, but it works."

"Thanks." I grab a mug sitting on the counter and pour myself a cup. "What's the plan?"

"The hurricane threat was lifted a few hours ago, so we should get going and continue north," Rocco says. "There's a clearing a couple of hours away. It's large enough for the plane to land."

I nod. "We should send out a team to make sure no one is coming after us."

"Already done," Rocco says. "Gumby and Fox went out just before sunrise.

That's good. I take a sip of coffee and almost spit it back out. "Damn, this is bad."

"We know," CT says. "But the caffeine seems to work."

Thunder and Lightning walk into the kitchen.

"There's coffee over there," I say with a smile. Yeah, I should probably warn them, but I don't.

"Thanks," Thunder says. "And Rocco, thanks again for relieving us last night."

He shrugs. "I couldn't sleep anyway."

Lightning coughs several times. "Holy fuck, this is bad," he says as he sets his cup of coffee on the counter.

Thunder slaps him on the back a few times until Lightning puts up his hand. "I'm fine."

Rocco laughs. "Since when did you guys get so soft when it comes to coffee?"

"Since I didn't have to drink that instant shit anymore," Lightning says.

Cara walks into the kitchen and stops when we all stare at her. She holds up her hand. "I'm fine, and yes, I slept well. Thank you."

Their eyes all fall to me.

I throw my hands into the air. "What? You heard her. She slept."

"Yeah? Then why do you look like shit?" Thunder asks.

I sigh. "You're a real ray of sunshine, you know that?" I tell him. "For your information, I didn't sleep well. The damn wind kept me up."

The front door flies open, and I jump, ready to run or attack.

"It's us," Fox calls.

Fox and Gumby walk into the kitchen.

"Bad news," Gumby says. "There are at least four men combing the hillside just south of here, all armed."

"We should have checked south first, but we didn't. They are close. We need to go," Fox says.

Rocco folds up the map on the table. "How far are they?"

"If they don't speed up, maybe ten minutes away," Fox says.

Rocco nods. "Let's move out."

"We should go back to the road and follow beside it in the trees until we're on the north side of this mountain, then we can move our way down," Gumby says.

Rocco tucks the map into his pocket. "Agreed. Let's go."

"You ready for this?" I ask Cara.

She nods. "The sleep helped."

We all make our way outside with Fox and Gumby at the front, making sure the men haven't found us yet. We reach the main road.

"Let's split up. Half take this side of the road, and the others take that side," Rocco says as he points.

"Sounds good," Phantom agrees.

Rocco leads one group with Thunder, Lightning, and Gumby.

Phantom leads our group with Fox, CT, Cara, me, and Bubba.

"Do you think the men in the chopper and the ones behind us now could be Max's men?" CT asks Cara.

"We haven't heard one way or the other if Max survived," I say. "I'd think anyone working for him would be relieved if he was gone."

"Max wasn't working alone. Whether he lived or died wouldn't matter to those who work for them," Cara says.

"I thought Trip was looking into whether he was in a hospital or not," CT says.

I nod. "He is. I didn't have any messages this morning." I'll check again when we make it back to civilization. The phone is off now to preserve the battery.

Bubba comes running up behind us. "We need to move faster. The men are sticking to the road and gaining ground."

As much as we want to surprise them and take them out, we know more would follow. It's best if we can get out of here without them ever knowing we were here.

Even though the hurricane warning has been lifted, it's

123

still very windy. A large gust of wind blows through, fortunately masking any noise we might make as we walk along.

Rocco leads the other group across the street and joins us. Bubba fills him in with what he told us.

"We need to start moving northwest," he says as he holds up the folded map.

"Good, that will get us farther from this road," Cara says.

Rocco takes the lead, and we all follow, with Bubba and Phantom in the rear. Fortunately, there isn't much underbrush here, so the hike isn't too tough.

The next gust of wind is strong, and a tree cracks above our heads.

"Look up!" Fox shouts.

We all do, but it's too late. A large branch falls from above. I dive and take Cara with me out of the way.

"Fuck!" CT yells.

We jump up. Shit.

"CT's been hit," I say.

Phantom catches up to us. "What the fuck? Why are you yelling? They're going to hear you!"

"Can someone get this damned thing off me?" CT says. His voice is strained, and I hope like hell he didn't break his leg.

"Oh shit," Phantom says. He takes one end, and I take the other as we pull it off CT. We help him stand up.

CT rubs his chest. "Pretty sure I broke a rib or two."

"They're in the woods!" someone shouts from the road.

We all still for a moment, trying to determine how far away they are.

"Run!" Rocco yells.

"Here," Bubba says as he hands me his pack. "I'll carry CT."

"No, I can make it." CT winces when he takes a breath.

"We have to run." Bubba picks up CT like he weighs nothing, even though he must be over two hundred pounds.

CT winces with each step as Bubba runs. We all run and spread out as we do so. I make sure to stick with Cara, although so far this morning, she hasn't shown any side effects of what happened to her. Though her hand must hurt like hell.

The wind continues to blow hard, but fortunately, no other branches come down. After we clear several miles, Phantom runs to the front of us and waves us all together.

"We finally lost them. They went north at that creek we crossed," he says.

I glance at Fox. It was a good call on his part for us to cross the creek.

Rocco pulls out the map. "A clearing should be just up that way," he points through the trees.

"Anyone have service yet?" Fox asks.

"I do," Lightning says.

"I need to call Stormy and see if a plane can still meet us," Fox says.

Lightning hands him his phone, and he takes a few steps away to make the call. Cara is leaning against a tree.

"How are you feeling?" I ask her.

She nods. "I'll be fine. Water would be great," she smiles. "How about you? You're going on no sleep."

I shrug. "I'll sleep when we get home."

Fox walks back to the group. "A plane will be coming to get us in forty minutes. That should give us time to get to the clearing and have some to spare." He hands the phone back to Lightning. "Thanks."

"I guess we're going again," Cara says as she pushes off the tree.

We are close to the clearing when the sound of sirens grows louder. Gumby holds up his hand for all of us to stop walking. He turns. "Let's take a break. Phantom said he's going ahead to scope out the clearing."

Bubba carefully sets CT down.

The wind has finally calmed down, and birds are chirping again.

The sirens continue to wail, getting closer.

"The plane will be here in ten minutes," Rocco says.

Phantom walks back to the group. "It's a no-go. The clearing is full of police."

"How the hell did they know?" I ask.

Rocco stares toward the clearing. "I don't know, but I will find out."

"That doesn't make any sense," Cara says. "If they were trying to catch up, they wouldn't blaze in making so much noise."

She's right.

"You think it's just a coincidence?" I ask.

She stares off for a moment. "No. I think whoever has been following us is trying to box us in. They probably figured out they lost us by now."

Rocco pulls the map out of his pocket and wipes the sweat off his brow with his shirt sleeve.

"We can't go north or west to the clearing." Fox is staring at the map. "I guess we go south."

"Either we find another option for a clearing, or we hit the water," I say.

"I'd rather fly out of here. I'd feel like a sitting duck on a boat," Bubba says.

And I agree with him. But we might not get much choice.

"Before I call and ask for another plane, I want to know how the hell the police knew about this one," Fox says. "We better get some distance between them and us."

Rocco heads south. Bubba bends to pick up CT, but Fox steps up. "I got him for this leg."

CT holds his hand up. "I can walk. As long as we're walking, I'm doing it."

CHAPTER SIXTEEN

Cara

"IT WAS THE PILOT," Rocco says as he walks back to our group.

After another couple hours of walking, we finally took a break and ate the small amount of food the guys had in their packs.

"He called a nearby tower to check on the wind conditions. Since his flight wasn't noted anywhere, that sent a red flag and his plane was tracked."

"It won't happen again?" Fox asks.

"No, it won't."

Gray holds his phone up. "I have an update from Trip."

All eyes turn to him as he reads the message to us.

"Max survived. He's at a local hospital."

I sigh. He's likely sending someone after me.

"It says he's in a coma. There was a woman found with him who was dead."

"It isn't him who's behind the men tracking us?" Cara asks.

"Let's not rule that out just yet. We don't know who he's tied to here. Who else would be after us?" Fox asks.

I turn my phone on and check my texts. "I got a message from Anderson," I say. "They lost the location of Alex Kralik. He was last seen getting off a plane in Costa Rica. Whoever his driver is, they lost our guy tailing them."

"Makes sense he'd come to see his brother," Thunder says.

"Or finish the deal his brother didn't," I say.

"How?" Fox asks. "We confiscated all his weapons from his boat."

I frown. "Are you sure about that? Where did you put it, and what exactly did you take?"

"We found about fifty long-range sniper rifles that appear to have been lifted from an Army truck. As for where, we buried them. That's why it took us so long to get to the hospital the other day."

I stand up and walk over to Fox, who's leaning against the tree. "Did you get any USB drives? Any passwords to accounts? Because if I were Ivan, I'd have secrets that valuable up in the cloud as well as saved in a few different places."

Fox's hands go to his hips. "You said to search for weapons."

"It's more than just weapons!" I yell. I knew the moment they said they arrested Ivan and took whatever was on his boat, this wasn't over. It's never over with him.

"Fuck Cara, don't you think it would have helped if you told us that?"

"And what would you have done differently?" I ask.

Fox stares at me. "We would have searched for a laptop, USB sticks, something more."

I rub my temples. "As long as we capture Alex and Ivan before they escape, we can worry about all the rest later."

Thunder walks up. "Capture? We can't even get ourselves out of this place. How are we going to get two hostile detainees?"

He's right. We're not in a position to go after Alex just yet. I need to talk to Anderson. He might be sending another team down to take care of Alex.

"I'm calling Anderson." I step away to make the call, but it goes to voicemail. I leave a brief message before powering my phone down to save the battery.

"Good news," Lightning says as he walks up to us. "I went ahead just a bit, and we're almost at the water."

"How is that good news?" Gumby asks.

Lightning smiles. "Because we're not too far from the marina where CT's yacht is sitting."

Gumby turns to CT. "That yacht we met you on is yours?"

"My parents. Lightning, don't you think that's the first place Max's men or anyone would be looking for us?"

Lightning shakes his head. "No, it's the last place. They already know we're trying to catch a plane. I'm sure they're checking out any areas where a plane could land. Not a large yacht."

"You know, I hate to admit this, but he might be right," Thunder says.

"Might be right?" Lightning asks, eyebrows raised. "Asshole, you know I am."

"Okay," I say to stop these two before they get going. "We need a plan."

Thunder nods. "Two of us could go down just after dark and make sure everything is clear. Then the rest of us make the trek in the night. We pull out while everyone is asleep. Hell, we could be up the coast to El Salvador before anyone realizes the boat is missing."

"We'll go to Panama," I say. "I have a contact there who can help us."

"No," Rocco says. "It would put us near the coast longer, and we'd be a target. I agree with Thunder. We're going to El Salvador." The man turns away from me as if that's the end of the discussion.

"Hey," Gray says to Rocco, and I step up to Grayson.

"I've got this. Rocco," I call out.

He turns around.

"You and your team can get your own boat and go to El Salvador. We're taking CT's yacht to Panama," I say firmly.

Rocco's brow shoots up in surprise before his expression

grows serious as he steps toward me. "What do you know that I don't?"

I smile, glad he's open to listening. "My contact in Panama is on the north-western coast. He's former CIA and can get us transportation back to the US. If we go to El Salvador, yes, we will get off the water faster, but then we're deep in the jungle with no contacts and possibly into the middle of a gang war. Also, I can assure the yacht will be safe in Panama. Can you say the same?"

Rocco stares at a tree as he weighs what I've said.

"Guaranteed transportation to the US is all I need to hear," Lightning says.

"Keeping the yacht safe would be good. I'm not sure how my parents would respond if it were stolen or destroyed," CT says.

From what I know of CT, he comes from money but very detached parents. Parents who put money before love.

"I agree. I've had some troubles in El Salvador and some people I'd rather not run into again," Gray says.

"Ditto," CT says.

Rocco nods. "All right. You're sure about this guaranteed transportation to the US?"

I nod.

"It sounds like we might have a safe place to stay for the short term as well in Panama while we wait for this trans-portation. We'll go there," Rocco says.

It's clear he's used to being the leader and seems to need to have the final say. That's fine with me as long as he's doing what I want.

I smile. "I'm glad you see it my way."

"Don't get cocky now." Lightning chuckles as he walks past me.

We make our way to a spot near the marina without running into anyone else. CT has managed to keep up with us but is getting grumpier by the minute. I'm really hoping he has some pain reliever on that boat of his. Both for him and me.

Phantom and Gumby went down to check out the yachts and marina to make sure it's clear for us.

"How are you feeling?" I glance up to find Gray staring at me as he takes a seat on the ground.

"Better."

"About what happened with Rocco—"

I hold up my hand. "I don't want you stepping in for me. I can handle Rocco. Believe it or not, I know what I'm doing." I avoid his gaze. I've had enough men try to step in for me on the job, and that's something I have to cut off right away.

He nods as he moves some hair from my face. "I'm sorry. It's hard for me not to say something if I think someone is disrespecting you."

I meet his gaze. "I can handle myself."

"You can. It's more my issue. There's something I should tell you."

"Hey, lovebirds, time to go," Lightning says.

That's when I realize everyone is walking toward the marina. "Let's go," I say. "We can talk on the boat." I jump up and fall in line behind Lightning.

I glance back at Grayson, who's still watching me. Now, I'm very curious about what he was going to say.

Silently, we walk to the marina and onto CT's yacht. Fortunately, Ivan's yacht isn't here. Hopefully, the police seized it. Although somehow, I doubt that.

Once we're all on the boat, I leave them and go in search of a bathroom. Fortunately, the first one I find has a first aid kit that includes gauze, tape, and some ibuprofen. Slowly, I unwrap the gauze around my hand.

"Let me help you," Gray is at the door.

I nod, and he comes in.

"I'm amazed how clean you kept this today," he says as he finishes unwrapping it. He tosses the old bandages into a nearby garbage can before he places new gauze on while I stare at my hand.

"What were you going to say before Lightning interrupted?"

He finishes taping up my bandage and stares at me in the

mirror. "I'll tell you later. When we're alone and not running for our lives." He grins, and dammit if I don't melt into a puddle right there.

We sway a little. "Are we moving? I don't hear the engine," I say.

"I hope we're moving since that's the plan," he says.

I glance up, and he's still grinning at me. "Smart ass." I push past him and walk back to the deck where the guys are.

I stop the moment I see him.

Gray runs into my back. "Why did you stop?"

I don't answer, but Alex answers for me.

"You're Max's girl. He'll be happy to know I've found you."

Alex is standing near the edge of the deck. Five men, all with guns aimed at us, are also on the dock.

"And you." Alex points behind me. "You were there that night, too. Ivan was surprised when the two of you showed up on the boat next to him. He called and told me he recognized you from your photo."

I frown. That damn missing person photo.

"What photo?" Thunder asks.

Alex grins. "Max takes a photo of all his girls. That's how he entices the men. I remember you. You're older than his other girls. I'm sure you got the attention of a few on his mailing list."

Mailing list? What the fuck?

Alex takes a moment and studies each of the guys. "Now you all look like military men. Or former military. Am I right?"

He shrugs when no one responds. "I'm right." He steps in my direction. "But Erica, you don't seem like you were in the military. Maybe I'm wrong? I didn't get a chance to really study you." He steps closer until he's in my personal space. "Perhaps you have a tattoo showing your military allegiance? Shall we see?" In one quick move, he yanks my shirt up, exposing my stomach and part of my bra.

Gray lurches forward and yanks my shirt back down. One of the men with a gun aims it at us.

"Ah, so your relationship isn't fake." Alex leans down, his hot breath on my neck. "He likes you. I bet I could get him to talk just by touching you." He stares at Gray while he trails a finger over my breast.

I grab his hand with my good hand and twist, causing him to turn with his back to my chest. I use my other hand to grab his gun from the back of his waistband, and before he knows what I've done, I have his gun pointed at his head. My hand hurts like hell from gripping like this, but he'll never know that.

"Drop your guns, or I'll shoot him."

Alex laughs. "You won't shoot me."

Damn, arrogant asshole. I shoot him in the foot.

He howls and tries to bend down, but I don't let him. "You bitch!"

"Drop your guns, or the next shot will hurt a lot more," I say as I aim the gun at his crotch.

The men's eyes widen as they struggle with what to do.

"What's it going to be, Alex?" I ask.

"Don't drop your guns. She won't do it."

Well, I guess Alex is going to be in for a surprise. "Last chance."

No one moves. "I warned you." I aim just outside of his balls and fire.

Alex drops to the ground holding himself.

"She's a dick shooter!" one of the men yells.

The other men back away and take off, running up the dock.

"Holy shit!" Bubba says. "You shot his dick off?"

"Nah. He's only got a flesh wound on his left thigh."

Alex screams in pain. "It's more than a flesh wound, you bitch!"

I hand the gun to Gray, then stare at my bandaged hand. "I guess with my injury, my aim might be off just a little."

While Alex is groveling in pain, I notice there isn't much blood, supporting that it likely is only a flesh wound. Besides, if I really had shot off his dick, the guy would have passed out by now.

"We need to tie him up. Got any rope?" I ask CT.

He gets us some rope, and we tie Alex to a bench on the deck.

"You want to take him with us?" Thunder asks.

"I do. This is how we'll get Ivan back in custody."

"Yeah, well, I want to know how he knew we were on this yacht," Thunder says. "I thought you guys said it was clear." He turns to Bubba and Gumby.

"It was," Bubba says."

"Well, they were waiting for us from somewhere. Where the hell were they?"

CHAPTER SEVENTEEN

Grayson

"HERE, I MADE SANDWICHES," Fox says as he hands me one. "Fortunately, the fridge is stocked on this boat."

I take it from him. "Thanks."

He sits down on the bench next to me. We're taking turns keeping an eye on Alex as CT is sailing us to Panama.

"So uh, you still want to date her after that," Fox says while nudging his chin in Alex's direction.

I laugh. "I'm not worried. She hates that guy and still didn't shoot it off."

Fox stares at the man. "You sure about that?"

"Yeah, there'd be more blood."

Fox recoils in horror. "How do you know that?" He gags. "No, don't answer that."

I finish my sandwich, quickly realizing how hungry I am.

Fox nods toward the bedrooms. "I'll keep watch if you want to go talk to her."

After we got Alex tied up, Thunder took Cara into the cabin. I needed time to cool down. When he put his hands on her, I wanted to kill him. Cara had asked me to let her handle herself, but I can't always do that. And what scares me is that might be a deal breaker for her. I really hope it's not because that woman is amazing. But I'm afraid my past might ruin my future before it even gets a start. Something I've worried about before but in a different way. It's why I've avoided relationships.

"Hey, you okay?" Fox asks.

"Yeah, thanks for the sandwich." I stand up. "I'll take you up on that offer. I'd like to talk to her."

He nods. "Take all the time you need. We're not going anywhere."

"Thanks." I walk into the cabin.

None of the guys, except CT, know about my family history. I've kept it private for a reason; I don't like to talk about it.

I pass Rocco.

"Hey, it won't take much longer to get there. But we might be stuck in a marina for a bit until Cara can reach her contact."

I nod. "Thank you for everything. If you guys hadn't come, Cara might be..." I couldn't say it.

He claps a hand on my shoulder. "She's safe now. That's what's important."

As he walks past me, I hear voices as I make my way deeper into the cabin. I follow the voices and find Cara lying on a bed and Thunder sitting in a chair. It's a decent size bedroom.

Thunder sees me and jumps up. "I need to talk to Lightning about something." He's out of the room before either of us can respond.

"That was subtle," I joke as I close the door behind me.

A suitcase is up against the wall. "Is that my stuff?"

"Yeah, mine's here, too."

I frown. "How?"

"Not sure."

I make a mental note to ask CT about that later. Then I turn my gaze to her and sit in the chair Thunder vacated.

"Cara, I'm sorry."

She sits up, frowning. "Sorry for what?"

"You had just asked me not to step in when it comes to your job because you can handle it. Yet that's exactly what I did when Alex touched you. I was acting on instinct, and it could have ended badly."

She swings her legs off the bed and leans forward. "You don't need to apologize. I understand why you reacted the way you did. He was purposely trying to set you off."

I take a deep breath. "And it shouldn't have worked, but he hit a nerve. I told you I needed to tell you something." I glance up, and all I see is concern in her eyes.

"Come here." She pats the bed next to her, and I move to it, taking her hand in mine. She intertwines our fingers.

"None of the guys except CT know about this, but my family history is rough." I laugh. "Shit, it's worse than rough."

This is harder than I thought it would be. "My dad beat my mom. He never laid a hand on me. My brother made sure of that. But what he did to my mom…" My voice breaks, and I close my eyes.

Cara squeezes my hand.

"When my brother was fourteen, he tried to intervene and stop my dad. My dad threw him into a wall. It knocked him out. He ended up with a head injury that began a long list of problems for my brother."

She moves off the bed and is kneeling between my legs. She takes my hand in hers. "I'm so sorry. That's terrible."

I nod. "I was younger and smaller, so I hid. But I heard him. He thought my mom made Jasper attack him. He was so angry I was afraid he was going to kill her. So, I ran out into the room and yelled, 'Stop!'"

Cara doesn't say a word. She waits until I can say the rest. I've only told this story one other time because I had to.

"My dad grabbed my mom's hand and pulled her out of the house. He said, 'We're going for a drive. Call your aunt to come get you.'" I can't stop the tears. Shit. I never cry.

"Did you call your aunt?"

I nod. "The next morning, the police came." The memory is still so vivid I can smell the cologne the officer was wearing. "My dad had driven off a cliff with both of them in the car. There was no sign of the brakes being used. It was ruled a suicide and homicide."

She climbs onto my lap and hugs me. I wrap my arms around her.

"I've only told what happened in that house to the policeman that morning. Never to anyone else."

"Not even your brother?"

I shake my head. "Months later, my aunt got a copy of the police report and let us read it." I hold on tighter, not wanting to see her eyes when I say the next part.

"This is why I can't help but step up if I think someone is going to hurt you or disrespect you. I know you can handle yourself, but if anything bad happened, I couldn't live with it." I move my gaze to the floor. "And if that's a deal breaker, just let me know."

She pulls back. "A deal breaker?"

I gently move her off of me and stand up. I can't sit still for this conversation.

"Yeah, this might be odd to bring up before we've even really had a first date, but there are certain circumstances where I can't step back if someone is trying to hurt you. I couldn't live with myself if I did." I walk to my suitcase and open the front compartment. Just where I packed it, I pull out my fidget spinner.

Trax once called it childish, but I find it soothing. And it helps me focus.

Cara comes up behind me and puts her hand on my back. I turn but keep my eyes on my spinner.

"Thank you for telling me. Now that I know where you're coming from, it's okay. In my past, I've had men step in because they didn't think I could handle the situation. They thought I was weak. I'm not weak."

I meet her gaze. "No, you're not."

"And no, this isn't a deal breaker. If anything, it shows me what a truly wonderful man you are. You look after those you care about. I can't tell you how incredibly sexy I find that."

"Yeah?" I grin, happy I didn't just ruin everything.

"Yeah."

She pushes up on her toes, and when our lips meet, all the adrenaline I've been feeling today, mixed with my deepening feelings for her, just give way. I pick her up, and she wraps her legs around me as she deepens our kiss. I press her against the wall, and as much as I want to take things slow, I can't even think straight right now.

My hand moves to her breast, and I pinch her nipple through her clothes. She moans the sexiest of moans as her hands move down and squeeze my ass.

Her mouth moves to my neck as she tightens her thighs around me. I'm so hard at this point that I think I'm seeing stars. I turn us around and toss her onto the bed. As I climb over her, she grabs my shirt and yanks me closer to her. I kiss her deeply. Then she pushes on my ass, and I oblige and grind into her.

"Oh fuck, Grayson. I want you so bad."

I'm about to come in my pants; she has me so worked up. "I want you, too." I take her mouth again.

A knock at the door startles us, but before we can get up, the door opens.

"Hey, we're near our stop—" CT stops as he sees us. "Sorry to interrupt," he says, grinning.

I jump up, hoping like hell this doesn't embarrass Cara too badly.

"Yeah, next time, knock, then wait before coming in," she says as she sits up.

Maybe not.

"Or you could maybe lock the door," CT says.

Cara crosses her arms, and I swear I see the man shake in fear.

"Anyway, we're in Panamanian waters and close to a town called David. Cara, can you see if you can reach your contact?"

Cara stands. "I can't reach him by phone. I'll need to go to his place."

CT's smile drops. "Oh. Will it be safe?"

"It will. If we're close, let me show you where you can dock this thing."

She walks past CT and leaves the room. Before CT follows her out, he gives me a shit-eating grin.

"I'm happy for you," he says.

"Thanks."

I follow CT out of the room. Cara shows Rocco, who's now driving the boat, where to go to avoid any immigration or officials. It's still dark, and I figure we'll wait until morning, but I'm wrong.

"Gray, why don't you come with me?" Cara asks. "Once I make sure my contact is here and ready for us, we'll come back for everyone else."

Rocco steps forward. "What do you mean, make sure he's here? He's the reason we came to Panama."

Cara smiles. "Don't worry. I'm sure I'll find him."

We walk into town, and Cara directs us to a taxi waiting on the street. She speaks to the driver in Spanish. She turns to me. "He'll take us."

She gets in the back, and I follow. The taxi takes us out of the city and out into the country.

"How well do you know this contact? Are you sure we can trust him?"

She stares out the window. "I'm sure."

I shift uncomfortably. I don't like going into a situation without more information.

"Who is he?"

She turns to me and smiles. "I'll introduce you when we find him."

Find him? I don't bother asking any more questions as it seems she doesn't want to answer them. I'm hoping it becomes clear why soon.

The driver pulls up to a long driveway. "You're sure this is it?" he asks, suddenly speaking English.

"Yes, thank you," Cara says.

I hand him some cash, and the driver nods.

We get out of the taxi, and it drives away. Cara stares down the driveway but doesn't move.

"Is it down here?" I ask, pointing.

She nods. "I just need a minute." She takes a few deep breaths. "Okay, let's go."

Now I'm curious. "Is this someone you don't want to see?"

We fall in step beside each other. "You could say that." She grabs my arm. "Stop here."

A house is now in view, but we are a good fifty feet from it still. I lean down. "Why did we stop?"

"Just give him a minute to check us out through the cameras."

Cameras? I glance around and notice at least five security cameras attached to the trees surrounding the driveway. Whoever this man is, he's either paranoid or has enemies.

The front door opens, and I'm instantly on guard. A man steps out. He appears fit but older with white hair. His serious expression changes to a smile.

"Cara!" he says as he walks down the porch steps. "I can't believe you're really here." He steps up to her and gives her a hug.

One I notice she doesn't return. He notices me.

"This is Peaches. We're working together."

The man nods and holds out his hand. "Thomas."

I shake his hand. "Nice to meet you, Thomas."

He turns back to Cara. "Well, if you're here, it must be you're in trouble."

"We need help getting back to the United States. We have a team back at the docks."

Thomas nods. "You need a plane. Okay." He sighs. "And here I was hoping you just swung by to see your dad."

Dad? I choke on my own spit. "What?" I ask.

Cara turns to me. "Peaches, Thomas is my father. He's also former CIA, and why he has all this security." She motions to the cameras. "But he can help us."

"Is your mom here?" I ask.

Cara glares at me. "No. If she was, I would have agreed to go to El Salvador."

Huh. I guess there is some family drama on her side, too.

CHAPTER EIGHTEEN

Cara

THE LAST PERSON I wanted to see is standing in front of me. Correction, the second to last person I ever wanted to see. When I joined the agency, I swore I would never contact my parents again. But my dad has made sure to keep me apprised of his whereabouts over the years in case I ever needed anything. And dammit, today I do.

I figured bringing Gray with me would prevent my dad from trying to talk about our history or feelings or any of that bullshit he could give a crap about. After I was transferred to Seattle to work under Anderson, my dad, all of a sudden, wanted to reconnect and make amends for everything.

I almost bought it. Until Anderson recognized my last name and asked me about my father. But that's not something I have time to dwell on. We need to stay focused on getting back to the United States before Max's men find us. Or Alex's men, for that matter. Although after seeing them run off the boat, I doubt they hold any real loyalty to the guy.

"How many people are we talking?" my dad asks as he leads us into the house and straight back to the kitchen.

"Ten," Gray says. "No eleven. We have someone in custody."

My dad spins around. "That's a shit load of people." He crosses his arms. "That's what happens when the agency makes you work with the military. Too goddamned many people."

Peaches frowns, so I fill him in.

"My dad isn't a fan of military men."

"No, I'm not. What are you?" he asks.

Gray opens his mouth but doesn't get a chance to respond.

"Let me guess. A SEAL. Yeah, Anderson always insisted on working with SEALs." He shakes his head.

I need to change the subject. There isn't much point in talking to my dad about anything. He's set in his opinions, and nothing will change them.

"How long will it take to get the plane?"

My dad sits at a kitchen table and motions for us to sit as well. "That depends on a few things. I'll have to reach out to an old contact. How soon do you need it?"

I sit down. "As soon as possible. There are men chasing us. Angry men."

He nods, then glances at Gray. "What did you do to piss the men off?"

I lean forward across the table. "You know we can't tell you."

"Sir, anything we can do to help speed up the process, we will do," Gray says.

My dad stares at Gray. "All right. I need to make some calls. I'll be right back."

Once he leaves the room, I close my eyes, trying to calm myself.

"So, that's your dad?"

I turn to find him grinning at me.

"And he doesn't like military guys, but apparently you do."

"You can psychoanalyze me later. Right now, we need to stay focused on getting out of here."

My eyes move to the walls where local art is hanging.

There are no photos or anything that could tie this place directly to him. That's how he lives. Light. Ready to go when needed. Except now, he doesn't have anywhere to go, and that must be hard on him.

I stand and walk into the living room. My eyes catch on a drawing. Touching the frame, I remember the day he hung it up on our wall. He'd been so proud of the picture my mom had done of our house. It was a simple sketch, but he gushed over it. I never understood why.

Gray comes up behind me. "Are you okay?"

I spin around. "I will be once we're on that plane. I'll likely never speak to him again."

"Well, I hope that's not true."

I spot my dad standing in the kitchen.

"A friend can fly you to Texas." He turns to Gray. "She won't land at a commercial airport, so you'll have to arrange your own transportation."

Gray clears his throat. "Could I use your bathroom?"

"Sure. It's down that hall on the right."

Once we hear the bathroom door close, I turn back to the drawing. "Thank you for setting that up."

"Of course. Anything for you."

I laugh. "That's bullshit, and you know it."

Next thing I know, he's beside me and puts his hand on my shoulder. I flinch and step back.

"Cara, I would do anything for you."

I point at the artwork. "Why do you have this?"

His brow furrows. "I love that drawing. I miss that house and the family we had there."

"Family?" I yell. I take a breath to control my temper and speak quieter. "We were never a family. You weren't there. You left me with her."

This isn't the time to bring this up, but dammit, seeing that picture, I can't hold it in.

He closes his eyes. "I had no idea what was going on until you were in high school. You know that. I've explained."

I take a few steps back and hold up my hand. "Don't. I don't want to talk about this now or ever."

"Everything all right?" Gray asks, stepping back into the room.

"Fine," I say and walk outside. I need to keep my distance from my dad. All these years and I'm still so angry.

I sit on the steps and close my eyes. I visualize myself lying on the beach. It's a technique that was recommended to us during our training. I can almost feel the ocean waves lapping at my toes when Gray's voice interrupts me.

"The plane will be ready to go in two hours. We need to get back to the guys and get everyone to this address." He hands me a piece of paper. "He says we can use his SUV. It won't hold everyone, but at least we don't have to try to carry Alex in a taxi."

He hands me the keys. "He said just leave it at the airfield with the keys under the seat."

"Okay, let's go."

I'm halfway to the car before Gray steps down the stairs. He's smart not to bring up my father again.

By the time we get back to the boat, Alex has a rag in his mouth.

"Don't ask," Rocco says.

We explain the plan and divide into two groups.

CT is still hurting, so he comes with me, Gray, Alex, Thunder, and Lightning. To say it's crowded in the back seat would be an understatement.

Fox goes with Rocco and his team to find a taxi or two. We agreed to all meet a few blocks from the actual pick-up location, and I'll shuttle everyone over there. If Max were to track us this far, all he'd find out from the taxi driver is that we all went to the same restaurant.

We get to the airstrip early. The guys climb out of the back seat.

"Holy crap, I'm sore," Lightning says. "I hope there's leg room on the plane."

"MMM!" Alex grumbles.

I'm pretty sure that's the first time he heard about the plane. We'd kept him out of earshot before so we wouldn't have to deal with his grumblings.

"MMM!!!" Alex yells as Thunder pulls him out of the car.

"He's yours now," Thunder says as he shoves him toward Lightning. "You weren't supposed to say plane in front of him."

Alex's face turns red. He's trying to scream through the rag.

"Not sure why you're so upset. We didn't say anything about throwing you out of it." Lightning smiles at him. "Yet."

Alex stops screaming, and his eyes smile. I wonder why until I hear it.

"Shit, he's peeing his pants!" Lightning says.

"Guess she didn't shoot your dick off," Thunder says.

I shout from the car, "I'm going to get the other guys. I'll be back."

I glance at Gray, and he gives me a nod. There's concern in his eyes, and I should tell him more about my family at some point. He's been open with me about his.

The rest of the guys are waiting outside the restaurant as planned, and I shuttle them to the airstrip as well.

"What do we know about this pilot?" Phantom asks.

"Not much," I say. "But if my dad trusts him, then we can."

"Your dad?" Thunder asks. "That's who your contact was?"

I nod.

"Holy shit. Is he still alive?"

I smile. I've told Thunder little about my family, but he knows I hold a lot of anger toward my father for essentially abandoning us and choosing to work all the time. Although now that I'm in the agency, I get it. If you're good, you get called on assignment after assignment. And from what everyone has told me, my dad was good.

"I hope that's our plane," Fox says, pointing up.

There's a plane in the distance. Too far to make out what type just yet. As it gets closer, we can all see the US flag on it. It's not an official decal but a flag that someone must have painted freehand style.

"That's interesting," Gumby says as we all watch it land.

The plane appears like it should hold about fifteen people, so at least we don't have to worry about that.

Once the engine cuts off, the door opens, and a woman with green hair jumps out.

"Howdy! I heard you all need a ride to Texas." She's all smiles.

"We do. Thank you," I say. "I'm Cara."

The woman's smile grows. "I'd recognize you anywhere. Your dad has a photo of you he keeps behind a drawing at his house."

He does? And this woman has been to his house.

"I'm guessing by the shock on your face, you didn't expect that."

I swallow hard. "No, I didn't."

"Well, he said you didn't have time to waste, so let's get going before the air traffic controller gets back from lunch." She nods to the control tower off to the side.

It's empty, and I thought it was abandoned.

"You know his lunch schedule?" Fox asks.

The woman turns around. "I do. I know all their schedules. It's why people like your dad call me when they need a favor. I'm Mary, by the way."

"Isn't there someone else in there, though?" Fox asks.

Mary shakes her head. "There are usually only a handful of flights scheduled to come in here each day. No need for backup."

Mary had to be at least sixty, or else she simply spent a lot of time in the sun. Her green hair set off her green eyes. She struck me as friendly but serious, too.

The guys loaded Alex onto the plane. He tried to scream the entire time, but fortunately, the rag kept it muffled.

Once we are all seated, Mary stands in the aisle. "All right. I'll spare you the safety-feature talk due to a shortage of time. But I will warn you that we will be landing in the Middle of Nowhere, Texas. It's harder to use airstrips without people asking questions there."

"That will be fine. Thank you," I tell her.

As I settle into my seat, it hits me how tired I am.

"Mind if I join you?" Gray asks.

"Sure."

He sits, latches his seatbelt, and takes my hand in his. I lean back and close my eyes.

"Cara." Gray squeezes my hand. "Wake up."

My eyes pop open. "What's wrong?"

I turn my head, and he's smiling at me. "Nothing. We're about to land. Figured you'd want to wake up a little before calling in help."

Help. He means calling in to have someone take Alex Kralik off our hands.

"Yes, thank you." I stretch my arms above my head and take a look around the cabin. A few of the guys are sleeping.

"Here, I found a charger while you were out." He hands me my phone, fully charged.

"Wow. Thank you." I stare at it for a moment. I'm not used to being taken care of, but I have to say it's nice.

As soon as we land, I call Anderson and explain what's going on. I send him a screenshot of our location on a map, and he sends a text that an agent will meet us at the plane to take Alex in an hour.

Mary takes off, leaving us to figure out how to get to civilization.

Exactly an hour later, a large Ford truck pulls up, and a man steps out. The first thing I see are cowboy boots. I guess we really are in Texas.

"Good evening." The man has a Southern accent, and immediately, I know he's not CIA.

Stepping forward, I ask, "What agency are you with?"

He grins. "US Marshall's Office, ma'am. I understand you have a suspect in custody."

I don't confirm. "Where would you take him?"

The man crosses his arms. "Well, for tonight, I'm going to take him to the local police station because they have a cell there that locks. Tomorrow, I plan to drive him to the airport, where we're both going to get on a plane. The details I cannot divulge, but he will be questioned by the CIA. My orders came from your boss, Anderson."

Oh wow, the man knows more than I would have thought. "You must know Anderson personally."

"I do."

We stand in silence for a moment.

Thunder steps forward. "Well, I think we're good here. The man is over there." Thunder nods to Alex sitting on the ground. "I'd like to hand him over, then get the hell out of here."

We all look around and see nothing but fields.

"Uh, I don't suppose Uber comes out this way."

The man laughs. "No, but I can give you a ride to our motel. We only have the one. Anderson said he would arrange for a ride to the airport for you all in the morning."

I glance at his truck. "You only have room for two."

He cocks his head. "Plenty of room in the back."

And that's how we ended up piled in the bed of his truck, bumping along, while Alex yelled into his rag.

When we pull up at the motel, I hold back my groan. This place makes The Bates Motel look like a five-star resort.

Boots, as I now call him since he wouldn't share his name, gets out of the truck. "Well, here you are. Make sure you get all your luggage." He smiles when he says this.

We have no luggage. It's all on CT's yacht in Panama.

The man checks the rope that connects Alex's hands to the sides of the bed of the truck.

"Thanks for the ride," I say as we hop out of the back.

"No problem." Boots gets back in the vehicle and drives off.

Rocco leads us into the office. We don't all fit as the space is only wide enough for the check-out desk and deep enough for a few people.

Rocco approaches the counter. "Hi, we need rooms."

The man glances up. "How many?"

Rocco turns and scans us. "Well, if the rooms are double beds, five will be fine."

Without blinking, the man says, "We only have three left."

"Then why did you ask us how many?" Bubba asks.

The man shrugs. "Maybe you only wanted one."

CT makes his way up to the front desk and pulls a credit card from his wallet. "We'll take all three."

The man processes the card and gets us keys. They are old-school keys, not modern motel keys. We step out and join the rest of the group in the parking lot.

"We got three rooms with two beds each. Two rooms also have a pull-out sleeper sofa. Let's figure this out."

I let them argue over who's bunking with who. I don't care as long as I can get some sleep tonight and some coffee in the morning.

"Okay, it's settled," Rocco says.

Gray takes my hand and leads me to a room. Once we walk in, he closes the door. "It's just us in here tonight," he says.

CHAPTER NINETEEN

Grayson

MY HEART IS RACING as I wait for Cara to respond to what I just told her.

"Even though we are sharing the room, there are two beds, so this isn't me trying to push you into anything." I run my hand through my hair, and sweat breaks out on the back of my neck, but she still hasn't turned around. Shit, did I say the wrong thing?

"I mean, not that I don't want to push you into something," I chuckle. Shit, what kind of asshole thing is that to say?

"That's not what I mean." I take a deep breath and sit on the foot of the bed. "I'm going to shut up now."

When she turns to face me, she's grinning. "Please don't. I enjoy hearing you nervous."

I fall back onto the bed. "You're just messing with me?"

She laughs. "Maybe. Have you always been this nervous around women?"

"No. Just you."

She sits down next to me. "Why just me?"

"Because you're special. I really don't want to screw this up."

She lies down and takes my hand in hers. "Grayson, we've already shared a bed. There's no need to be nervous about sharing a room now."

I turn my head to glance at her.

"What I'm more curious about is how you managed to talk eight large men into sharing two motel rooms and us getting a bed for each of us."

I turn my gaze to the ceiling. "I promised them things. A lot of things. I don't even hand wash my own socks. Fuck." The idea of washing CT's socks makes me gag. Maybe he'll forget. Hell no, he won't.

"Wow, hand washing another man's socks? You really wanted to be alone with me."

"I do. But not for sex." I scratch the back of my neck. "I keep saying the wrong thing. Of course, I want to have sex with you. But you know when the time is right."

The bed shakes, and I glance over. She's laughing but covering her mouth to try not to make noise. I grab a pillow from above my head and hit her in the side with it. She falls off the bed, laughing.

"It's not that funny," I say, a bit sour.

Next thing I know, a pillow smacks me hard. "Yes, it is."

I jump to my knees and grab another pillow. Why are there so many damn pillows on each bed? At least they serve a purpose here today. She fakes me out, and I fall for it, only to get hit on the right side.

"You're not laughing," she says.

She's standing beside the bed. I move as if I'm going to hit her waist with the pillow. She dodges to her right, and I grab her thighs, pulling her onto the bed. In an attempt to break free, she ends up lying on top of me, and our lips are inches apart. I grow hard instantly.

"You know, for someone you're not even dating yet, you're awfully handsy," she says while grinning.

"Oh, is that right?'

"It is."

154

I grow serious. "There's something about you Cara. You're different. I want to be near you, touch you, all the time. And if CT hadn't walked in on us, I'm not sure how far I would have taken things."

"I know. I feel the same way."

My hand goes behind her neck, and I pull her to me. The moment our lips meet, the same jolt is there. Her mouth opens and I sweep my tongue in. She lets out a small moan, and it sets me further on fire.

I flip us both over so she's on her back and I'm settled between her legs. My hand moves from her neck down her front finding her hardened nipple through her shirt. I give it a small pinch.

"Grayson, yes."

Fuck, I love when she says my name. I kiss from her jaw to her neck. She bends her head the other way, giving me full access as her hand moves down my back until it's on my ass, which she gives a squeeze.

My lips move back to hers, and I can't get enough of her.

Her other hand finds its way to my ass as well. Despite her bandage, she uses both to urge me to grind against her. Part of me says slow down, but the part that wins obliges, and I grind.

Her grip tightens. "Yes, right there."

I put my hands on either side of her and push myself up just far enough to watch her as I continue to move against her. She smiles at me and lets out another moan. Her hands move to the bottom of my shirt as she tries to pull it off. I sit up and tug it over my head and toss it to the floor. Her eyes widen as her hands trail over my chest and abs.

"I want you, Grayson. So bad."

"I want you, too."

I lean down to kiss her again when there's a loud knock at the door.

"Hey, it's Thunder."

I sit up. "How the hell does he know?"

Cara laughs as she gets up. "I'm sure it's just a coincidence."

I run a hand through my hair as Cara goes to the door. She opens it, and Thunder is standing there, holding a pizza box.

"CT ordered pizza delivery for us, and here's yours. Hope you both like pepperoni."

Cara takes the pizza. "Thank you."

"And here are some waters." Thunder hands over a couple of bottles with his other hand.

He spots me sitting on the bed without a shirt. His eyes travel to Cara, who has bedhead. Then his eyes go to the mattress. I glance too. Yeah, it's a little rumpled. That's when it hits me what we almost did. I really like Cara. I meant what I told her, that I want to date her. But dammit, I get alone with her in a hotel and I attack her like the horny bastard I am. Maybe Thunder's arrival was a sign that I need to slow the fuck down.

"Want me to stick around?" he asks Cara.

She laughs. "No, not at all. Thank you for the pizza, though." She tries to close the door, but Thunder stops it.

"In that case, you should know I'm staying in the room next door."

"Next door?" Cara asks.

Thunder leans against the door frame and crosses his arms. "Yeah, on the other side of the wall from your headboard. You might consider moving the bed away from the wall next time." He pushes off the frame and walks away.

Cara closes the door and sets the pizza on a chair near the door.

When she turns back to me, her face is red. "Well, that killed the mood, didn't it?"

I stand up and pull her into my arms. "I want nothing more than to get you in that bed and do all sorts of things to you, but I don't think our first time should be with Thunder and the other guys listening in."

Her mouth opens in an O. "Do you think they heard you moaning?"

I laugh. "Me? You were the one moaning."

She cocks her head and grins at me. "Uh, maybe a little, but you were the one who was loud."

I stare at her. Is she fucking with me, or did I really moan? I mean, I was into it.

Her arms wrap around my neck. "Okay, so we'll take this slow and wait until after our date before we get hot and heavy again."

"I really moaned?"

Her face grows serious as she nods. "You really didn't notice?"

I shake my head. "I was too focused on you."

She lifts onto her tiptoes and gives me a quick kiss. "Well, that's all you get, for now, so you can focus on yourself again." She steps back and grabs the pizza, bringing it to the bed.

"I really doubt that will change my focus." I wink at her as I grab a slice.

"Oh, man!" Lightning's voice comes through our wall, and our eyes immediately lock.

"Holy shit, that wall is thin," she says.

"It is. Maybe I'll tell the guys we had the television on."

She laughs. "What? You turned it on to porn? You think that's better?"

I finish swallowing my bite. "Nah, I'll tell them it was *Animal Kingdom.*"

She spits out the water she was sipping on. "I'd like to listen in on this conversation."

"Listen in? You don't want to be there?"

She cocks her head. "Grayson, they aren't going to grill you when I'm standing right there. Wait till you all get back to the office."

My smile drops. Shit. I scratch my head. "You're right."

"I know these guys. CT will lead the charge."

I stare at her. "What about you? Will Thunder grill you?"

She takes a bite and thinks a moment. "I'm not sure. On any other topic, I would say yes, but he treads lightly on this subject. Well, usually."

I finish my bite. "Why is that?"

"I dated his brother for a while, and things didn't end well. Now he's protective of me. I think he's worried I'll get hurt again."

I finish my slice, hoping she continues, and she does.

"Caleb, his brother, and I met when we were both young and fell madly in love. Or so I thought. We didn't see each other as much as we would have liked between my assignments with the CIA and his tours. He was in the Navy."

"Just like his older brother."

She smiles. "Yes, I think there was a little competition there." Her smile fades. "Caleb came back from his last tour, changed. I thought he'd seen something, but he wouldn't talk to me. I found out from Thunder he'd been discharged for a medical reason."

I finish off my water as I take in her sad eyes. "Caleb didn't tell you himself?"

She averts her gaze. "No. I didn't find out until afterward about the discharge. Apparently, he'd begun to hear voices. They deemed him no longer fit for duty."

"I'm sorry. Afterward?"

Tears well in her eyes. "I've never told anyone about this. Thunder already knew, and frankly, I didn't want to talk about it."

I move from my side of the bed to where she's sitting and put my arm around her shoulders. "I'm sorry, I don't mean to push. You don't have to tell me."

She shakes her head. "No, I do. You need to know why it's hard for me to open up."

When she turns to me, a tear runs down her cheek, and it guts me to see her in pain. I can't say I've ever seen her cry. With her job, she never gets emotional. At least not that I've ever witnessed. I wipe away her tear, and she wraps her arms around herself.

"A week after he came home, he disappeared. Thunder found him." She sniffles. "He killed himself."

"Oh shit. Cara, I'm so sorry." I pull her onto my lap, and she leans into me.

"He didn't leave a note, and it devastated his family. I

sensed something was wrong and tried to talk to him. But he wouldn't take my calls. I had no idea it was that bad. Thunder got angry about it all for a while but took care of me. He's always been there for me since."

We sit there a moment, holding each other. Then she sits up and wipes her eyes.

"I've always regretted only calling him. I should have gone to see him and forced him to talk to me. Maybe I could have stopped it."

I take her hand in mine. "No. You didn't know because he didn't tell you. It's not your fault."

She turns away from me, closing her eyes. "But if I hadn't been so focused on my job…if I'd focused on him, maybe I could have seen it."

I reach out and move her chin gently until she's facing me. "Look at me, Cara."

She reluctantly opens her eyes.

"Don't take that on. I'll bet Thunder is thinking the same thing of himself. You can't second guess yourself like that."

She wipes her eyes again. "I'm sorry. I didn't realize I'd get emotional."

"Don't ever be sorry about opening up to me. I'm here for you any time you want to talk."

She leans in and hugs me. "Thank you." Then she pulls back, and I follow her eyes as they take in the other bed. "Would it be all right if we slept in the same bed tonight? I want to be close to you," she says.

"I would like that as well."

CHAPTER TWENTY

Cara

THE NEXT MORNING we're all outside, waiting for our rides. None of us were willing to stay in those rooms any longer than we had to.

"Thank you again for everything you did. I really appreciate it," I say as I shake hands with Rocco, Gumby, Bubba, and Phantom.

I swear Gumby leaned in for a hug but glanced at Gray and stuck his hand out instead. I bite back a laugh wondering if Gray gave him some sort of look.

"I'm happy we could help," Rocco says.

"Yeah, it was good seeing you guys again," CT says. "Gumby, Bubba, and Phantom, you should come visit Pine Valley sometime. It's not too far out of Seattle."

Rocco crosses his arms. "What? I'm not invited?"

CT laughs. "You always are, but you came up last December. These guys need to come see more of the area."

"I'll think about it," Phantom says.

A car pulls up outside the motel where we're all standing.

"That's our ride," Gumby says.

The guys all say their goodbyes, and I watch as the four

SEALs get into the car. I'll have to let Anderson know if we need to call in anyone again that those are the guys we want.

"You know they're all taken, right?" Lightning says, leaning down.

Without turning to him, I whack him in the stomach. "I'm not looking at them like that."

"Uh-huh. Well, don't let your boy toy see your eyes, or he might get jealous."

Lightning has always liked to tease me. It goes both ways. I turn to him.

"Speaking of toys, is this new girlfriend real or a blow-up doll?"

"Oh, no, she didn't!" Thunder says as he turns to listen to our conversation.

Lightning grins. "Why? You jealous, Harding?"

I laugh. "If you can't get a real woman, that doesn't speak much for your skills. So no, I'm not jealous. More like relieved I dodged that bullet."

"Oh shit!" CT laughs. "I hope our car doesn't come too soon. I gotta see this play out." CT glances from me to Lightning. "You gonna take that man?" he prods.

Lightning's hands go to his hips. "Dodged a bullet? Like you had a chance with this." He motions his hand from his shoulders down to his thighs.

I nod. "Egypt. Three years ago. I had a chance. Like I said, I dodged a bullet."

Lightning's smile falls, and his cheeks redden.

Shit, maybe I went too far. "Hey, you know I'm just kidding around, right?"

He stares straight ahead. "Yeah."

The air shifted from fun to uncomfortable.

"Hey, anyone seen our car?" I turn to stare at the road.

"You hit on her on the Egypt assignment?" Thunder asks as he steps beside me.

"No, I was kidding." Please, everyone, drop this. This is why I don't flirt. I'm not good at that, either.

Lightning coughs. "No, we were just flirting. You know how we do."

A minivan pulls up and stops in front of us. A man gets out. "To the airport?" he asks.

"Yes, thank you," CT says.

We all get into the car. Thunder, Lightning, and Fox take the back seat. CT is still in pain, so we motion for him to take the front seat. Gray and I get in the middle.

To say I'm uncomfortable is an understatement. I wish I could talk to Lightning about this. He's been a good friend, and I didn't realize how he'd react. I really was kidding about dodging a bullet. Twenty minutes into the car ride and I can't let it go. I glance at Grayson. He's sleeping. CT is sleeping in the front seat, too. Guess they didn't sleep well last night.

I turn to find Lightning staring at his phone.

Perfect.

I send him a text.

Me: *Sorry about earlier. I was kidding but didn't realize it would sound so harsh.*

I send it and wait. And wait. Nothing.

Ten minutes later, a notification comes in.

Lightning: *I know you were kidding. Just surprised you brought that up. I thought we agreed to never speak of that again.*

Me: *We did. I'm sorry. It won't happen again. Can you forgive me?*

I send him a gif of a puppy with big eyes saying please.

Lightning: *I forgive you.*

I stare out the window, remembering that night in Egypt. We'd just finished our assignment, and he helped me get the broken curtains closed in my room. I thanked him, and he leaned down and kissed me. He moved slowly, but I didn't stop him. The kiss didn't last long. He pulled back, and we were both frowning.

"Is it me, or do we have no chemistry?" he asked.

I laughed then he laughed. "We don't."

He grinned. "Okay, this never happened. Agreed?"

"Agreed."

He held out his pinky, and I held out mine. We shook on it.

While Thunder has been like a brother to me for many years, Lightning is like that good friend who won't bullshit me. Even though I don't see him often, I truly value his friendship and opinions. He's not someone I want to lose out of my life.

Me: *I do want to meet your new girlfriend. You know, make sure she's good enough for you and all.*

Lightning: *Maybe we can double date sometime.*

I smile. I like that idea.

"Hey, you look happy."

I turn to find Gray stretching as he wakes. "Yeah. I can't wait for our date. When is it again?"

He laughs. "You're impatient, aren't you?"

I reach out and intertwine my fingers in his. "Maybe a little."

After a long drive to the airport, Thunder and Lightning head to a separate terminal for their flight to New York. Fox and CT go ahead, leaving Gray and me alone.

We walk together hand in hand until we find an empty gate waiting area.

He walks me backward, pressing me against a wall. "I'm glad we got a little time alone before we are back in Seattle."

I grin. "Why's that?"

His thumb caresses my chin. "So I could do this," he says as he leans in and captures my lips with his.

This kiss is tender and not like in the hotel room where we couldn't get enough of each other. That is until I press my body up against his. His hands move to my hips and grip tight. Then he pulls back.

"Damn, I want to kiss you, but whenever I'm close to you, it's hard to not lose control."

"No one said you couldn't," I say as I run my hand under his shirt.

His breathing picks up, and he looks around. "While it appears no one is around, we both know there are cameras everywhere. And I refuse to be the cause of you having a sex tape that goes viral."

I laugh. "Interesting place your mind went."

He grins, then leans in and kisses me again. I move my other hand around and squeeze his ass.

"Okay," he pulls back, breathing hard. "We should probably find our gate so we don't miss our flight."

"One more kiss." I step up onto my tiptoes as he meets me halfway.

Once again, we get lost in each other, but I don't want to stop. However, the sound of applause has us jumping apart.

Our once-empty gate is now full of what appears to be a soccer team and many of its fans. They are all staring at us, cheering.

"Damn, you two are hot!" one of the guys yells.

"If you want privacy, check out one of the family bathrooms," another guy yells.

I scrunch my nose. "Gross."

Gray grabs my hand and leads me away as we both smile and wave at the crowd. We run to our own gate, laughing.

"Hey, what's so funny?" Fox asks when he sees us.

I glance at Gray, who squeezes my hand. "Nothing."

CHAPTER TWENTY-ONE

Grayson

SHORTLY AFTER LANDING, CT, Fox, and I are summoned to the office to explain to Stormy what the hell happened.

"That sounds like a hell of a mess. Thank you for giving me the summary, but you know you still have to do the paperwork," Stormy says. "The CIA has requested a copy of it for their records."

I chuckle. "For an agency that's supposed to be secretive, they sure require a lot of paperwork."

Stormy laughs. "That is true."

"Stormy, I'd like to take this week to retrieve my parents' yacht. We had to leave it in Panama."

Stormy nods. "Yes, of course. But you should go see a doctor about your ribs first."

"I could help him," Fox offers.

"Nice try, but no," Stormy says.

A knock on the door has us all turning to Rover standing in the doorway. "Sorry to interrupt, but there's something you need to see, Stormy. Right now."

Rover walks in and hands Stormy his phone.

Stormy's smile falls as his eyes narrow. "What the fuck is

this?" he asks Rover as he scrolls. "How the hell did they get this information?" He stands up.

"What's going on?" CT asks.

Stormy goes to his desk and opens the bottom drawer. He removes a box and opens it. "It's gone. Shit!" He throws the box against the wall, and some papers fall out.

"SeattleNow posted a story about Stormy purchasing an interest in Reed Hawthorne Security," Rover explains.

"Did you not want anyone to know that?" I ask.

Rover turns his phone so I can see it. "It's not that. The article states what he paid for it and details some of Stormy's finances, including who some of our clients are."

Fox stands up. "Fuck! That's confidential." He goes to the box Stormy threw and picks up the papers. "What was in here?"

Stormy sits down and rubs his face. "I had all my financial information on a USB stick. I was going to give it to my accountant next week when he comes in."

CT frowns. "Why wouldn't you just upload it to the cloud? Doesn't he have secured folders online?"

Stormy glares at CT. "I couldn't get it to work, so he told me just to do this." He motions to the drawer.

"Next time, I can show you how to do it," CT says.

Rover puts his hand on CT's shoulder. "I think the bigger issue now is who stole the files and leaked it to the press. And why?"

"Either it was someone inside, or someone broke in. And there's been no evidence of anyone breaking in," Stormy says.

Shit, it couldn't have been one of the guys. We're all like family here.

"Can you pull the door logs?" I ask. We all have our own code to punch into the door to get in. "See if anyone came in at an odd time?"

Stormy scratches his beard. "It's worth checking." He sits down at his computer and starts typing. A moment later, the printer fires up. Stormy hands us each a page of the log. "Look for anything outside our usual hours. This is for the last two weeks."

I go over the list, and all of the timestamps are within reason.

"I got something," Fox says.

All eyes are on Fox.

"Right here. Someone came in at two in the morning a couple of days ago." He holds up the paper, pointing to the line item.

"What was the code used?" Stormy asks.

"2997."

Stormy stands up and walks over to Fox. "Let me see that." He practically rips the paper from his hands.

"Do you know whose code that is?" Rover asks.

Stormy sets the paper on the table. "Yeah, it's mine. But I never come in at two in the morning."

"Who knows your code?" I ask.

He scratches his beard. "No one. The only people who have access to these logs are Cowboy and me, and he never logs into the security." Stormy sits back down at the conference table, staring at the paper.

"Is it a pin or code you've used before that someone could guess?"

He arches a brow. "Trust me. No one would know it."

"Are you certain?" Rover asks.

He pounds his fist on the table. "I'm damned certain. It's the date I lost my virginity. Not exactly something I share or that others know about."

We're all silent. I never thought to use that date as a pin, but actually, that's a pretty good one. Hell, I don't even remember the date.

"What about the woman you lost it with? She would know the date," Fox asks.

Stormy laughs. "Maybe, but this is from when I was eighteen. After I went into the service, we never spoke again."

"Maybe her parents? Or a jealous boyfriend of hers who can't stand you were her first?" Fox says.

Stormy arches a brow. "An ex going after an office full of former SEALs because I had sex with a woman all those years ago?"

Fox leans back in his chair. "Yeah, it's a stretch."

"Okay, forget for a moment how this got leaked. The issue now is what are we going to do about it?" Stormy asks.

Someone sings something about peach jam, and it comes from my pocket.

"Motherfucker," I say as I pull out my phone. "Okay, it has to be one of you because this never happens on assignments. It's someone who knows when I'm in this damn office. Which one of you is it?" I stare at each one, but dammit, none of them look guilty.

They all hold up their hands. "It's not me," they all say except Stormy.

I stare at the man. "Stormy, is it you?"

His brows shoot up. "Really? I have better things to do than to fuck with you."

He's right. And it's likely not him, but dammit, who is it?

I put the phone back into my pocket. It was Cara, and I really want to talk to her but not until after we deal with the current situation.

"I need to call Cowboy and Shaw to discuss. Once we have a plan, I'll let you know," Stormy says.

Shaw is Cowboy's wife and a damn good attorney. Hopefully, she'll be able to get this so-called news source to pull their story. Although, the thing appears to have gone viral already.

We all stand up to leave.

"Don't forget about the paperwork," Stormy says.

I'm the first out of the room, but I hear Fox and Rover talking behind me.

"Did you tell Trax, Maverick, and Cody about this?" Fox asks.

"No, they're still on assignment. We can tell them when they get back."

I have no idea what assignment they're on, but I hope they don't see this. Distractions can get you killed.

I go into my office and close the door, itching to return Cara's call.

"Hey," she answers.

"I saw you called."

She sighs. "I did. Have you seen the news?"

I sit in my chair. "Just did."

"How the hell did someone get Stormy's financial information?"

"We're still trying to figure that out."

Maybe someone watched Stormy punch in the code from a distance. It's a long shot but about the only logical explanation. But how would they know he kept his financial data on a USB stick in a drawer? The more I think about it, the more personal this feels.

"If you need any help let me know. I'm off the next few days."

That caught my attention. "Oh yeah?"

The sound of birds chirping comes through the phone. "Yeah. I've been sent home for the rest of the week to 'help my hand heal faster,' as Anderson put it."

"Home—is that why I hear birds?"

She laughs, and I can imagine the way it lights up her eyes. "Good ear. I'm on my back deck. It overlooks a green belt with a lot of birds."

"Sounds nice."

"Yeah, it is. You should come over sometime."

"Hmm. You did agree to a date. Maybe I could pick you up tomorrow around six?"

She doesn't respond right away.

"Or not. I don't mean to push."

"Grayson, I'd love to go out with you tomorrow. I'll text you my address. See you at six."

I grin. "See you at six."

I end the call and sense someone watching me. I glance up, and CT is standing in my doorway, wearing a grin. "Why the hell are you always lurking around my office."

"I'm not lurking. I need to ask you something."

I sigh. "Fine, come in."

CT walks in and sits in the chair across from me. "Do you think I should stick around and help with this leak business?"

I lean back. "I thought you needed to pick up your parents' yacht."

He nods. "I do. I just feel shitty leaving now."

Staring at the man, I take in that he seems genuinely concerned about letting everyone down.

"You know there isn't much you can do. With the client's names leaked, Shaw or some other attorney is likely going to handle this. It's probably better if you aren't here. Something tells me this could become a circus."

CT's leg starts bouncing. "It just feels like I'm abandoning the team."

"You're not. Now go get that yacht out of Panama while you can. And enjoy the trip." I grab my stress ball from my desk and toss it at him.

He laughs as he catches it. "How the hell do you not fidget on assignments? You seem to only do so in the office."

Guess he didn't notice me using the fidget spinner on the yacht. But that was because I was nervous to talk to Cara, not about the assignment.

"It's my superpower."

He stands up and walks to the door. "Thanks for the advice. And I hope everything goes good for you tomorrow night."

Me too, which means I better plan something she'll really enjoy.

CHAPTER TWENTY-TWO

Cara

I CLOSE MY BEDROOM DOOR, hiding the pile of clothes on my bed. After my shower, I put on what I planned to wear for the date but then decided a dress wasn't really me, so I tried on everything I own—twice. I finally decided to go with dark-wash jeans and a silky red top with booties. Since I have no idea what we are doing tonight, I'm ready for anything. I hope.

There's a knock on my door. Right on time. Taking a deep breath, I smooth my top as I reach for the doorknob. When I open it, I just stare.

Grayson is wearing a fitted blue tee that not only makes his blue eyes pop even more, but the T-shirt also shows off how muscular he is. His jeans are fairly snug, too. He gives me a sexy grin when my eyes make their way back up to his face.

"You're beautiful," he says as he moves forward and kisses my forehead.

"Come in," I step back and give him space to enter. "I wasn't sure what we're doing. Is what I'm wearing okay?"

His eyes move down my body, setting it on fire as they go.

"It's more than okay." His gaze works its way back up, and I can't believe how turned on I am just from that.

"We should go. In public. Soon," he says.

I must look confused because he clarifies. He leans in. "If we stay here, I'm going to want to pin you to that wall over there and do all sorts of things to you."

I glance at the wall in question. I turn back to him, arching a brow. "That doesn't sound like a bad idea."

He laughs as he takes my hand. "As tempting as that is, I promised you a date, and I don't go back on my word."

"That's something I really like about you," I say as I squeeze his fingers.

After I lock up, he leads me to the parking lot, and he walks up to a minivan. I stop.

"You drive a minivan?"

He nods.

"Do you have kids?"

"Why does everyone think that? No, I got it because I transport most of the band's equipment. It's easier using this."

I stare at it for a moment. "It's not the typical choice of a young, single guy."

He rolls his eyes. "I'm not typical."

I grin but let it go as we get in. "Where are we going?"

He turns to me. "You'll see."

For the entire drive, I keep guessing. And I make sure to pick wildly unlikely options.

As we drive out of town and into a rural area, I slap my leg. "You're taking me to a farm where we get to milk cows for fun."

He laughs. "You think that would be fun?"

I shrug. "I've never done it, so I don't know."

"Okay, I'll add that to the list."

"List?"

"Uh-huh."

"You already counting on more dates?"

He grins. "I am."

I stare at him, and damn, he's so good-looking it almost hurts to stare.

"What?" he asks.

"You're an enigma."

He turns down a new road, and I see a silo. "Are we going to fill a silo?"

"No, we are not going to a silo. How do you fill those anyway?" He glances over. "Never mind that. Why am I an enigma?"

I stare at the cows in the field as we continue down the country road.

"Well, you're very confident and competent, yet you rely on a fidget spinner at times. You like to make jokes and tease the other guys, but the changing ringtone on your phone seems to anger you. And you seem like a sexually confident man, yet you waited a long time before even flirting with me."

His brow shoots up, and he blinks many times. "Wow, that's a lot to take in. Okay, first, I am confident, but I get antsy sometimes. As for the ringtone, it was funny at first, but it's been going on since last year. I mean, shouldn't there be a cut-off time for a joke?" He glances at me, and I turn away to hide the fact I'm laughing.

"You know who it is, don't you?"

I hold up my hands as I turn back. "No, I don't. I swear!"

"As for the last item, what do you mean I waited a long time?"

I grimace, realizing I just gave something away.

"Cara?"

"Thunder might have mentioned you had a thing for me."

His brows shoot up. "Thunder? How the hell did he know?"

"I don't know."

He sighs. "I swear I can trust my teammates with my life but not a damn crush."

"He only told me because he knew I was interested in you."

Grayson smiles. "Yeah?"

"Yeah."

"I guess I can forgive him. And to answer your question, I only hesitated in asking you out because I wasn't sure I could do this. And this is nothing to do with you. It's because of what happened with my parents and my fucked-up family in general."

I rub his shoulder. "I'm so sorry you went through that."

He glances at me. "I get the impression your family life wasn't all roses, either."

I stare out the front window. "No, it wasn't. But let's save that story for another time. I've already brought down the mood, and this is supposed to be fun."

He turns down another road. "You haven't brought down any mood. You were being open and honest. I really appreciate you telling me that."

I think about what he said and start overthinking. "This reluctance, do you feel it now?"

He smiles. "No. After what we've been through together, we're a good team."

I nod. "It really was just you keeping your word back at my apartment and not a reluctance to take things too far?" I realize what I've asked after it's out of my mouth. Dammit, now I sound insecure. "I'm sorry, I didn't mean to ask that."

He takes my hand in his as he continues to drive down the road. "It's all right. Keeping my word is my reason for leaving your apartment. But don't think for a minute I haven't stripped you down and made you come hundreds of times in my mind. I've been fantasizing about you for the better part of a year."

He speaks so calmly, yet I'm a bundle of nerves with my heart beating so fast I'm surprised he can't hear it.

"Do you talk like that when you are having sex?" My eyes widen then I turn and stare out my window. "I apparently have no filter tonight."

He laughs. "Well, this isn't the first date conversation I was expecting, but I guess I did open myself up there. Let me ask you, do you like dirty talk?" He steals another glance at me.

"I don't know. I don't have a lot of experience. Caleb and I didn't do anything like that."

"Well, something we can experiment with." He winks.

And despite being a CIA agent, despite the dangerous situations I've been in and what I've had to do to escape, this man, with one wink, has turned me into a puddle of mush. Heat creeps up my neck to my cheeks, and I turn away again, hoping he doesn't notice.

We pull into a parking lot, and he stops the car.

He sweeps my hair off my shoulder and smiles. "You're blushing."

I swallow. "I've survived a lot of things in my life, but I'm not sure I can survive you. Please don't hurt me."

His smile turns to concern as he places his hands on my cheeks. "Never." He leans in and gives me a gentle kiss. "We're here."

All I see is a warehouse. "What's inside?" I ask.

He grins. "You'll see."

As soon as we step out of his van, I hear engines. I'm intrigued. He leads me into the building, where the back doors are open, and running both inside and outside is a large track. And on that track are a few go-carts.

"You want to race me?" I ask.

"I do." He takes my hands in his and winces. "Uh-oh. I'm sorry. I forgot about your hand. You won't be able to hold the steering wheel."

I pat his cheek with my bandaged hand. "Don't worry about it. I can beat you at any race with a hand tied behind my back."

He takes a step back, surprise all over his face. "Wow, you're a big talker. I'll have you know I'm a go-cart champion."

I nod. "We'll see."

A man comes out and shakes Grayson's hand. He sets us up in two go-carts and explains the course in more detail than necessary. By the time he's done, I'm itching to show off my skills.

We put on our helmets and get strapped in. A loud whistle

blows, and I pull ahead. On the first lap, Gray comes up and tries to pass me on the inside, but I cut him off. By the second lap, I've gained a couple hundred feet, and at this point, he doesn't have a chance to win. We do three laps, and I'll give him credit; he tried his hardest to catch me, but he never could.

After we cross the finish line, he yells to me, "Best two out of three!"

"You really want to embarrass yourself two more times?"

The guy running the place is laughing.

"Let's just go," Grayson says.

After I win the second race, he finally concedes.

"Okay, you have to tell me how the hell you learned to race like that."

I stare at the track. "My dad."

The manager comes up. "Wow, that was fun to watch. Here, thought you two could use some water." He hands us each a bottle.

"Thanks," Gray says. He takes a sip, watching me.

"When my dad taught me to drive, he also taught me some racing and evasive moves in case I was ever in a car chase. That, plus I've been in a car chase or two."

"Damn, you're a badass, Cara Harding. A sexy badass." He finishes his water, then tosses the bottle into a recycle bin. "Ready for dinner?"

"I am. Where are we going?"

He walks backward toward the door. "It's a surprise."

"Another surprise?"

"Yep." He takes my hand and leads me outside and to the van.

The wind has picked up, and I shiver. Why didn't I think to bring a jacket? Oh yeah, because Gray's sexiness distracted me.

We get into the car, and he reaches into the back seat and comes back with a flannel shirt.

"Here, it's getting chilly."

"Thank you." I put it on, and then he pulls out of the parking lot.

We drive back to Pine Valley, and he pulls up in front of Kelly's.

"Wait here." He jumps out.

I check my phone, and I have a message from Thunder.

Thunder: *How's the date going? Need me to call in an emergency?*

I laugh.

Me: *No need. Going great so far.*

Thunder: *Not too great if you have time to text me.*

Me: *Well, if that's how you're going to be, I'll only talk to Madison about it.*

Madison is Thunder's girlfriend, and I already claimed her as my new best friend. She's amazing, and I'm so glad they finally worked out their differences and got out of their own way.

Thunder: *Go ahead. She'll just tell me.*

I roll my eyes. Gray walks out of Kelly's, carrying a large bag. He hops back into the van and puts the bag in the back seat.

"Now to the next destination."

I know better than to ask, so I lean back and enjoy the ride. When he turns onto the campus for Havenwood University, I'm curious what he has planned.

"We're here."

We parked by a building I'm not familiar with. I follow him as he leads me inside and up several flights of stairs. Once we hit the top floor, we turn a corner, and in front of us is a large window. I step up, and I can see all of Pine Valley from here.

"How do you know about this place?'

"From Cody. His woman is a professor here. She told me about this place."

"His woman?"

Grayson shrugs.

"You mean Lucy?"

"You know her?"

"I do."

"Well, she suggested this would be a nice place for dinner as long as there weren't too many students hanging around."

There's no one else here. "I like it."

We sit on the window seat, and he opens the bag.

"It's not fancy, but the food is good." He hands me a warm item wrapped in foil. "It's a calzone. For these, just peel the foil back as you go. It can get messy." He pulls out a large pile of napkins.

We eat in silence as we stare out at the town. My mind is racing with thoughts about this man. Everything about him and us feels right. I'm hoping he's feeling it, too.

Once we're finished, we clean up, and he pulls me next to him.

"Why did you leave the service?" I ask. "If you don't want to talk about it, that's fine."

He's silent for a moment, so I take it he doesn't want to discuss it. "My brother. He needed me. He'd been arrested on drug charges and was forced to go to rehab. I thought if I was around, it would stick."

"But it didn't?"

He stares out at the town. "No. And I hate to say this, but now he seems worse."

"I'm sorry."

"It's okay. I really enjoy working at MTS."

"Yeah, that's a good group of guys there. Even if they do mess with your phone."

Shaking his head, he turns at me. "I will find out who's responsible. And if you know, you are now obligated to tell me."

"Obligated?"

He nods. "You're my woman now."

I roll my eyes. "Not if you call me that."

He laughs and pulls me closer. We spend the rest of the evening enjoying the view and sharing a few work stories, well, what we can share, of course.

Now we're nearly to my apartment, and I'm nervous. Will he come up? Do I want him to come up? Hell yes, I do.

He parks and rounds the hood to my side to help me out of the van.

"Such a gentleman," I say.

"For you, yes."

He walks me to my door. I'm going to invite him in.

"I'd like to take you out again sometime."

"Yes, me too."

He leans down and presses a light kiss to my lips. "Goodnight," he says, then walks away, leaving me wondering what just happened.

After all that sexy talk in the car, I thought for sure something would happen. Maybe he thinks this is the gentlemanly thing to do. I'm going to have to convince him it's not. I pull out my phone as I step inside my door.

Me: *It's too bad you didn't get to see what I wore under my clothes for you.*

He's almost to his car as I watch him pull his phone from his pocket. He stops as he reads it. He tips his head up to the sky. But instead of turning around, he continues on.

Damn, that didn't work. I unbutton my blouse until the blue lace of my bra shows and snap a photo. I send it.

He opens the driver's door, and he stops. His hand goes to his forehead as he rubs it. Then he turns and glances up at my building.

Grayson: *I'm trying to be good here.*

Me: *I don't want you to be good tonight.*

CHAPTER TWENTY-THREE

Grayson

THAT PHOTO FROM CARA. That was hot. I've got a war in my mind. On the one hand, I want to take this slow and do the right thing. On the other, I want her—badly. My phone buzzes with another incoming text.

Cara: *I don't want you to be good tonight.*

I don't want to be, either. By the time I get to her door, she's standing there, smiling at me.

"Are you sure about this?" I ask her.

"Very."

I walk in as she backs up. I kick the door closed with my foot and keep walking forward. When her back hits a wall, her eyes widen. I cage her in with my arms on either side. The fire that's been brewing between us is fully ablaze as I crash my lips to hers. The moment her mouth opens, I move my tongue in. Her hands are grasping at my back as I wrap my arms around her, pulling her closer until we are fused together.

She pulls back from our kiss with a mischievous glint in her eyes. Then she yanks up my T-shirt, and I oblige and take it off. Her fingers trace over my chest and my nipples. I groan and start trying to unbutton her blouse. It's taking too long, and we both grow frustrated. Finally, she pulls it off over her head.

I stare at her in the blue lace bra. "You're gorgeous."

She kisses me again. Hard.

I free my lips long enough to ask. "Where's the bedroom?"

She points down the hall. "Last door."

I pick her up, and she squeals as she wraps her legs around me. I kiss down her jaw to the bottom of her ear and to her neck.

"Yes, right there," she says on a particular spot on her neck.

I step inside the dark bedroom and lay her on the bed. Her hands immediately go to the zipper of my jeans, but I stop her.

"Not yet. First, I want you to lose the bra."

I sit up, giving her space to remove it. To my surprise, she sits up and slips off the bed. She walks to the nightstand and turns on a lamp.

"I want to be able to see you," she says.

And fuck, that is hot. I move toward her, and she holds a finger up.

"Your turn."

I glance down, then back at her with a smirk as I take off my socks. "Now you."

She shakes her head and unbuttons and unzips her jeans. Interesting. She's waiting on the bra. As soon as the jeans are off, I'm admiring the matching blue lace panties.

"Spin for me," I say.

She does a slow turn, revealing that her underwear is indeed a thong.

I'm growing harder by the moment, something I didn't think was possible, just from staring at this woman. She arches a brow at me, indicating it's my turn. I remove my jeans. The look of surprise on her face is priceless.

"No underwear?" she asks.

"Not tonight."

Her eyes move down again. "I wasn't expecting that." She keeps staring at my cock.

"Wasn't expecting what?" I stalk toward her. When I reach her, I reach around and unhook her bra.

She tilts her head up to meet my eyes. "You're bigger than I expected."

I smile. "Well, thank you, I think."

I lean forward and take her nipple into my mouth. I lick it, bite it gently, and then suck. I continue my onslaught as she moans. My hand moves down her hips and between her legs. As it moves up and reaches her panties, I discover she's soaking.

"You're so fucking wet." I get down on my knees and pull off her panties; she steps out of them, kicking them away. "I have to taste you."

Before she can respond, I lick her slit. She stumbles a little bit and grabs the nightstand for support. I take hold of her hips.

"You okay?"

She nods. "Very."

I chuckle, turn my attention back to her, and then I feast. I suck and lick as she's moaning and pulling on my hair.

"Yes!"

My grip on her ass grows tighter as I move my tongue faster. I insert two fingers inside her, and we both groan. She's so tight.

I return to sucking her clit as I curl my fingers ever so slightly. She lets out a loud moan and yells, "Yes, yes, yes!"

She squeezes my fingers as her orgasm takes over. I continue to lick until it's done.

She's dazed, so I lay her down on the bed. I climb over her and kiss her, letting her taste herself on my lips.

She wraps her arms around my neck. "Grayson, I want you inside me. I don't know how you feel about this, but I'm on birth control. And I'm safe."

"Are you sure? I'm safe."

She wraps her legs around my waist, urging me closer. "Very sure. Please fuck me now."

Damn this woman. She knows what she wants, and I love that about her. But after I felt how tight she is, I need to go slow. My control is barely holding on by a thread, and sweat is beading on the back of my neck, but I line up with her and slowly push in.

"Yes, more!"

Next thing, her hands are on my ass and pushing me in until I'm fully seated. I watch her. "You okay?"

She nods. "Just don't move for a minute."

I stay as still as I can, which feels like a herculean accomplishment right now.

"Okay, please move."

And I rock, slowly at first. The way she feels is so perfect. I lean down to kiss her, planning to take it easy, but when our lips meet, it ignites something more, and I thrust hard and faster. She's urging me on both with her hands on my ass and her legs as they tighten around me. I reach down and find her clit. I pinch it, then rub it as I move in and out.

She growls into my mouth. "Don't stop. Right there," she says.

I don't stop.

And seconds later, she screams out my name. "Grayson!"

Her body clenches me as her orgasm hits her, and I follow her as mine takes hold as well.

I moan loudly but it can't be helped. I'm holding myself up, breathing hard, waiting for some blood to get back to my head. Holy shit. That was by far the best sex I've ever had.

Cara's breathing heavily and staring at me with a question in her eyes.

"Ask," I say.

"It's never been like that for me," she says.

I lean my forehead to hers. "Me either."

"You're not just saying that?" she asks.

"No."

I lean down and gently kiss her. "I'll be right back." I stand up and walk toward the bathroom.

"Damn," she says.

I turn back. "What?"

"Rover wasn't kidding about how you got the name Peaches. That is one fine ass."

I laugh as I grab a towel. I return to the bed and clean her up. The way she's watching me right now, I could get used to it. She has pure satisfaction written on her face.

Cara is the whole package. And we've only been on one date, but fuck, I'm pretty sure I'm falling in love with her.

She sits up. "Wait. Why didn't you wear underwear tonight?"

I lie down beside her, laughing. "You really want to know?"

She nods.

I blow out a breath. "I miscalculated and ran out of clean boxers."

Her brows shoot up. "You ran out of underwear?"

"Trust me, this isn't normal for me. I thought I had some packed in my extra bag, but I didn't. And by the time I showered and discovered the problem, there wasn't time to do laundry before our date."

She grins. "So, you are human."

I take her hand in mine and intertwine our fingers. "I am. But I have to say I have a few questions for you right now."

The bedroom has the basics, with a bed, two nightstands, and a dresser. But what catches me off guard is the large whiteboard on one wall. It appears she's kept track of Ivan's movements on that board.

"Is that an Ivan board?"

She hides her face on my chest. "Yes," she says muffled. Then she sits up. "Sometimes thoughts about cases come to me at random times. I have a wall here, just like at work, so I can keep track of everything."

"You have a wall just like that at work?"

Her thumb caresses the back of my hand, and it feels good. "I do. And whenever I make a change, I take a photo of it so I can keep them identical."

I rub my nose to hers. "You're a workaholic, aren't you?"

She rubs her nose to mine, too. "Maybe. Can you deal with that?"

I shrug. "I think so." I pull her so she's on top of me.

Her eyes widen. "You're ready again?"

"Just being around you turns me on."

She rolls her eyes. "A line like that isn't going to get you what you want."

"No? How about this." I sit up and take her nipple into my mouth.

"Yeah, that'll do it."

CHAPTER TWENTY-FOUR

Grayson

WHEN I PULL into Morgan Thompson Security, I spot Rover and Maverick outside looking up. I park and join them.

"Hey, welcome back, Maverick," I say.

He doesn't even glance at me. "Thanks."

"What's going on?" I ask.

Rover points to our roof. "Wild peacock."

I glance up, and sure enough, there is a large peacock on the roof. "You sure it's wild? Maybe it's someone's pet," I say.

"No, it's wild. I heard a couple of guys talking about it over breakfast at Kelly's. Apparently, it was on top of the strip club terrorizing anyone who went in."

I arch a brow. "Terrorizing?"

Rover nods. And as if the damn bird understands, it starts screaming.

Fox comes out, holding a bag of Cheetos in one hand and a couple of the golden, cheesy treats in another. "What the hell is that?"

Rover points to the roof. "Wild peacock."

Fox shoves a couple Cheetos into his mouth. "Hmm."

"It's loud. Maybe we should shoot it down," Maverick says.

"Don't even think about it," Stormy says as he walks out the door. "As far as I'm concerned, that bird is welcome here."

We turn to Stormy. I can't say I've ever seen him excited about wildlife in the area. Quite the opposite, as he normally complains about the raccoons.

"Did you lure the bird here?" Maverick asks.

Stormy crosses his arms and stares at us. "Maybe I did. I figured you could all handle getting around a damn peacock, but if that thing can be a deterrent to anyone else trying to get in, so be it."

"How the hell do you lure a peacock?" I ask.

Stormy shrugs. "I may have put some bird seed on the roof."

The bird flies down to the parking lot. Then it approaches Fox.

He backs up. "Hey now, stay back. Shoo!"

But the bird keeps going after him. We stand there, not knowing what to do. Fox is a large man who has taken out many enemies. He wouldn't let a peacock take him down, would he?

Fox stops backing up and stands his ground. "Shoo, I say!"

The peacock runs forward and grabs a Cheeto out of his hand.

"Ouch! The damn thing bit me."

The peacock finishes off the food he stole and approaches Fox for more.

"Drop the bag," Stormy says.

Fox drops the bag, and the bird descends on it. "What the hell?" Fox asks.

The bird locks eyes with Fox with a Cheeto hanging out of its beak, and I swear it proceeds to eat it in slow motion.

Rover laughs. "Well, it's official. His name is Cheeto, and he's our defense peacock."

Stormy shakes his head. "Show's over. Let's get inside and get back to work."

I follow Stormy, leaving the rest of the guys outside. After

I grab a cup of coffee, I start up my laptop. Before I even take a sip from my mug, Rover and Fox walk into my office with stupid grins on their face. Without invitation, they plop down in two other chairs across from my desk.

Fox points at me. "Based on your glow, I'd say your date last night went well."

I lean back, crossing my arms. "I'm not glowing." I'm smiling. I've been smiling since I woke up this morning with Cara in my arms. To say last night was magical would be an understatement.

And this morning, too. We were both almost late for work because we couldn't keep our hands off each other. But I'm not going to tell these guys about it.

"The peacock encounter put me in a good mood." Maybe they'll buy that.

Rover leans forward. "I know for a fact it wasn't Cheeto. Cara and Connie are friends. Apparently, Cara was nervous about her date last night and gave Connie a call. Maybe Connie can give Cara a call today and see how she's doing."

"Shit, I can't get away from you guys, can I?" I say, laughing.

"Nope. Brothers for life," Fox says.

I shake my head. "Well, it did go well, but there's a more important matter we need to discuss."

Both Rover and Fox lean forward. "What's going on?" Rover asks.

I grin at Fox. "I believe you owe me a clean minivan." I toss him my keys, and he catches them.

"Damn. I was hoping you'd forget."

Rover looks back and forth between us. "Do I want to know?"

Before I can fill him in, Stormy knocks on my open door. "Meeting in my office. Right now."

He takes off, and we follow him down the hall. I'm the last one in the room. As I go to take a seat at the large conference table, my phone rings. Another damn song about peaches. This is getting ridiculous.

I drop my head and sigh. "I know it's one of you. For the love of everything, make it stop."

Fox tries unsuccessfully to muffle his laughter.

I turn to him. "It's you. I've already ruled out Maverick. CT and Rover couldn't keep it up this long."

"That's what she said," Fox says.

"I can, too, keep it up a long time. Just ask Connie," Rover says.

I close my eyes. This is what I'm dealing with.

"Peaches, we'll deal with your phone issues later," Stormy says. "I have an update." He carries his laptop over to the table and turns it around. "This is footage of someone entering our office at two in the morning last week. They used my passcode to get in, but as you can see by the figure, it isn't me."

He plays the video, and we all focus on it. Someone wearing dark pants and a dark hoodie walks up to the building and stands there a moment, punching a passcode. The door opens, and the person walks in. There is no car visible in the parking lot. The person is clearly thinner than Stormy. But I can't tell from the video if it's a man or a woman.

"The person stood at the door for a moment, and I checked; a few other numbers were tried."

"What numbers?" Fox asks. "It might help narrow down who it is."

Stormy stops the video loop and closes his laptop. "My birthdate and the date I entered the service."

All dates from a while ago. But anyone in security would know he'd never use something public. I pull a fidget spinner out of my pocket and spin it as I think this through. "It's someone who doesn't know you well," I say.

Fox taps his fingers on the table. "Or someone trying to throw us off. They did get the right number, after all. And it's such a personal fucking number."

"Those numbers are all from a long time ago. Do you have someone in your past who may be trying to get revenge?" I ask.

Stormy shakes his head. "Not that I know of."

The video was too damn grainy to really make out much on the person. No logos on the clothes.

"All we know is that someone broke in, knew to go to Stormy's office, and what to take," Rover says. "We need to question anyone who would have an interest in that information."

"Well shit, Rover. That opens up competition security firms, anyone who hates the military, and a hell of a lot of other people," Fox says.

"Is there any other video?" I ask.

Stormy nods. "There is the video of this person leaving, but I'm afraid you can't see much more."

"How long was this person inside?"

Stormy sighs. "Thirty minutes."

Wow, we could accomplish a lot in thirty minutes. "Odds are they stole more than just this file."

"It's possible," Stormy says. He purses his lips.

"What aren't you telling us?" Maverick asks.

Stormy stands and walks to the window. "It could be a coincidence, but at the edge of the building, out of sight of the camera, was a cigarette butt." He turns to us. "Have any of you started smoking? I have to know if this could be related."

Holy shit. Part of this building was burned down earlier this year, and the only evidence found at the time also happened to be a cigarette butt. Sadly, it was too burned to get any evidence, but maybe this one has some.

"That's great!" I say. "We can send it in to get DNA off of it."

Stormy shoves his hands into his pockets. "I'm hoping for that, too. I've already sent it for testing. But that's why I'm asking you, is anyone here smoking?"

I shake my head, as do all the other guys.

"Okay, good. I'll let you know if we get a match. In the meantime, someone is coming today to install more cameras on the exterior of the property."

I glance at the other guys. "And what? Are we supposed to

wait for this person to drop the next bomb? There must be more we can do."

Stormy sits back down. "Trip has the video. He's going to blow up some still shots and see if we can see anything else. For now, I'm denying the information out there regarding our clients. If any reporters manage to track you down, send them to me."

Fox clears his throat, and all eyes move to him. "Should we postpone next weekend's paintball game?"

We often play paintball on the property behind our building. But a few times a year, we set up something bigger that we call the championship.

"No, there's no reason you guys can't all blow off some steam," Stormy says.

I plan to ask Cara to join us. She's played with us before, and she's one of the best.

"That's all for now."

We all walk to the kitchen and grab some coffee.

"Do you guys have any idea who this suspect might be?" Fox asks.

I pour a cup of coffee and take a sip. Then I turn and lean on the counter. "We keep focusing on how well this person knows Stormy, but what if it's this business or one of us who is the real target?"

The guys turn toward me.

"Like someone we pissed off on an assignment?" Rover asks.

I shrug. "Maybe."

Fox whistles. "That's a long list of suspects."

Yeah, it is.

Fox takes a sip of his coffee, then spits it out. "What the fuck did you do to my coffee?" He glances at each of us.

Rover does a terrible job of hiding his smile. "What's wrong with it?"

I push mine away somewhat, not wanting to know.

"That is not vanilla creamer," Fox says as he gags. "I need water." He runs to the sink, bends down, and drinks directly from the faucet.

"What the hell did you do?" I ask.

"There might be a little cayenne in the creamer," Rover says with a smile.

Fox pours the rest of his cup of coffee into the sink. "Why are you so childish?" Fox asks Rover.

I take another sip. I like my coffee black, which is a good thing around here.

"And when did you decide it was okay to mess with the creamer? I thought the kitchen was off limits," Fox mutters.

"Lightning told me a story or two about the New York guys the last time he was here. It gave me a few ideas." Rover's face was lit up.

Great. Guess I won't be using the kitchen for my lunch.

"It's funny, right?" Rover asks.

"No!" Fox and I respond.

I grab my coffee and head down the hall.

About an hour later, Rover runs into my office. "Lover-boy, you have a visitor," he sings out.

I glance up, and Cara is staring at him. "I can't say I've seen this side of you, Rover."

He grins. "Hey, I'm happy for you two."

Cara walks into my office, and Rover steps out, closing the door behind him. But he opens the door and pops his head back in.

"Hey, just remember these walls are thin. I found out the hard way, if you recall." He grins before he leaves.

Cara glances at me. "Rover?"

I smile. "You don't want to know."

Rover got a little hot and heavy with Connie in his office, and unbeknownst to them, many of the guys could hear them.

"I hope it's okay that I stopped by. I wanted to see you again," she says.

I stand up, walk around my desk, and plant a kiss on her. "I'm happy to see you. Sorry about Rover. He can be obnoxious."

She snorts. "I've worked with him before. I'm fully aware."

As if on cue, Rover squeals as he runs down the hall. Cara's brows go up.

"Rover messed with Fox's creamer, so based on that squeal, I'm guessing Fox just got revenge."

"Uncle!" Rover yells.

Cara smiles. "I think you're right." She hooks her hands around my neck. "I want to see you again tonight."

I pull her close to me. "Good, because I do, too."

"I need to go into the office briefly, but do you want to come by around six?"

"Sounds good to me." I lean down, and when our lips meet, she lets out a little moan.

"You can't do that," I say.

"Do what?"

"Those little moans. They drive me crazy." I press her body right up against mine, and she smiles the moment she feels my erection.

"Good to know. I'll save them for tonight." She kisses my cheek, then backs away. "Bye, Gray."

"Bye."

I watch as she opens the door and walks out. If I had it my way, I'd spend every minute with her. And that's when it hits me. I'm not just falling for her; I've fallen.

CHAPTER TWENTY-FIVE

Cara

"Good morning, Harding. I wasn't expecting you in." Anderson is standing next to his desk, holding a cup of coffee.

He made it clear I should stay home for a few days and rest, which surprised me, but I need answers. He moves around his desk and sits. "Please have a seat."

"I can't sit at home not knowing what is going on with Max, Ivan, and Alex. Do you have any updates?"

"I do." He clasps his hands on his desk. "As you know, Alex is in custody. We are still waiting to hear from the Costa Rican police about Ivan. With what was found on Ivan's boat and what we have on Alex, they won't be free anytime soon. Hopefully never. It was a great job you all did."

I nod. "Thank you. If the police don't turn over Ivan—"

He holds up his hand. "I'll take care of it. I don't want you to worry about it."

I swallow. He's been my assignment for several years now, but frankly, I'm ready to move on and away from Ivan Kralik. "And Max? Is he still in the hospital?"

Anderson takes a deep breath.

"Is he dead?" I ask, now worried about what this will mean for Gray if it's determined he killed the man out of rage.

"Neither. I just found out last night that he left the hospital."

I sit up straighter. "What? But I thought he was in critical condition."

"He was unconscious when they brought him in, but soon after, he was in stable condition. He was released and told to take it easy."

I sit back in the chair, and my eyes go to the photos on the walls. Anderson has pictures of himself with a couple of past presidents and a few high-ranking military officials. The agents refer to it as his brag wall.

"He left. So, he could be…"

"Anywhere. Yes. I'm sorry. I was going to call you today to tell you."

He'll come after me. But all he has is the fake identification which said my name was Erica and gave a false address in Florida. But if Ivan knows CT and all the guys are former military, he might have told Max. Although there is still no reason for him to suspect I'm not Erica. Regardless, I'm going to be extra vigilant until we catch him.

Anderson leans forward. "Seriously, you can take a few days off and rest until your hand heals."

I glance down at the bandage. Yeah, like I'm going to rest knowing Max is out there somewhere, probably hurting more girls.

"I have emails I'd like to answer before I head home."

He nods. "Okay, sounds good."

I leave his office and go to my desk. We don't have too many agents in this building, and right now, most of them are gone. It's sad to say that despite working here for several years after transferring out of New York, I still don't really know my coworkers that well. I guess it comes with the territory. We're all lone wolfs in our own way.

Instead of checking email, I search for any activity on

Max. I worked his file, and I know the circles he runs in. After an hour, I have nothing. I show no flight information or record of his passport anywhere in the last week. Either he's still in Costa Rica, or he found his own way to travel.

The man has access to money and to men with even more money. He could be back in Brazil doing business, or he could be in the United States searching for me.

I grab my phone and smile when I see another text from Gray.

Grayson: *What do you call a bunch of raspberries playing guitar?*

Me: *What?*

Grayson: *A jam session.*

I roll my eyes. That was a good one.

Me: *Max left the hospital. I've searched but can't find any hits on his passport.*

I set down my phone and stretch my arms above my head. My phone buzzes.

Grayson: *Send me any details you have on him—birthdate, full name—and I'll ask Trip to run a search.*

I smile. The man really does have my back. I send him everything and thank him. He responds immediately.

Grayson: *Anything for you.*

I turn my attention back to my computer, smiling as my stomach flutters, picturing this man. I've worked with Peaches before, and I admit I've had a bit of a crush on him. But after the last couple of months, he's managed to work his way into my heart. A feat I didn't think was possible anymore.

I leave the office, grab lunch to-go, and head home. I find myself smiling, thinking of Grayson while I eat. Finally, I text Madison to see if she can chat via FaceTime.

I'm so happy Thunder and Madison are together. She's perfect for him. And for me. She doesn't hold back her opinions and is a great friend.

A notification comes in on my laptop. It's Madison, so I click accept.

"Hey, Spy Girl, how's it going?" Madison asks, wearing a huge smile.

"Ugh! I know that smile. I don't want to know you've just had sex with Thunder. He's like a brother."

Madison laughs. "How do you always know?"

I point at the screen. "It's the goofy smile you have."

"Whatever, you're just jealous." She rolls her eyes.

"No. I don't want the picture of Thunder doing anything like that in my head."

Madison chuckles. "Tell me, how was your date?"

She'd messaged a couple times to tell her about it, but I wanted to wait until I could tell her in person. Or at least face to face.

"It went well." I don't even try to hide my grin.

She claps her hands together. "You look so happy! Does this mean you're opening up to him?"

I nod. She knows about my history with Caleb and my reluctance to get close to anyone again.

"And I'm seeing him again tonight."

Her eyes light up. "Oh, where are you going?"

I carry my laptop to the couch and sit down. "I'm not sure."

"What did you do on your first date?"

Thinking back to our date, I smile. "He took me to a go-kart place and thought he was going to win."

She smiles. "Damn, you showed him up on the first date?"

My stomach drops. "What? Was I not supposed to do that? Dammit, I figured because Gray knows what I do for a living that I could be myself."

She laughs.

"Madison!"

"I'm sorry. No, it's fine. You should be yourself around him. I'm laughing because I'm sure he's used to winning."

He probably is. "Well, if he wants to be with me, he'll have to get used to losing."

Madison shakes her head. "Please, please, let me be there when you tell him that."

"I called you for advice but not that kind of advice."

Suddenly, she's walking, holding her phone. Then a door clicks. "What's going on?" she asks.

I jump in. "I know this will sound crazy coming from me, but I'm scared. I've known Gray for a while, but these last couple of months, while working on assignments together, my feelings have grown so fast—too fast. I've spent years never letting anyone in, and somehow, he is all the way in already."

"Well, not unless something happened you haven't told me about," she snorts.

My cheeks warm. "I'm pouring my heart out and you're snorting?"

She waves her free hand in front of the screen. "I'm sorry. You're right." She narrows her eyes. "Wait, you're blushing? Why? Oh, Cara! Did you have sex with that man?"

I feign innocence and blink a few times. "What do you mean?"

She grins. "You did! After the first date? Wow, Cara. You go girl."

I grin. "Part of me thought maybe we should have waited, but dammit, the chemistry between us... I didn't want to stop."

"I'm so happy for you!" Madison is beaming.

I pinch my brow. "Thank you, but on the other topic, how do I slow down my feelings?"

Madison tilts her head. "Oh, Cara, you don't. I'd say the reason you feel so much, so fast, is because you finally opened your heart to someone. To Grayson."

"I didn't mean to open it."

"Yeah, you did. You said he asked you out when you visited Thunder and me at Lightning's cabin."

I cross my arms and stare at her through the screen. "Thunder told you that?"

She smiles. "No, I overheard it. Don't worry; I didn't overhear everything. Due to my concussion, I was sleeping a lot."

"I don't know if it was a date. He asked me to watch his band play."

Madison nodded. "Okay, so maybe not an official date, but he was trying to see you outside of work. That still counts."

She's right. It does. Then he said sweet things in the jungle after jumping out of a helicopter, and he spooned me to keep me warm.

"What are you thinking about? I've never seen you smile like that."

"Just realizing why I opened up to him."

"Thunder says he's a good guy. Enjoy this."

I stare up at the ceiling. She's right. I should enjoy this. He is a good guy, and he gets me. "Thank you. I really appreciate it."

"Anytime." She looks to her left and then smiles. "Again? Okay, but I'm going to talk to Cara first."

"Ugh! You two. Go, have fun."

Madison laughs, and Thunder's mug comes into the screen. "Thanks, Cara," he says.

"I'll talk to you later," Madison says.

I nod and close my laptop. She's right. I'm going to enjoy my time with Gray. Go with the flow. Well, it wouldn't hurt to ask for a hint as to what tonight's date will be.

I set my laptop beside me on the couch and stand up to get my phone. I hear the noise behind me too late. While attempting to spin around, someone grabs my hands, pins them up against my back, and slams me to the floor in one swift move.

"Don't move," a man's voice says.

He binds my wrists with some kind of fabric before jerking me up. Shit, I have nothing on me that could help. But we're close to the wall, so I step closer to it. Then I lunge.

As expected, he grabs my hair since it's the only thing he can reach. I run up the wall and flip over the top of him. It's a move I've done in training, but he's expecting it. And he's taller than I anticipated. He grabs me mid-flip and a second man puts duct tape over my mouth. How the hell did I not hear two people in my room?

"Let's go."

The man slings me over his shoulder and walks out my door. Wait, someone will see this and report it. I try to scream, but the tape is muffling it.

The second man grabs a fistful of my hair. "If you don't shut up, I'll rip this out by the roots."

I turn my head in his direction, but all I see is the side of a hoodie. But that voice.

"Max?" I try to say. It comes out muffled, but he must know what I was trying to say.

The hoodie turns until I see his face. He has black eyes and stitches across his cheek. His nose is crooked. He smiles and is missing a couple of teeth.

"You're my girl. You don't leave until I tell you to."

Shit. I can't let him get me into his car. As we near it, the man holding me sets me down. This is my chance. I take a step back, and Max turns.

"Don't—" Before he finishes his sentence, I do a roundhouse kick as hard as I can. Max grabs his nose. "Fuck! You bitch. My nose is already broken!"

The second guy comes at me, so I fake stepping right. He follows then I bounce on my left foot and kick him hard, too. He goes down fast.

I twist my wrists together and discover the fabric isn't too tight and I'm able to slip one hand out. I run to my car while ripping the tape off my mouth. Thankfully, my keys are still in my pocket. While I wish I had my phone, I'm not about to go back to grab it.

I unlock my door and glance back. Max is chasing me. I get in and lock the doors. The key misses the ignition because I'm staring at Max.

"Get out of the car!" Max turns to the other guy. "Dan, get your ass up and help me!"

Finally, the engine turns over. I glance back, and Max is holding a large rock and slams it into my window. I hit the gas pedal and turn away as the glass smashes in on me. I hope like hell no one is behind me. After I back up, I turn, and the tires squeal as I speed out of the parking lot.

Gunshots fire, and I duck and press harder on the gas pedal. As I turn on the road, I glance back to see Max getting into his car. I've got to lose him. Fast.

How the hell did Max figure out where I live? He must know my name isn't really Erica.

CHAPTER TWENTY-SIX

Grayson

I STARE at the house I grew up in, memories flooding back that I don't want when my phone buzzes.

Jasper: *Are you going to sit in the driveway all day like an asshole?*

I chuckle. There are a lot of issues between my brother and me, but it's nice to see his familiar smart-ass side. Besides, I don't have all day since I stopped by on my lunch break.

Grabbing the folder from the passenger seat before I exit my van, I walk up the front walkway. He's standing in the doorway, smoking a cigarette.

"Wow, my little brother stopped by for a visit. Did hell freeze over?"

Shit. I can smell the liquor from here. I thought coming over before noon would give better odds, but I was wrong.

"There's something I need to talk to you about." I hold up the folder.

He nods, tosses the cigarette onto the porch, and steps on it. That's when I notice a pile of them. I bite my tongue to keep from saying anything.

It's been a year since I've been inside this house. The house we were raised in after my parents died. My aunt and uncle took us in and, when they passed, left us the house. They had kept it in great shape, and my aunt had been so proud of her rose garden. But now, all the bushes are dead. I tried to keep up on the maintenance, but my brother doesn't want me around, so it's been hard.

He follows me inside. I walk into the kitchen and toss the folder onto the counter.

"What's that?" He nods toward it as he opens the fridge and grabs a beer. He doesn't offer me one. He knows better.

"The neighbors have complained several times over noise. I just found out about this last week."

He chugs his beer and sets the can on the counter. "I have to earn money somehow. Tell them to mind their own fucking business."

"Jasper, you do have to follow the law, and based on these complaints, you're revving engines and making all sorts of noise too late at night."

He sits in a kitchen chair. "So, they complain. Let them."

I sit across the table from him. "Mr. Buchin said the next time he'll sue. Come on, just get along."

My brother laughs. "Let him sue me."

He's not following. "If there are enough nuisance complaints, the city can condemn the property. That means you won't be able to live here."

His eyes widen. "They can do that?"

It's more complicated than I'm letting on, but dammit, he needs to take responsibility. "Yeah, they can do that."

"I'll call Drake. He's been saying I can move the cars to his garage." He shrugs. "He's got more tools there than I have here anyway."

I breathe a sigh of relief. Drake is my brother's best friend who happens to have a huge garage and property where no one cares what they do with it.

"Thank you." I stand up to go.

"That's it? You only came by to tell me what to do?"

I sigh. I don't have the energy for this fight again. "No. I came by to visit but based on how strong the liquor smells, I'm guessing you aren't up for a friendly chat."

He laughs. "You condescending prick. Not only do you have the nerve to steal my life, but you're going to insult me in my own home, too?"

And here we go. "First, I didn't steal shit. Second, this is *our* home. *Our* home. If I didn't keep up on taxes, you'd have been homeless a long time ago." I know better than to engage, but dammit, I'm tired of this shit.

He stands up. "You didn't steal anything? I was playing guitar on stage before you even knew what one was. You copied me. I was going to enlist. But when that didn't work out, you made sure not only to enlist but now you're a fucking SEAL." Turning, he stares out the window. "If it weren't for me, you wouldn't have shit."

He's right, and that's what makes all of this so hard.

"I'll always appreciate what you did for me as a kid. That's why I keep this place up. And why it's important to me that we don't lose it."

He does pay for utilities, but that's it. I've kept up everything else.

He shoves his hands into his pockets. "Yeah, well, some of us aren't made of money like you are."

I grab the folder and walk toward the door.

"I saw your girlfriend."

His words stop me cold. I turn. "What?"

He smirks, knowing he's got my attention. "Your girlfriend. I saw her. Long, dark hair. Cute. Reminds me of Laura."

Laura is his ex, and Cara looks nothing like her.

"You can't even be original when picking women, can you? Do you do it to rub it in my face?"

I ignore his taunt. "Where did you see her?"

He gets a second beer from the fridge. "At the go-kart place. I stopped in to talk to Simon. And imagine my surprise seeing you there with a Laura lookalike. I shouldn't be surprised. But it will never work, you know. We're broken. She'll see that soon enough."

I storm up to him. "Enough. She looks nothing like Laura. If you stopped drinking for a minute, maybe you wouldn't be so damned bleary-eyed and could see that."

He guzzles his beer, then turns his cold stare to me. "You can see yourself out." Without another word, he walks down the hall to his bedroom and slams the door.

I leave, making a mental note to call Drake tomorrow to see if he heard from my brother.

As I drive, I turn the music up loud. The last thing I need is to be in a foul mood for my date with Cara tonight. I smile, thinking about everything I have planned. I've never gone to this much trouble planning dates, but I have to say, I like it. Especially when she lights up the way she did for the go-kart racing. I should have known she'd be great at it.

As I walk to the front door of Morgan Thompson Security, Cheeto screams at me. I give him a wave and continue inside. Fox runs past me, grinning like a fool. Trax tears around the corner, chasing after him. Well, that's new. Trax is usually not one to partake in any of the office shenanigans.

"Welcome back, Trax!" I call out.

"Thanks!" he yells back.

CT and Rover are in the break room, arguing as usual. But this sounds more serious than their normal bickering.

"Amber's an adult. At some point, you have to stop trying to control her," CT says.

I step up to the doorway of our break room. Rover is pacing.

"I know she's seeing someone. Twice I've caught her holding her phone with that stupid look on her face. But she won't tell me who he is."

"Why does that bother you so much?"

Rover stops. "Because I need to run a background check on this guy. After what she went through last year, I'm not taking any risks."

CT sighs. "Would you feel better if I talked to her about it? She might talk to me."

Rover nods. "Yeah, thanks. And if he's a creep, you'll let me know, right?"

"Of course," CT says. He smiles, but it doesn't make it to his eyes.

But I'm not about to peel that onion, so I go for a change of topic instead. "Hey, CT, you made it back fast."

He crosses his arms. "Yeah, I wanted to get back and help with the leak. I flew a red-eye last night." He yawns as if to confirm it.

"Why is Trax chasing Fox?" I ask.

CT grins.

I chuckle. "What did you two do this time?"

Rover shrugs. "Wasn't our fault, really."

I cross my arms. "Really?"

CT stands and walks toward me. "Trax may have said something about not touching his special coffee blend before he left on assignment."

Rover grins. "And we may have forgotten to mention that to Fox, who just happened to use it all this past week."

"So, you see, it really wasn't our fault. Trax should have told Fox," CT nods to confirm his own statement.

I shake my head. "Have any of you made any progress in finding out who broke in here? Or have you been too busy causing problems?"

Rover pours himself a cup of coffee and sits down at the table. "We don't cause problems." He takes a sip. "Oh wow, CT, this special blend is good. Now I get why Trax is so upset. You should try some."

I roll my eyes and walk to my office. My phone rings. Another fucking song about peaches. "Motherfuckers!" I yell.

Rover and CT giggle from the break room.

I check my phone. My brother. At this point, he's definitely drunk, so I ignore the call.

After a few hours at the office with no luck getting any closer to knowing who broke in, I head home and get ready.

Before I shower, I check again to make sure I didn't miss a call from Cara. She hasn't responded to any of my texts since she left here this morning. Even if she was sent out on an assignment, she could at least text. And besides, she told me she wasn't going anywhere until her hand healed per her boss's orders.

She could be busy, but I'm still feeling uneasy about it. As I head out to my van, I call her. It rings and goes to voicemail. Odd, but she hasn't canceled, so I drive to her apartment.

After knocking on her door, I stare out at the parking lot. Her car isn't there. I knock again and check the time. I'm not too early. Something doesn't feel right. I try the door, and it's unlocked. Something's wrong. Cara would never leave her door unlocked. She mentioned that while we were hiking through the jungle in Brazil.

Slowly I open the door. "Cara?" I call out.

Silence. I place my hand on my gun as I walk farther into her apartment. Several items are on the floor that had been on the table last night. I spot her phone on the kitchen counter. She would never go anywhere without her phone.

I call Stormy.

"Peaches?"

"Cara's gone. Her apartment was unlocked, and her phone is here. There are some items on the floor. I have a bad feeling."

"Is it possible she went for a walk?"

I swallow. I'm not one to talk to my boss about my personal life, but he needs to know. "We're supposed to go out on a date. She's expecting me. So no, I don't think she went out on a walk. Besides, she would never leave her phone behind, and the door unlocked. Her car's not in the parking lot, either."

Stormy's chair squeaks against the floor. "She could have another phone, but I agree about the door. I'm going to call Anderson and see if he knows anything. I'll call you right back."

He ends the call, and I walk through her apartment, searching for anything that might tell me where she could be. I find nothing.

Stormy calls back. That was fast.

"Yeah?" I answer.

"She checked in with Anderson this morning. Apparently,

Max and one of his guys tried to kidnap her. She got away and is hiding."

And she didn't call me.

"Anderson gave me the number of the burner phone she's using. I'll text it over. If you find her, let me know."

"Thank you. I will."

Once Stormy texts the number, I call it. Someone answers the phone but doesn't say anything.

"Cara?"

"Grayson?"

Thank God.

"Gray, I'm in trouble."

CHAPTER TWENTY-SEVEN

Cara

As MUCH AS I dislike my father most days, today, I'm thankful for him and for this cabin. After I transferred to Seattle, he bought it under a pseudonym and told me if I was ever in danger to come here.

I lost Max and Dan within the first mile, but then I drove fifty miles out of my way to be certain no one was following me. I secured my car in the garage and was staring out over the forest from the large cabin window when Grayson called.

I almost didn't answer the unknown number, but my gut said I should. He insisted on knowing where I was, so I gave him the address but made him promise to memorize it and not write it down.

The bigger issue is that Max knows where I live. Does this mean my entire identity is compromised? How else would he know where my apartment is? I grab a notepad and retrace my steps.

I went to MTS to see Gray. Afterward, I stopped at home to get some ibuprofen and park my car before walking to the CIA office. That means someone would have had to have followed me from MTS in Pine Valley to Seattle. Why would Max know about MTS?

The leak. It put MTS in the news. And someone posted photos of some of the guys online. One photo was of Gray. Max would recognize him if he saw him.

But any online search of Gray would have come up with little to no information. The more I think about it, the more it makes sense that Max had MTS watched, and once he knew where I lived, he planned to kidnap me.

But if that's true, anyone coming or going from MTS could be in danger. I call Gray back, but it goes to voicemail. I call Anderson.

"Harding?"

"All the employees of MTS are in danger. The only way Max found me would have been if someone was watching MTS and then that person followed me home."

"You didn't notice someone following you?"

I bite my lip to keep from saying something snarky. "I'm afraid not."

Anderson sighs. "Harding, you always have to watch your back. You know this."

"Can we save the lecture and warn MTS? Since I don't have my phone, I don't have their numbers on me."

He doesn't respond right away.

"Anderson?"

"You're right. I'll call Stormy right away."

"Thank you."

He ends the call, and I pace the room. The man with Max, who he called Dan, I've never seen him before. Not that I should be surprised, I'm sure the man has a lot of people working for him.

My stomach drops. I lost him in the first mile while driving. But maybe that was on purpose so I wouldn't notice who was really following me. The window creaks, and I turn my head to see a branch rubbing against it. I realize if someone knows I'm here, I'm a sitting duck.

Just in case, I go to the pantry and make myself comfortable on the floor. I listen for any sounds of doors or windows opening. The window continues to creak as the wind picks up. Thunder roars above. Great, that will make it harder to hear anything.

I sit there and stare at my phone. Ten minutes have gone by. I have no idea how long it will be until Gray gets here. But then I hear the unmistakable beep of the keypad at the door. Someone's trying to get in. The door creaks open.

I stand, readying myself.

Shoes click-clack on the floor. I strain to hear. It sounds like a woman's heels.

"Hello? Anyone here?" a woman calls out.

Who the hell is this, and why does she have the code?

I don't move. This could be a trick. I crack the pantry door and see a woman with long, dark hair walk past. She's pulling a vacuum and holding a bin of cleaning supplies. She's not wearing a uniform. I cannot imagine my dad hiring a cleaning service without telling me. That would make this place useless if someone saw me here.

White earbuds are in her ears, and she sways her hips as she wipes down the counter.

Is she going to come in here? Thirty minutes into her cleaning, she turns on the vacuum cleaner. Hopefully, this is a quick clean and she leaves soon.

She's in my view again as she vacuums the tile floor of the kitchen. A loud pop sounds. The woman stills and falls forward, and that's when I see the bullet hole in her back.

Fuck, please, Grayson, tell me you didn't kill an innocent woman. But it isn't Grayson who steps into view. It's Dan. The one I tried to knock out by kicking his nuts. He turns off the vacuum, and it's eerily silent in the house now.

He flips the woman over. "Fuck!" He retrieves his phone from his pocket and holds it to his ear. "It's not her."

A man's voice is yelling through the line, but I can't make out what he's saying.

"Too late," this man says. He holds the phone away from his ear as there is more yelling.

"No, her car is gone. She's not here." The man nods. "I

followed her here. She pulled into the driveway, but she must have left while I was getting lunch."

He went for lunch? Guess he's not a professional hitman. Luckily, I had to idle in the driveway while I looked up the passcode for the garage.

"Yeah, I can meet you there in twenty." The man ends the call and walks out of the room. The front door opens and closes.

I don't leave the pantry because I have no idea who is on their way or where Dan went.

Another ten minutes go by with no sounds except the wind. Even the thunder seems to be gone. My phone lights up.

Grayson: *I'm here.*

Me: *A man was just here and killed the maid. He called someone, likely Max. And that person is on their way here, too.*

Grayson: *Got it. If he's here, I'll find him.*

I slowly exit the pantry. There are still no sounds coming from within the house. I make my way out of the kitchen and down a hallway toward the front entry.

The movement of the front door opening catches my eyes, and I jump behind it.

"Cara?" Grayson calls.

"I'm here," I say.

He closes the door and pulls me into his arms. "Is there anyone else here?"

I nod. "The maid, but I'm sure she's dead. The guy who shot her was the one with Max when he abducted me from my apartment. He's still here somewhere."

He nods. "I saw him sitting in his car. I parked farther down and hiked in through the woods. We'll go out that way."

He turns to open the door but instead spins around, pulling me in the other direction. "The man is walking up the driveway."

I take the lead and go to the back door. We manage to get out before Dan enters the house. We creep around outside the perimeter. Gray points to a small path in the trees. He counts his fingers down from three so we can run on one. But when he holds up two fingers, a car pulls up. I recognize it immediately—Max.

He exits the vehicle and limps up the driveway. From here, I can see the dried blood on his face from when I kicked his nose.

Dan walks out the door. "No sign of her."

"Fuck," Max says as he takes in the property. His gaze stops on the garage. "Did you check in there?"

"Isn't that another house?" Dan asks.

Max stares back at the cabin. "Same paint. I think it's a garage."

It does look more like a cottage from this side because you can't see the large doors, and it has more windows than your average garage. But if they go in there, they'll see my car and know I'm still here.

The men walk to the garage, and I nudge Grayson, letting him know we need to go. He nods. We enter the trees at a point at the back edge of the property.

He leads me through until we pop out onto the road farther down. His car is right there. We get in, and he drives off, away from Max and Dan.

"I think MTS is in danger. The only way Max could have found my apartment is by following me home from MTS."

Gray is staring in the rearview mirror.

"Are they following us?"

"No, just being careful. But you know, we do need to get them in custody for your safety." He turns out of the property development and onto a main road.

"I'm still not completely sure if he really did follow me from MTS or if he knows my true identity."

He glances at me. "If he knows your real identity, what would that mean for you?"

I shrug. "I could get relocated to work in another area. I could be let go. Depends on a lot of factors. Not something we need to discuss right now. Besides, it's much more likely he followed me."

He nods but still glances over a few more times. "Did you call Stormy?" he finally asks.

I turn to him. "I called Anderson, and he said he would. I don't have my phone, so I don't have anyone's numbers.

"Here, you can use mine."

I take it from him and call Stormy. It turns out Anderson didn't call yet. After filling him in on everything, he told us to keep driving for now. He'd get back to us with a safe place soon.

"Where do you think he's going to have us go?" I ask. I don't know if MTS has any safe houses, but at this point, I really hope they do.

Gray frowns. "I don't know, but he'll find somewhere secure. Then we're going to hunt down Max and anyone working with him."

"We need to lure Max somewhere so I can question him."

"You think he'll talk?"

I turn and stare out the window. "Yes, I'm sure I can make him talk."

CHAPTER TWENTY-EIGHT

Grayson

"Got it!" Fox says as he walks in the open door.

After we left Cara's cabin, I called the guys and explained what was going on. Fox offered us a solution to our problems.

It's a warehouse outside of Fisher Springs that apparently was confiscated in some kind of drug raid a couple of years ago. Frankly, I don't care about the history. I'm simply happy to have a place we can all gather. It's a bit of a drive for the guys from MTS in Pine Valley, but odds are, Max won't search this far out for us.

"Trip found a hit on one of Max's credit cards. He rented two rooms at a hotel south of Seattle."

"Good. We can get eyes on him."

Fox grins. "Already done. Trax is on his way there and will report what he finds."

Cara's been pacing the space since we got here, and suddenly, she stops. "Once we find him, we need to lure him here."

I glance at Fox, who is frowning. "Why here?" I ask.

"Because I can get him to answer my questions without interruption here."

I take a step toward her. "Do you mean torture?"

She cocks her head. "Whatever it takes to get him to tell us the names of everyone involved in his sex trafficking ring."

"Have you talked to Anderson about your plan? Is he on board?"

Her hands go to her hips. "He knows I want to take Max down."

I'm surprised when I see Cody walk in. When Trax returned, he said Cody would likely be out for another week.

"Hey, I thought you were still on assignment." I walk over to shake his hand.

"Just got back this morning. I just talked to Trax."

Cara walks up to us. "Glad you're back."

Cody nods. "Me too. He said Max is with two men. He got some photos from a distance." Cody holds up his phone, and we look at the pictures.

"That's the man who was with him in my apartment." She points to a tall blond. "I heard Max call him Dan. But this man, I've worked with him before." She points to the man with brown hair.

"Another agent?" I ask.

"No. His name is Eduardo. He's an officer in the Brazilian military. Why the hell is he with Max?"

Cody pockets his phone. "It appears he's helping him."

"No," Cara steps back and rubs her temples. "He can't be. He told me about his wife and family back home. He has daughters. He couldn't be a part of this."

"Maybe Max lied to him about why he's here. Did you see him in your apartment?" I ask.

She shakes her head. "No."

"Trax said Dan drove off, and then Max and Eduardo drove off a moment later in a separate car. He's going to follow Max. Hopefully, we'll know more soon."

"We need to get all three of them here. Question them separately," Cara says.

"I have an idea. Let's call Rover, CT, and Maverick as well. We all need to be on the same page," I say.

Fox arches a brow. "I'm not going to like this, am I?"

I shrug. "This won't be like that time in Monaco."

"Right. It better not."

"What happened in Monaco?" Cara asks.

"I'll tell you later."

We reach the other guys and discuss my plan. By that evening, everything is set up.

According to Trax, both cars drove to Cara's apartment. Dan remained there, and Max and Eduardo are now parked near the MTS building.

Cara volunteered herself as bait to lure the men here. I objected, but she had a decent plan, and now I'm pacing the warehouse, reminding myself she's well trained. And she's not alone.

My phone buzzes, and I grab it.

Maverick: *Cara just picked me up at MTS. We are headed your way.*

Rover: *Max and the other man are following Cara and Maverick.*

Rover and CT are following Max in case he tries to run them off the road instead of simply following them.

I spin my fidget spinner. Fuck, I'm nervous, and I'm never nervous on an assignment. But this is more. These men want to harm Cara.

Fox grabs the spinner from my hand. "It's going to work out."

I nod, really wanting to believe those words.

Fox sits on the ground and leans against the wall. I sit near him.

"Have you asked Julia out yet?" I ask.

Fox shakes his head. "I was going to a few weeks ago when I went to see her at the station. But this big, burly guy came up and kissed her. She introduced him as her boyfriend."

"Ouch."

"Yeah. I didn't think she was dating anyone. Found out she's only been with him for two months."

"Double ouch."

He sighs. "Yeah, I waited too long." He turns to me. "I'm happy things are working out for you and Cara, though. Maybe she has a friend you can set me up with."

I laugh. "You'd do a setup?"

He shrugs. "Why not? Better than sitting around, doing nothing."

"I'll ask her about it."

"Thanks."

Fox stares at me.

"What?"

He smiles. "You really care for her, don't you?"

Just thinking about that woman makes me smile. "I do."

"Have you told her?"

"No, she seems skittish at times. I don't want to scare her off."

I sense his eyes, and I turn to find him staring at me. "What?" I ask.

"I can feel your hesitancy. She probably can, too. She's trained to read people."

"Hesitancy? No," I chuckle.

But as I sit with his words, I realize he might be right. My brother's words won't stop running through my head. *We're broken.*

I swallow. "My brother said something that's been bothering me. He says I stole his life."

Fox leans away from me. "How does he figure that?"

I shrug. "Well, he was planning on going into the service. I joined and moved up as fast as I could. He used to play guitar in a band, and now I do."

Fox hands me my spinner. "That's bullshit. That's the addiction talking. Yes, he planned to do those things, but he got in his own way. Just because you've been successful at life, it doesn't mean you've *stolen* anything from him." He stands up. "Him saying that pisses me off."

"He said more."

Fox stares down at me, but I don't meet his gaze.

"He saw Cara from a distance. He said we're not cut out for relationships. We're broken. I'm worried he might be right."

Fox slides back down the wall and sits next to me again. "Hey, look at me."

I meet his eyes.

"I'm sorry your brother is doing this, but you have to know he's lashing out. Let me guess, after he made you feel like shit, he asked for money, right?"

I shrug. He did in a text after I left. He always does, and I always give it to him.

"You have to stop supporting him."

I throw up my arms. "And what? Let him die on the street?"

Fox clenches his jaw as he stares straight ahead.

"What?" I ask.

He turns to me. "He's not spending your money on food or necessities. You know this. Tell me you know this."

I pick at some dirt on my shoe. "But I owe him so much. I can't say no."

"You don't owe him your life. That's what he's asking for by making you feel bad for the choices you make. Hell, so what if you're broken? We're all broken in some way. It's how you move forward that matters."

I shrug. "Maybe. But what if I really did choose everything he wanted? Subconsciously."

Fox doesn't respond right away, and I think our conversation is over. But after a couple minutes, he takes a deep breath. "Does this mean you aren't going to pursue things with Cara because he wishes he had a relationship?"

When he says it like that, it sounds stupid. But in my head earlier, it made more sense.

Fox stands up again. "I can tell by the look on your face that's what you're thinking. Don't go there. You and Cara are good for each other. We can all see it. I don't know why it's so hard for you to recognize."

He walks out the door to where Cody is waiting to see headlights approaching.

I stew on his words. I see what a fantastic woman Cara is. She has it all. She's smart, beautiful, strong, and she might know more ways to kill a man than I do. That mind of hers will challenge me. But fuck, Jasper got into my head, and now I'm not sure if I can give her what she needs.

I'm circling these thoughts for about the tenth time when Fox runs back into the warehouse.

"We see headlights."

That means they are less than five minutes away, so we get into position.

Cara pulls up right in front of the open garage door as planned. She and Maverick get out and casually walk into the warehouse. Then they assume their position as well.

"Coming down the road, headlights off," Cody reports to us through the walkie-talkie.

The sound of the wheels on gravel is soft as the car moves slowly. As expected, they pull around to the opposite side of the building from where Cara parked.

What they won't be expecting or seeing is Cody.

A gunshot followed by a tire popping lets us know Cody hit his target. Another tire pops.

We make our way outside. Max is still in the car, but Eduardo is gone.

"The other guy ran into the trees," Cody says through the walkie-talkie.

I'm not surprised. Cara said that man was military. He wouldn't wait and be a sitting duck like Max.

I carefully make my way into the trees and listen. The night is eerily silent. The backside of the warehouse is bordered by a green belt of pines. A stick cracks behind me, and I whip around. Trax is standing there with his arms up. I let out my breath in relief. He scared the shit out of me. He must have followed Rover and CT up here.

He points to his goggles. Night vision. He points at himself and then toward the trees. I nod. If that man is in these woods, Trax will find him. Instead of interfering, I slowly make my way back toward the car, careful to remain quiet.

Cody's gun is trained on Max, but the man hasn't gotten out of his car. None of the other guys nor Cara are in sight. Hoping Trax has a good read on where the other man is, I take a chance and speak to Max.

"Max, get out of the car."

The man frowns and moves fast. He reaches for something and aims it at me. I drop to the ground as Cody shoots.

I roll onto my back, keeping my gun aimed at the car.

"He's hit," Cody yells as he runs to Max.

Jumping up, the first thing I see is Max breathing heavily.

Cara and Maverick come running out of the building. I open the car door, and Maverick yanks Max out and onto the ground. The bullet grazed his shoulder. It likely hurts like hell, but the guy won't die.

Cara steps over him. "Get him inside," she orders.

I can't imagine how angry she must be with this man. After knowing what he planned to do with Cara, what he's done to other women, I want to rip him apart myself. But Cara needs answers, so I take a step back and let Cody and Maverick drag his sorry ass into the warehouse.

"Shit! It hurts!" the man yells as he is dragged by his arms, likely pulling on his wound.

Cara turns, walks to him, and slaps him hard across the face. "Don't speak unless you are asked a question."

My heart breaks for her, knowing that was probably a sample of the shit he put her through. I want to know what all he did to her, but I've been afraid to ask, and she hasn't volunteered it.

The guys tie Max to the chair as we had planned. What we hadn't planned on was the knife Cara pulls out from a sheath on her leg.

"Now, we can do this the easy way. Or the hard way," she says, holding the knife in front of the man.

Max's eyes widen.

I'm not sure how far to let this go before I step in. Yes, she is a trained professional, but this is beginning to feel personal.

In one swift motion, she whips the knife up, ripping open the man's shirt. "You know what? It's better you are awake for this. And believe me, it will be worse than what you have Trudy do to all the girls."

I glance at Cody, who appears concerned. Maverick leans against the wall as if he doesn't have a care in the world. Fox walks in and takes in the scene.

"You need any help in here?" he asks.

Without turning around, Cara responds. "Nope. Not at all."

She leans forward and moves the knife's blade down his chest, past his stomach, to his pants. The man's eyes widen.

"Worried I might cut you in the wrong place?" she asks as she pushes the knife into his clothes right next to his zipper.

"Please, don't cut off my dick," Max says. Tears are now streaming down the man's cheeks.

Either she pressed the knife harder than I realized, or Max knows what happened to Alex. But how could he?

Cara takes a step back and reaches her hand back to her waistband.

"No!" Max shouts. "Please, don't shoot it off, either!"

Cara simply scratches her back, taunting Max about whether she may or may not have a gun on her. But all I can focus on is how the hell Max could know what happened to a man who has been in custody since Cara shot him.

"Fuck, we have a leak," I say.

CHAPTER TWENTY-NINE

Cara

GRAY'S WORDS are ringing in my ears. A leak. Max shouldn't know that I almost shot off Alex's penis. But all of Alex's men witnessed it and likely shared it. I'm not clear why Gray jumped to the conclusion there must be a leak. But now isn't the time to discuss it with him.

Focusing back on Max, the fear in his eyes as I run the straight-edge blade down his stomach tells me I'm close to breaking him.

Honestly, I was worried my plan wouldn't work. I figured a guy like Max would be hairless. I was wrong. I slowly work my way down his chest, dry shaving him. The sheer terror on his face when I pulled a straight-edge razor out of my back pocket was priceless.

I might have nicked him a few times. Trust me, I want to do more. But I'm hoping he'll tell me the names of everyone he's working with.

This is going to work. I see the fear every time I move down. The asshole actually laughed after I cut off his shirt.

"You can't torture people!" Max shouts as the razor keeps moving down.

I cut off the button of his pants with my knife. I grin while holding the knife in one hand and the razor in the other.

His eyes widen. "You can't torture people. I watch the news. My government will tell everyone."

I lean down as I unzip his pants. Cutting through the zipper is risky. It might dull my blade. "Good thing I'm not torturing you. You see, shaving you falls under grooming. And that's allowed. I checked."

I yank down his pants, revealing that Max likes to go commando. Makes my job easier.

"And Max, you need a lot of grooming down here." I move the blade close to his balls.

"Jesus, maybe we should discuss this first," Cody says.

I glance up, and the poor man is turning green. "You guys are welcome to leave," I say, then bend down and get to work.

"Fuck!" Max shouts. "That hurts!"

What can I say? I'm not going easy.

"Tell me what I want to know, and maybe I'll be gentle."

Gentle is the best he can hope for because this hair is coming off. When I woke up after Trudy drugged me, I was hairless from the neck down. Everywhere. I'm all for a good trim, but I've never been hairless in my pubic area. Whatever she had done, my skin hurt like hell. By the time I made it back to Seattle, it was growing in and itching like crazy. That was one of the main reasons I didn't fight being stuck at home for a couple of weeks.

I move the razor to the top of his penis. "I see you have some hair here."

"No! I'll tell you!" the man yells.

Tears are falling from his eyes. "Please, just don't cut off my dick."

I take a step back and set the razor on another chair as a show of good faith. "Tell me who you're working with. I want all the names."

Max swallows. "I can give you some but understand there are others; they will kill me if I tell you."

My phone buzzes in my pocket. I check it. Anderson. I turn back to Max. "I'll give you five minutes to change your mind."

I walk out of the warehouse and answer. "Anderson?"

"Harding. I got your message. I need you to hold off any further questioning on Max Acrile."

I must have heard him wrong. "What?"

"There is a situation with the Brazilian government right now, and we need to tread lightly."

I scratch my forehead. "Sir, with all due respect, I am treading lightly."

"No more questions, Harding. That's an order. I'm on my way to your location with a team. We'll bring Max in until we get clearance to question him."

I take several deep breaths. I've never been shut down like this before, and I don't like it.

"Harding, understood?"

"Yes. Understood."

He ended the call, and I wanted to scream. But I heard footsteps coming around the building. Before I can run inside, Trax comes into view. I breathe a sigh of relief. He's dragging Eduardo. The man's hands and feet are bound.

Trax gives me a nod, drags the man inside, and drops him.

"I need a word with all of you," I say.

There's no way I'm going to let Max know I can no longer question him.

The guys gather outside, leaving the two men in the warehouse in view. I explain what Anderson said and how we are supposed to wait for someone to take these guys away.

Gray steps up beside me. "Hey, you okay?"

I shake my head. "I had him. He was going to tell me the names."

"You literally had him by the balls."

I glance up and see the big grin on Gray's face. I smile despite my foul mood. "Damn you."

He winks, and my stomach flutters. Only this man could make me smile moments after I got bad news.

We stay out of earshot of the two men until Anderson arrives. He's not alone. Agent Canton is with him, and the two men walk up to me.

"Harding," Anderson says.

"Anderson. Canton. The men are inside."

Anderson nods. He takes in all the guys standing around before focusing on Canton. "Let's get them in the car."

They walk into the warehouse but stop when they see Max.

"What the fuck?" Canton asks.

Anderson's face turns a lovely shade of red. "Harding, why are this man's pants around his ankles?"

I step forward. "He needed grooming, sir."

Anderson read my report. He knows what was done to me and likely why I did this to Max.

"You can all leave. We'll handle this from here," Anderson says.

I frown.

"It's an order, Harding. I need to clean up your mess."

I clench my jaw. This isn't a mess, but he gave an order, and I don't have a choice. I follow the guys outside.

I'm pissed, but I keep walking to my car. Two gunshots go off. Several of the guys pull their weapons as they run back toward the warehouse door. I'm right there with them.

Anderson is standing between Max and the other man, who are both on the ground. Canton is standing behind the chair Max was in, holding a gun. I run up to Max. He's dead.

"No! Fuck! He was going to tell me the names. What the hell happened?"

"He came at me with a razor," Anderson says.

The razor I used to shave him is lying on the floor near Max.

"How the hell did he get that?" Maverick asks.

"Canton untied his hands, and he went for it. Then this man tried to charge me at the same time." He points to Eduardo, who I'm certain is also dead. "I had no choice."

Anderson turns to me. "I'm sorry, Cara. We'll find out who his associates are some other way."

I stare at the men on the floor. "You shot Max?" I turn to Anderson.

He puts his hands up. "No, Canton did. He saved my life."

I swivel to face Canton. He shakes his head. "Like Anderson said, we had no choice."

No choice? Now everything Max knew died with him. Wait, the blond. Dan. I need to get out of here and find him. He'll know something.

"Cara, I'm worried about you."

My gaze shoots to Anderson. He never calls me by my first name.

"What the hell were you going to do with that razor? And don't say nothing because the man's pants were down."

"I was only shaving him. That's all."

Anderson stares at me for a moment. "Go ahead and go home. Canton and I will deal with this."

"I'll make sure she gets home, sir," Gray tells Anderson.

"Thank you," Anderson says.

I let Gray drive as I go over everything that happened. Halfway to my place, he pulls over.

"What are you doing?" I ask.

"Checking on you. You've been silent."

"I'm thinking," I say as I stare out the window.

"How about I take you to my place?"

"No," I say.

He winces.

"I don't mean it like that. What I mean is we need to find Dan. Odds are he's still waiting at my apartment."

He nods. "Okay, but if we find him, are you all right?"

I'm starting to get mad at all these questions about my mental state. "Why the hell do you and Anderson think I'm so fragile that I can't handle questioning a couple of suspects? This is my job."

He turns in his seat to fully face me. "I can't speak for Anderson. But the reason I'm concerned is that I don't know exactly what the hell that man did to you in Brazil. And I've questioned terrorists and war criminals, but I've never pulled their pants down and waved a razor in their face. I'm sorry, but that concerns me." This man is staring at me with compassion in his eyes.

I take a deep breath. "Max had his assistant, Trudy, remove all the hair from my body. I was unconscious, but I'm pretty sure she used hot wax. I was told to wear a dress they gave me. Then they tried to drug me, but I poured the drink out when they weren't looking. After that, I was led to the room where you found me. That's it."

He studies me, I suspect, to see if I'm telling the whole truth. Finally, he nods.

As he pulls back out onto the road, he says, "Let's find Dan."

CHAPTER THIRTY

Grayson

ON THE DRIVE from the warehouse to Cara's apartment, I kept glancing at her. She spent most of the ride staring out the window except for when I pulled over and shared my concerns.

When she pulled down Max's pants at the warehouse, all of us guys cringed, worried about what was coming next. The last thing we wanted to do was question her in front of the man.

I'm in love with this woman, and I have to make sure she's all right. In my time working with her, she comes across as the most levelheaded, cool-under-pressure agent I've ever known. And I'll admit, she never did lose her temper in the warehouse.

We're almost to her apartment when she turns to me.

"I would never cut off a man's dick. I want you to know that."

I swallow. "Uh-huh." What the fuck am I supposed to say? Good for you? I glance over, and she's narrowed her eyes at me.

"You don't believe me." It's not a question; it's a statement.

"No, I do," I say.

She crosses her arms. "I wouldn't throw my entire career away on a man like Max. I was just giving him a taste of his own medicine. And if he thought I might do something else with the razor, well, that was on him." She slouches. "But it doesn't matter now, does it? He's dead along with all the names we need."

I park two blocks before we get to her apartment. "You don't think Dan will know any of the key players?"

She unfastens her seatbelt. "I hope he does but odds are he won't know them all."

"Time for us to find out."

We both exit the car and approach the parking lot.

"That's him," she says. "In the black SUV in the front row."

I spot him. The man is staring at his phone from the driver's seat.

"What are the odds the doors are unlocked?" she asks.

"Guess we'll find out."

While the guy continues to be distracted by his phone, we make our way to his vehicle. Cara walks to the passenger door, and I go around to the driver's. Luck is on our side because the driver's window is down.

I push my gun against his temple. "Unlock the doors."

The man's fingers twitch.

"Don't even think about it. I'm not alone."

His left hand hits the button and unlocks the doors.

Cara climbs into the passenger side and removes his weapon from his coat. She pats him down for any other weapons. "That was it."

I get in the seat behind him and keep my gun aimed at the back of his head.

The man looks at Cara. "I know you."

He doesn't have an accent which surprises me.

"American?" I ask.

He glances at me in the rearview mirror. "Yes."

"We have some questions for you about your work with Max," Cara says.

The man smiles. "Who is Max?"

Before I can wipe that smile off his face, Cara punches the man.

"Shit! I think you broke my nose," he cries.

"I'll break more than that if you don't start answering our questions."

Damn, is it wrong if that turned me on? I shake the thought from my head. One minute this woman scares me; the next, she's got me hot and bothered. There's no other woman out there like her, that's for certain.

"I barely know Max."

Cara hits him again.

"What the fuck? I answered your question!"

"You lied."

The man winces and turns to Cara.

"I want the names of the men Max provided girls for."

The man leans his head back on the headrest. "I don't know them all, but giving you those names could get me killed."

Cara arches a brow. "Not giving me those names *will* get you killed."

The man glances back at me again. "You should be asking Max. He has all the names."

"Max is dead," I say.

The man's eyes widen as he turns back to Cara.

"How?" Dan asks.

"I'm the one asking questions. Now give me names," Cara says.

He's still holding his nose. "All right. In my pocket, there is a list of the men I'm supposed to contact. We were supposed to grab you and then get back to Brazil for a party tomorrow night."

"Keep your hands up," I say.

The man lifts his hands, and Cara reaches into his pocket to pull out a piece of paper. She opens it up. Her brow shoots up.

"There are only two names on this list."

"Yes, but they bring friends," he says. "But they will only show up if I call."

Cara grabs the man's phone from the console and hands it to me along with the list. "Call the first name about the party."

She's calling this man's bluff. She takes my gun and keeps it pointed at the guy as he stares straight ahead. I call the first number.

"Hello?" a man answers.

"The party tomorrow is on," I say.

"That's good. Thank you for the confirmation." The man hangs up.

I smile at Cara. "It worked."

She smiles back. "Good. Now we better take him in. We have a party to get ready for."

"You want to go back to Brazil?" I ask.

"No, but I will."

Fortunately, Cara has a contact with the Seattle Police Department, and they are willing to take Dan and hold him until Anderson can transfer him.

The man tried to complain we were illegally detaining him. Cara quickly listed quite a few laws he'd broken and said it would take some time to sort through all of the witness testimony. It was a speech I'm sure she's given before.

I called the other name on the list using Dan's phone. He answered and seemed happy to hear from me.

After that was all set, we each called our bosses to update them on the current situation and the need to go to Brazil. Stormy was understanding and told me if Anderson approved it, he would, too.

Now I'm leaning against Cara's car, watching her. As she finishes up, she's staring at her phone.

"Are we good to go?" I ask as she returns.

She smiles. "We are. I just need to grab a few things."

We both glance in the direction of her apartment.

"I'm coming with you."

She nods.

While she packs, I book two tickets for us. A few hours

RESCUING CARA (SPECIAL FORCES: OPERATION ALPHA)

later, we're on the plane, and we're both ready to get some sleep.

Our layover lasts several hours, and we concoct a plan. We would arrive early at Max's house to give us a chance to go through his things to see if we could find any additional names. Cara called a contact she has in the area to help us detain the men at Max's place.

Our rental car is small, but at least we have a way to leave this time if we need to.

I park down the road from Max's place and unfold myself out of the vehicle.

Cara laughs, and I glance up as she covers her mouth. "Sorry, but you really don't fit in there."

My brow shoots up, and I grin.

"Don't say it."

"You didn't give me a choice. That's what she said."

She rolls her eyes. "Why do all you guys use that line? It's old."

I laugh. "Because it's funny."

She shakes her head as we approach Max's house. It's large, but fortunately, there are no guards or gates. We go to the back of the home and get in easily.

The décor is not at all what I expected. The place is covered in floral wallpaper, and hanging on the walls, is what I can only assume is cross-stitch art. Whoever did those loves cats and Bible verses.

"Do you think this was Max's parents' place?" I ask.

Cara is taking it all in, too. "Kind of looks that way."

"Any preference on how to split this up?" I ask.

"Yeah, you should take the bedrooms. I'll start at the other end of the house."

Well shit. I should have thought of that. Who the fuck knows what we will find in a bedroom here. "Okay."

She heads in the opposite direction.

Twenty minutes later, I'm wondering if this really is where Max lived because there is a serious lack of personal items.

"Gray?" Cara calls.

I find her in what appears to be an office.

"I found something," she says.

She's sitting at a desk, staring at a laptop. I walk behind her and find she's staring at photos of herself.

"He was stalking you?"

"I don't know. These are dated from before I went to Chile. I remember this day, too," she says, pointing at one image. "I was out for a run, and a car splashed a large puddle on me. That's why there's mud on my legs."

I squint and see the dirt covering her skin.

"Gray, I had no idea anyone was watching me. I usually sense it."

I squat down next to her and take her hand in mind. "Yes, but you were off duty and relaxed. You weren't expecting anyone to be watching you."

She brings her eyes to mine. "I'm never off duty. Someone from my past could be watching me at any moment." She clicks the mouse and moves to another picture taken moments later. "But this wasn't my past. The assignment to catch Max hadn't been assigned to me yet."

"You said he worked with Alex Kralik. Maybe that's how he knew about you."

She shook her head. "Max had no history of dealing with weapons. And Alex didn't know who I was."

She opens the desk drawer and digs through it. Then slams it shut and opens the next one.

She holds up a USB stick. "Found one. I'm copying this entire folder and hoping Trip can get some information off of this for me."

I walk over to a bookshelf where a stuffed teddy bear sits. I examine the bear and find what I expected. "There's a camera in this thing."

Cara stills. "Someone could be watching us."

It's not a question; it's reality.

"And listening."

We both immediately search the room for any additional cameras or listening devices but come up with nothing.

I place Teddy outside the back door and do another walk-through of the bedrooms.

"There's a teddy bear in each bedroom," I tell her.

"Do you think Max was recording what happens in those rooms?"

I swallow my disgust. "Somehow, I wouldn't doubt it. He was a sick fuck."

She returns to the computer. "Yeah, but that sick fuck might lead us to all the men involved. I just need to find the videos."

"Hello?" a man's voice calls.

I still. "They're early," I whisper to Cara.

She shakes her head. "That's my contact. He's okay."

We walk toward the kitchen and find a man almost as tall as I am, with dark hair and a huge smile.

"Cara! It's so good to see you again." The man takes her into his arms and hugs her... for a little too long, if you ask me.

He finally releases her, and she turns to me. "Peaches, this is Malone. We've worked together in the past."

I frown. Why is she calling me Peaches again?

"Work, play, it's all been good." The man winks at Cara.

"Ah, let's go to the office and discuss our plan," Cara says as she walks ahead of us.

Malone follows her. "I was so happy to hear from you again. Maybe after this, we can catch up for old times' sake."

I clench my fists, wanting to shut this man up. Did Cara sleep with this asshole?

Malone's phone rings. "Oh, I need to take this first." He walks back the way we came holding the phone up to his ear.

I turn to Cara and arch a brow.

Her hand goes up. "I did not sleep with that man. We worked together and went out for a drink once. It was clear he wanted something more. I didn't. And I never called him again. Until today."

I cross my arms. "You don't owe me any explanation."

She places her hand on my arm. "I don't want you

239

thinking something happened when it didn't. You're important to me."

I nod. "Why is he here?"

"We need someone from the Brazilian government involved so these men can be taken into custody. Officially."

Now I understand why he's here, but I still don't like him.

"Why are you calling me Peaches?"

She smiles. "Because that's what you go by on assignments."

Malone steps back into the office. "Ah, sorry about that. It was a work thing I had to take."

I stare at the man. "You work for the Brazilian government?"

"Yes, I work at the US Consulate's Office here in Brazil."

I turn to Cara. "I thought that office was compromised."

She smiles. "Malone doesn't work in San Paulo." She turns to the man.

"Here's the plan."

The doorbell rings, and we all still.

Cara goes to the window. "A new car is parked out there. And three men are standing at the door."

"I'll let them in," I say. "You both go into the first two bedrooms, and I'll lead a man into each room. The third, I'll take care of in the room at the end of the hallway."

Malone frowns. "And what are we supposed to do with these guys?"

"Restrain them. Cara will explain."

I approach the front door from the side and peer out the window. Three men, all in suits, are standing on the front porch. They're all over forty, and none appear to be in great shape. Placing my gun behind me, I open the door.

"Good evening," I say.

The men startle. "Oh, we're here to see Max."

"Yes, he's finishing up some business in his office. Please come in."

The men walk in, glancing around.

"Where are the girls?" one asks.

Girls? Fuck, these men disgust me. But I keep a straight

face. "In the bedrooms. Please come this way." I lead the men down the hall and open the first door for one to enter. "Please wait in here," I say.

I open the second door for the next man. And I bring the third down to the final bedroom.

As soon as he's in the room, I close the door. I pull a wire tie from my back pocket while the man's back is to me.

"There's no girl. This isn't how Max normally does things," he says. Then the man whips around, and a sharp pain goes up my arm. He stabbed me.

Where the hell did that come from?

He still has a hold of the knife and swings it down again, but this time, I'm ready. I gain control of it as he's swinging down, and it connects with his stomach. I shove him away, and he falls to the floor.

His glassy eyes are staring straight up. "Don't let me die. I'll pay you."

"Motherfucker!" Malone yells.

I run to the other room and find Malone in a headlock. The guy is at least trying with his arms, swinging at the other man but missing. I storm up and punch the asshole, and he goes down, releasing Malone. I spin on my heel and go to find Cara.

The room she's in is very quiet. Slowly, I push the door open. Cara is sitting on the back of the guy, adjusting the wire ties to his wrists. The man's eyes are closed.

She stands. "He fought back, had to knock him out. You?"

"Think mine's dead."

"Fuck, no. We need them alive." She runs to my room and bends down to check on the man. "He's dead."

Malone runs in. "Two more guys just pulled up."

"You two stall them while I move everyone into this room," I say.

They both leave, and before I do anything, I pull up my shirt. My arm hurts like hell, and I'm losing a lot of blood. I rip a piece of the sheet off the bed and tie it around my arm as a tourniquet. Hopefully, that will last long enough.

CHAPTER THIRTY-ONE

Cara

MALONE OPENS the front door and steps out. I return to the hall as Grayson is dragging Malone's man across. I go to my room and find my guy. Once we have them all together, I turn to Grayson.

"I've imagined doing a lot of things with you, but I can't say this is one of them."

He grins, but his smile fades.

"What's wrong?"

He sighs. "If we're dating, Stormy isn't going to want us working together."

He's right. And that's sad because we work so well together.

"We'll deal with that later. Maybe he'll make an exception," I say. "I'm going to let Malone know we're ready."

I leave the room but can't shake the fact this is probably our last assignment together. Although, when he finds out Anderson didn't actually approve our coming down here, he might not want to date me. I try to shake those thoughts from my head. Right now, I need to be present and ready for the next group of men.

I return to the front door, lean my head out and announce, "They're ready."

Malone smiles. "Great. Let's go inside."

The two men follow him in. And just like last time, I take one down and bind his hands behind his back. When I finish, I find Malone is still pussy footing with his guy.

"Need help?" I ask.

Malone grunts, so I secure the man. Then we move them into separate rooms, where I begin to question the first guy.

"What's your name?"

He's glaring up at me from the floor. "My wallet is in my pocket. Just take it."

Another American based on the lack of accent I hear. I retrieve his wallet and check his identification.

"Walter Ford." I toss the wallet onto his lap.

He frowns down at it. "Don't you want my money?"

"No."

He glances at the door. "But that is the man from the consulate's office. I already paid him to extend my visa."

I blink a few times as what he says registers. "What do you mean?"

He frowns. "What do you think I mean? He asked for money. Is this about that? He wants more?"

I sit on the bed and study Walter.

"Can we just get these questions over with? I'm supposed to be meeting someone here."

He can't be serious. "Who are you meeting here?"

Walter glares at me again. "I don't know her name, but it's supposed to be a blind date."

I stand up and walk toward him. "How old is this date?"

His face flushes red. "I don't know."

I nod. "But you did request she be underage, right?"

There's panic in his eyes now. "Who the fuck are you?"

I pull out my badge. "CIA. And you just got busted going to a house owned by a known sex trafficker. To a party where you expected to find underage girls."

The man frowns. "Fake badge."

"What?"

He nods to it. "That's a fake badge. If you were really CIA, there would be more of you, and you'd have me in handcuffs, not whatever the hell this is."

I bite back a laugh. Because this isn't going down like a television show he saw, he figures I must be fake. Yet, I didn't take his wallet. Okay, so he's not the bright one here.

I nod. "All right. I was giving you the first chance to come clean. The first man who does usually gets the best deal. I'll move on."

I walk to the door, and the asshole doesn't stop me. I hope the next guy makes a better choice.

As I enter the room Malone is in, he hands me a wallet.

"I got this out of his pocket. He panicked when I found out his real name—Joe Parker—and threatened to call his wife." Malone holds up a cell phone. Then he nods at the man. "Tell her what you told me."

Joe has tears in his eyes. I don't feel one ounce of sympathy. And now he's worried about what his spouse will think? I take the cell phone. As soon as this Joe talks, I'm calling her.

"Walter set up this trip. He says he meets with this guy, Max, all the time, and it's always worth his while. He said there would be women here, but I swear to God I didn't know they'd be underage."

I take a moment, staring down Joe. Is he serious? "Let me get this straight. You didn't find it odd that you had to fly to Brazil to meet someone as opposed to finding them in your own town?"

"Walter said the women here were looking for wealthy Americans."

More like Max was looking for suckers.

"Who all came on this trip with you?" I ask.

Grayson enters the room and steps up beside me.

"Just Walter and me. He's brought others before."

"I need names."

Joe nods. "There are a couple guys from our office, but there's one Walter says introduced him to Max. His name is Pat Anderson."

I take a step back. No, it can't be him. Shit.

"Are you sure about that name?" Grayson asks.

The man nods. "Yeah. Walter brags he's a big whig in the government."

Grayson instructs Malone to stay in there with the guy, and then he leads me to the other end of the house.

"You all right?" he asks.

I shake my head. "No, I'm not all right. My fucking boss might be a client of Max's? Why the hell was I put on this assignment?"

Grayson puts his hands on my shoulders and stares into my eyes. "Maybe Anderson found out about Max and put you on the assignment to bust him."

I nod. "I hope you're right and that Walter is lying about Anderson having introduced him to Max."

"But we also have to be open to the possibility that Anderson used Max's services."

I squeeze my eyes shut. "But why assign me to the case?"

"That's something we need to figure out."

"Max had photos of me on his computer. He knew where I lived and found me at my apartment. Before he could give me any names, Anderson shot him." My head is spinning as the pieces fall together. "Anderson is supposed to be one of the good guys. Did he send me after Max to get me out of the picture?"

Grayson grabs my shoulders. "It does no good to specu-late. We need more facts."

I nod. "You're right. Walter is the man in the other room. He won't answer any of my questions."

Grayson nods. "Let me talk to him. Alone."

I nod again. He leaves me, and my mind is racing, thinking through all my interactions with Anderson on this case. Nothing stands out except for the voicemail.

I called and left a message for Anderson about returning to Brazil and told Gray the trip was approved. I didn't doubt for a moment Anderson would approve it so I could finish this case. And I didn't want to miss the next available flight.

Anderson returned my call and left a voicemail just before we got on the plane. He didn't approve the trip.

But by then, everything was in motion. I had to know who else was involved and take them down. But maybe Anderson simply wanted Max dead.

Stop. I can't let my mind race on guesses. Like Grayson said, I need facts. And I need to know how those other three men are tied to Walter and Joe.

I walk back down the hall, ignoring the noises coming from Walter's room. I step into the bedroom across the hall. One of the men has his eyes open. Another has his eyes closed. And the third is on the far side of the bed, out of sight of these two.

"What do you want?" the first guy asks me.

"What's your name?"

"Peter."

I nod. "Peter, do you know the two others you arrived with?"

"Yes, we've known each other since college. Carl set all this up, and we just showed up. I swear I've never done anything like this before. It was supposed to be a guy's trip."

"Having sex with little girls is your idea of a guy's trip?" I yell.

His eyes widen. "What? Little girls? Carl told us we were meeting friends of a woman he already knew."

Either Peter is a great actor, or he really didn't know.

I nod to the man on the floor next to him. "Is that Carl?"

"No, that's Mike."

Fuck. That means Carl's dead. We won't be getting any more information from him.

I turn to leave.

"Are you going to let us go?" Peter asks.

I ignore him and close the door behind me. Grayson is standing in the hall. There's fresh blood on his shirt.

"He talked," Gray says as I approach. "But you aren't going to like what he said."

Malone steps out. "What's the plan now?"

"You call the local police, explain why they're here, and take them in," I say.

I turn to Gray. "We're going home."

"You're going to leave me here with five men?" Malone asks.

"They're tied up. You can handle it," Gray says.

"Malone, thank you for your help. I really appreciate it," I say as I walk down the hallway.

"Wait!" Malone says.

Gray and I turn back to him.

"Are you at least going to pay me for my services?"

"Your payment is that I'm not turning you in for taking cash bribes to extend visas."

He takes a step back. "What are you—"

"Save it. Walter told me all about your agreement."

I spin back around and keep walking until I'm in the office.

"I'll get the laptop," I say.

Gray comes up behind me. I turn and touch his arm. He winces.

"You're hurt. How bad?"

"Let's get out of here."

My eyes catch on the blood again. "That's your blood, isn't it?"

He nods. "The first asshole stabbed me in the arm. We can grab some bandages, and that should hold me till we get back to the US."

I touch the crease that's formed between his eyes. "You're in pain. I'll drive."

He nods. We leave without any more complaints from Malone. Gray gets into the passenger seat, indicating he must be hurting. He insisted on driving here. I find a local hospital.

"No. I'm not going in there."

"You're not. I am. Supplies."

I go inside and scope out the layout. I ask for the bathroom, and fortunately, it's back where they take the patients. Instead of going into a bathroom, I go into one of the exam rooms and find what I need in the upper cabinet. Shoving it all into my pockets, I rush out before they notice.

I get back to the car and drive us a few blocks away.

"Get out of the car; I'm going to patch you up."

Gray reluctantly follows my instructions. He slowly removes the fabric tied to his arm as I lay out my stash on the hood of the car.

He winces as he peels it back. Some blood has dried, and it's sticking to his arm. But he finally gets it off.

"Gray, you need stitches."

He glances at his arm. "I'll get them when we get home."

I grab the alcohol swabs. "This will sting."

He nods, and I gently wipe down the area. I grab the surgical tape.

"I'm going to push it together and hold it closed with this."

"Just do it. I don't need a play-by-play," he grits out.

I work fast to try to close the open wound the best I can with what I have. Then I put a bandage over it all as well. I wrap it several times to secure it in place.

"Fuck. Could you use more tape?"

I step back. "You think it won't stay?"

He lets out a chuckle. "No, I don't think I'm going to have any arm hair left when I remove that."

"Better to lose arm hair than get it infected."

He smiles at me.

"What?"

He shrugs. "I've never seen this nurturing side of you. I like it."

I arch a brow. "Well, don't tell the other guys. Now, let's go to the airport and get the hell out of here."

CHAPTER THIRTY-TWO

Grayson

By the time we land in Houston, I'm dizzy. It's probably the lack of rest. My damn arm fucking hurts like hell, and I couldn't sleep on the plane.

"Our layover is eight hours," Cara says. "Let's get you to the emergency room."

She grabs my bag and hoists it over her shoulder with her own. I take it from her.

"I can carry my own damn bag."

"Uh-huh. And if I were CT, would you let me carry it?"

I grin. "Yeah, but he's an asshole, though. I like you."

She shakes her head as we walk out of the airport. "I requested an Uber." She holds up her phone to show me.

I follow her and get into the car, not as aware of my surroundings as I'd like to be. The car drops us at the emergency room of some hospital, and as I follow Cara inside, my vision starts to go black.

"Uh, Cara," I say as I start to fall.

She catches me and helps me inside. "I need help here," she says as we walk in.

Amazingly, there aren't many in the waiting room.

Someone ushers me into a wheelchair and pushes me back to a room.

"I'll be here waiting," Cara says. "I have to deal with some paperwork."

I reach out for her, but she's gone.

"Mr. Walsh, I'm going to put an IV into your arm now," a nurse says.

I close my eyes.

* * *

I WAKE TO A BEEPING SOUND. I reach to my side, but instead of finding my phone on my nightstand, I connect with wires. Wires? I open my eyes and sit up.

I remember Cara taking me to the hospital.

She stands from a chair and stretches. "You're awake," Cara says.

"What happened?" I ask.

"You passed out as soon as I got you into the emergency room. I thought it was due to loss of blood, but the doctor says it was more likely a combination of the trauma combined with no food or water."

I frown, realizing I haven't had anything to eat or drink since our flight down to Brazil.

She takes my hand in hers. "I'm sorry, I didn't realize."

"I'm in the hospital because I forgot to eat?" I ask.

She grins. "Kind of. That combined with your injury."

I lean back. "Let's tell the guys it was a loss of blood. All right?"

She laughs. "Whatever you want. I'm just happy you're awake."

A man in scrubs pushes the curtain aside and walks into my space. That's when I realize I'm not even in a room.

"Mr. Walsh, how are you feeling now?"

"Better."

"Good. We got your arm stitched up and gave you liquids via IV. As soon as you can walk around, I'll sign your discharge papers." He gives me a smile before he leaves.

"What time is it?" I ask.

"We missed our flight. But I got us booked on another one in a few hours."

I sit up again and swing my legs to the side with the IV machine. "How did you know I'd be released in time?"

"It was a guess based on what the doctor told me earlier."

I stand up and feel a bit woozy, so I don't move for a moment. "Thank you for taking care of that." Once I'm stable, I take a few steps forward. "You want to get that doctor? I want him to see me walking so we can get out of here."

She eyes me closely. "Are you sure you're ready?"

"Yes."

Cara was able to get the doctor's attention, and an hour later, I'm released. Fortunately, we made the new flight, and this time, I ate on the plane. With an hour left in the flight, I glance over, and Cara is staring out the window, clenching her jaw.

"What are you thinking about?" I ask.

"Anything I could have missed with Anderson. And the fact that the man I was supposed to put away is running free."

"Ivan will resurface."

She turns to me. "After he's sold more weapons and more secrets." She sighs. "I'm just feeling…I don't know. Useless, I guess."

I intertwine my fingers in hers. "You're not useless. What happened with Ivan and the local police in Costa Rica was unfortunate. As for Anderson, maybe Walter introduced Anderson to Max and that's when he assigned you to the case."

"You're right, but I can't stop going over it in my mind."

I squeeze her thigh. "I know something to take your mind off of it." I wink.

She smiles. "Are you trying to get me to go into the bathroom with you?"

I make a face. "No, gross. It's something I need to tell you."

She grows serious. "What?"

I glance around to make sure no one is listening. I lean down to whisper into her ear, "I don't trust stairs. They're always up to something."

She blinks several times before she bursts out laughing. "That's terrible."

"It is!" I'm laughing, too.

"Where do you get these?"

I shrug. "Internet."

We trade bad jokes until we land. As we're walking through the airport, she stops.

"What's wrong?"

"I don't want to go back to my place. Max may be dead, but what if any of his guys decide I'm to blame? If they even know he's dead. I didn't ask Anderson what he did after we left."

I wrap an arm around her shoulder and squeeze her to me. "You're staying with me, and don't try to argue."

A smile plays on her lips. "You sure?"

"Very."

"Thank you." She gives me a quick kiss and then pulls out her phone. "I'll get us a ride there."

Once we get to my place, she walks into the living room, taking it all in.

"Wow, Gray."

"What?"

She turns, smiling. "Did you decorate yourself?"

"Um. Yeah."

"It's amazing. The colors all tie together, and it feels like a real home."

Her words make me smile. That's what I always wanted growing up—the feel of a real home.

"You have plants. How do you keep them alive when you're gone a lot?"

I walk over and move some leaves away. "These little gadgets will keep the plant moist if you set it up right."

"And you have so many pillows. I love it."

I walk to her and take her in my arms. "Well, I didn't just

get my pillow fighting skills overnight. I have to practice regularly."

She laughs as she pulls away and walks down the hall to my bedroom. She stops at the doorway. "This is so different."

She's right. My bedroom is minimalist. There are no extra pillows or blankets. The walls are white. I have no real décor.

"I like to keep the bedroom simple since I only sleep in here."

She turns and arches a brow. "Only sleep?"

I shrug. "Before you, it had been a while since I'd been with anyone, and even then, I didn't bring anyone here."

"I like that." She stands on her toes and kisses me.

I show her the bathroom, and she gets ready for bed. I send Stormy a message to let him know I'm back in town.

Instead of a quick text reply, he calls.

"Stormy? Is something wrong?"

"Just a minute, I'm going to get Anderson on the line. Is Cara with you?"

I glance toward the bedroom. "She is."

"Perfect. Put this on speakerphone."

Well, that doesn't sound good. I step back into the bedroom. Cara has changed into one of my shirts.

"I hope you don't mind," she says.

"Not at all. Stormy wants to talk to both of us. He's calling Anderson, too."

Her eyes widen. "Gray, there's something I need to tell you."

"Anderson, you on?"

"I'm here."

Cara closes her eyes.

"Do you know why I wanted to speak to you both?" Stormy asks.

"No," I say as Cara says, "Yes."

"You want to fill Peaches in?"

I glance over at Cara, and I swear I see fear in her eyes. "What's going on?" I ask.

She licks her lips. Everything feels wrong all of a sudden.

"Cara, what's going on?"

She takes a deep breath. "I told you we had Anderson's approval because I thought for sure he would give it. I left him a voicemail. We were nearly on the plane when he called back. By then, it was too late, and I'm sorry I didn't tell you."

I process what she just said, and I couldn't have heard it correctly. "Wait. You didn't have Anderson's approval when you said you did?"

She nods.

"And he called you, but you didn't take it?"

She shakes her head. "No, I missed the call, but he left a voicemail."

I turn away from her, my anger brewing. "Cara, did you hear the voicemail before we got on the plane?"

She runs to me and grabs my arm. "Just before we got on. They'd already boarded half the plane. We had to go if there was a chance to find out if anyone knew who Max worked with."

I'm so angry at her for lying to me. And risking not only her job but mine.

Stormy clears his throat. "I'll admit I'm happy you didn't defy my order, Peaches. But since this was not approved, this expense will fall to you."

"Understood," I say.

"Harding," Anderson says, "did you discover any of Max's associates?"

"No," she says.

I turn to face her, confused.

She mouths to me, "Not over the phone."

I nod. I get it. She needs to see Anderson when he answers her questions to see if he gives any indication of lying. But if she reveals what she learned and he is indeed guilty, he might not hesitate to eliminate her the way he did Max. That's all I can think about now. Cara is likely in danger not only from Ivan, wherever he may be, but her own boss.

But fuck, I'm pissed at her for lying to me about Anderson's approval.

"Get some sleep. We'll talk about this more tomorrow," Anderson says.

"Thank you," Cara says.

Stormy ends the call, and I stand there staring at Cara. She lied to me.

"Gray, I can explain."

I hold up my hand. "Not tonight. I'm too tired and too angry. I'll sleep in the guest room."

I grab a few things and close the door behind me. Once I'm set up in the guest room, I lie there, staring at the ceiling. I value honesty above all else. Cara knows this, doesn't she?

As my anger slowly fades, I have to admit I understand why she pushed ahead with the trip. This was her chance to possibly shut down Max's operation. Unfortunately, instead of finding his associates, we only learned of some of his customers.

I really hope Anderson is not truly a customer. But the evidence so far is pretty damning. And if he thinks for a moment Cara knows about him, she isn't safe. And that's why I need to try to put my anger aside. I can't leave her alone.

CHAPTER THIRTY-THREE

Cara

I TOSSED and turned all night. The pain and anger in Gray's eyes after he learned I lied was too much. It hurt. Not that I can blame him. I hope I can make him understand why I did it.

My phone buzzes, and I grab it. A text from Anderson.

Anderson: *Meet me at the pier at nine.*

The pier. It's on Seattle's waterfront and usually fairly busy. We've met there before. Anderson refers to it as his thinking spot. At least it's out in public. Throughout the night, I kept imagining Anderson requesting a meeting in some remote place. And that I would end up wherever Max did.

I remind myself that Anderson doesn't know what I know. But he must suspect; otherwise, why would we meet there and not in his office?

My eyes fall to the laptop I took from Max's house. Maybe it will have something more on it.

After a shower and coffee, I finally get the courage to go to the guest room to see Gray. I knock on the door.

A moment later, he opens it. He's only wearing his underwear. Damn, this man is so sexy, but I swallow down that thought.

"Anderson wants to meet me at nine."

"Where?"

"The pier."

He frowns. "I'm coming with you."

I place my hand on his chest. "That's not necessary. This is a public place. Besides, he would wonder why you were there."

He crosses his arms. "I'll stay out of sight."

I frown.

"It's non-negotiable."

"Okay. Listen, Gray, I really am sorry. I was so focused on this case that I let everything else slip aside."

He runs his hand through his hair as he stares at me. "I understand why you did it. But I don't like it. Honesty is important to me. So is trust. And by lying, you abused that."

Tears well in my eyes. I hadn't thought about what effect this could have on us. This is why I don't let myself fall for anyone. One mistake and it's over.

"I'm sorry. I promise I'll never withhold information from you again. Please don't let this ruin us."

He places his hands on my shoulders. "I will admit I was very angry when I found out you lied. But last night, I thought about it. A lot. And I understand. I don't agree with it, but I understand why you did it."

"You do?"

He wipes a tear off my cheek as he nods. "I do. As for ruining us, as far as I'm concerned, that won't happen. Cara, I'm falling for you. Hard." He leans his forehead to mine.

"Me too," I say.

He grins. "Yeah?"

"Yeah."

He kisses me, and it turns heavy fast. "Fuck I want you," he says. "What time is it?"

I push him down onto the guest bed. "We have time."

He watches as I strip off all of my clothes and then yank

off his underwear. I straddle his waist as I kiss him. He flips me onto my back.

"One minute, I'm so angry with you; the next, I want you more than anything in my life. What are you doing to me, Cara?"

I spread my legs. "The same thing you're doing to me." I kiss him, and he enters in one thrust.

We both moan.

"You feel so damn good," he says between kisses.

We pick up speed. His thrusts are hard, causing the headboard to slam against the wall.

"I can't get enough of you," he says.

"Harder!" I yell.

He pulls out and flips me over. I get on my hands and knees, and he drives into me.

"Yes!" I say as I move against him.

His balls slap against me, lighting my whole body on fire.

"Don't stop. Right there," I say.

He continues to pump into me while reaching around and finding my clit, and my orgasm hits fast.

"Gray! Yes!" It takes over my body as he pumps several more times before letting out a loud groan.

We collapse onto the bed, breathing heavily. Finally, I find the strength to turn over, and he moves to my side.

"Why are you grinning?" he asks.

"I think we just had our first make-up sex."

He laughs. "If that's what that was, then get ready for some more arguments."

I laugh as I climb on top of him. "I really want to stay here with you, but we should probably get moving."

"Okay, wait here." He slides me off him and gets up. He returns with a towel and cleans me up.

"I'll shower and be ready in ten," he says.

"I'll be ready." I watch him walk away naked, and damn, I really do love that man's ass.

He grins at me from over his shoulder. "Stop staring."

"Can't help it." And I can't. I could stare at him all damn day.

* * *

I SPOT Anderson as I make my way down the pier. Gray assured me he would always have eyes on me. I walk up and stand beside my boss.

"Anderson," I say.

He turns to me, and his eyes are red-rimmed. Has he been crying? No, that can't be right. I've never seen this man show an emotion in his life.

"Harding. Thanks for meeting me here. I needed somewhere more private than the office to discuss this."

"Are you all right?" I ask.

He takes a heavy breath. "No, I'm not."

I don't respond but wait for him to tell me what's going on.

"Last year, before my promotion, I was assigned to work undercover on a case. A senator's daughter had been taken, and when she was found, she told her dad about Max Acrile and what he made her do. I was supposed to infiltrate Max's circle and obtain as much evidence as possible."

I lean against the railing. "You were working the Max case before I was? Why didn't you tell me?"

He stares out at the horizon. "Somehow, Max made me. He drugged a drink of mine. I woke up the next morning in bed with an underage girl."

"But if you were drugged and nothing happened, you can explain that."

His face turns red, and he shakes his head. "Something happened. I have no memory of it, but Max has photos of the girl doing things to me, and in the photos, I'm smiling."

I process what he's told me. Max set him up.

"When I realized what had happened, I got sick. I couldn't believe it, but he had the photos."

I turn my back to the water and watch the people walking by. "What happened next?" I ask.

"After Max showed me the photos, he said I was part of his organization now. I can't leave. He left me alone in his house for a few hours to think about it. I found his computer and hundreds of photos similar to mine. I copied them for the agency to evaluate."

"Wait, you went into his office at his house?"

Anderson nods.

"Did you see a teddy bear on the shelf?"

Anderson frowns. "Yeah, the sick fuck has stuffed animals in the house, probably for the kids."

"No, they all have cameras in them. He likely saw you at the computer."

Anderson turns around. "I left the country after that. Even if he wanted to, he couldn't have found me."

I spot Grayson on the sidewalk at the end of the pier. He's wearing a hoodie, and his head is down. He's staring at his phone, but I'm sure he's using the camera to watch us.

"So, you assigned me to get evidence on Max. Weren't the photos you had enough?"

He shakes his head. "No. Max wasn't in any photo. And I had no way to prove he took them."

His eyes meet mine. "Even though the photos weren't enough to take down Max, I still got the promotion I had applied for months before."

But Max had photos of me.

"Why did you give Max photos of me?"

He frowns. "What are you talking about?"

"He had photos on his computer. They were taken when I was out on a run. Before I was assigned to his case.."

Anderson stares above my head. "I never gave him photos. I never communicated with him after I left. You're sure he had photos of you?"

I cross my arms. "Very. And Max found me at my apartment. Any idea how that happened?"

His mouth opens. "No, but Cara, I may have assigned you to watch Max, but it wasn't my idea."

"Whose was it?"

"Whitlock. He said after the fiasco with the Kraliks, you needed some easy surveillance work. That's all it was supposed to be."

My mind races. That day I went running and a car drove

through a puddle, soaking me, it was a workday. I went in. I joked with Anderson about the fact he was already drinking a pumpkin spice latte. Deputy Director Whitlock walked in and commented how he finds pumpkin disgusting. Shit. He was in town that day. Had he been following me and taking photos?

I need to go through Max's laptop as soon as possible.

Anderson pulls his phone from his pocket. "I need to go. Do you need a lift anywhere?"

"No, I need to walk and think. Thanks."

Anderson nods and walks down the pier to the sidewalk. I follow. He turns right, and I go left but stop next to Gray. I turn and watch as Anderson gets into his car.

"Is he behind everything?" Gray asks.

I meet Gray's gaze. "No. I think Wh—"

My words are cut off by an explosion. I turn to see Anderson's car in flames and pieces soaring in the air.

"Anderson!" I scream.

Gray grabs my hand and pulls me until we are running away from the explosion as pieces of his car begin to fall all around us.

He grabs my arms and pulls me into the first door we find. It's a souvenir shop with Seattle T-shirts and mugs everywhere. I try to get free.

"We have to see if we can save him," I yell.

"Cara, it's too late." Gray wraps his arms around me both as a comfort and so I can't go anywhere. "No one could survive that."

He's right. I stop fighting him.

"Cara, we need to get out of here. You might be the next target."

CHAPTER THIRTY-FOUR

Grayson

CARA STOPS FIGHTING me and falls to her knees in front of the window. We watch as several onlookers run to Anderson's car, but there's no way he survived that.

"We have to get you out of here," I say as I take her hand in mine.

We go out the door to the sidewalk, where people are running and pushing to get by. We follow the crowd in the opposite direction of the explosion.

I parked in a garage a few blocks away. As we run there, we pass a bus stop. Pedestrians are pushing and shouting to get on.

"You have to get us out of here. A bomb went off! There may be more!"

By the time we make it to the garage, several others apparently have the same idea, and there's already a line to exit. Shit. The last thing I want to be is a sitting duck.

"We can go out the entrance," she says as she walks to the passenger side of the car.

"Works for me."

As I approach the back of the line, I move to the left and

drive toward the entrance. "Hold on," I say as I run through the barrier gate, and it breaks off. I glance in the rearview mirror, and there are cars now exiting the entrance, too.

Traffic isn't great, but at least it's not at a standstill. I drive us back to Pine Valley and to my place. Cara nearly jumps out of the car before I get it into park. She beats me to the front door. I follow and unlock it. She runs to the bedroom and returns with the laptop.

"If we can access Max's email, we might find who sent him the photos of me. Because I don't think it was Anderson."

"Who do you think it was?"

As the laptop powers on, she sets it on the coffee table and sits on the couch. "Deputy Director Whitlock, Anderson's boss and the man I reported to for the Kralik case."

I pace the room. "A deputy director? Are you sure?"

She nods.

"Why? How?"

"Anderson told me it was Whitlock's idea to send me out on the assignment to collect evidence against Max. He also denied sending Max any photos of me. And I remembered that the day I was splashed with mud Whitlock was in town."

I sit down on the couch. "Or Anderson could have been lying to save himself."

Her brows go up. "And he blew up his own car?"

"Max is after you. Anderson and Canton kill Max. Then someone kills Anderson. And you believe that someone is Whitlock? But why? It doesn't make any sense."

She scoots closer. "Anderson explained he was at Max's house. At one point, he was left alone, and he went into the office and took some files off the computer."

As I picture this, I remember the teddy bear. "The camera."

"Exactly. Max would have known, which would have put a target on Anderson. Unless Max didn't see what Anderson did for some reason. Anderson was back here for well over six months and didn't appear to be a target."

I stand up as I think through what she says. I go to the kitchen and grab a couple of fizzy waters and return.

I hand her one. "Are you suggesting someone else put the teddy bear camera there?"

She takes it from me. "Thanks. If Whitlock put the camera there to keep an eye on Max and he sent Anderson on an assignment, he would expect to see Anderson at the computer. And by promoting Anderson immediately upon his return, Whitlock had an excuse for Anderson not to continue on the case. That way, Whitlock got to view all the files and delete anything he didn't like first."

I take a sip. "Okay, but what if Anderson saw something as he was copying the files?"

She shrugs. "Maybe Whitlock questioned him and decided he didn't know anything."

This still isn't adding up. "Why send you?" I ask.

She leans back. "That's a good question. Maybe agent Canton knows something. He and Anderson were close."

I set down my water. "Canton might be in danger."

"Or he might be the one behind the explosion."

Fuck, she's right. We don't have enough information yet. I point at the laptop. "Let's see what we can find."

Fortunately for us, Max wasn't great about security and didn't password-protect his files. But after an hour, Cara shoves the laptop across the coffee table.

"How can there not be more here? The photos of me were so easy to find."

I pull the computer to my lap. "That is odd."

We've gone through about half of the folders and deter-mined Max loved to cook based on how many recipes he saved. I scan the folders again, but this time, one catches my eye. It's called My Pet Cat.

"Did Max have a cat?"

She shakes her head. "Not that I ever saw."

I open the folder. "Bingo."

She leans in closer. The folder contains thirty-two photos and one text document. I open the photos first. Neither of us is prepared for what we see. All the photos are of Whitlock, and in each, he is with a different girl. Yes, *girls* who are clearly underage.

"Open the text document," she requests.

I open it, and we read through it together. It lists the names of men and the dates they came to Max's parties. There are a few well-known figures on the list.

"If Whitlock saw the files Anderson copied, he's known that Max had this file on him. Maybe that's why he sent me to bring him down."

I set the laptop back on the coffee table and turn to her. "But if Max had been arrested or brought to the US, what would prevent him from telling everyone about all this?"

She chews on her lip. "Maybe Whitlock had a plan to intercept him."

That's possible. "But when Max showed up in the US, Whitlock must have been nervous." I stand up and stretch as I try to work this out.

"Shit. That's why Canton was there with Anderson," she says.

"You think Canton was working with Whitlock?"

She nods. "I do."

"But his name isn't on this list."

She stands, too. "True. But maybe Whitlock had something on Canton and he was forced to comply."

"Okay, but until we have more facts, we're just guessing here. We need to find Canton."

She pulls her phone from her pocket and calls Canton on speaker phone. "We do."

Three rings and I think it's going to voicemail when he answers.

"Canton, it's Harding. Are you at the office?"

"No, I took a sick day."

She arches a brow at me. "I wanted you to know Anderson's dead."

"What? Shit! How?"

"A car explosion."

Canton is silent, but we can hear his breathing through the phone.

"Canton, I think you might be in danger, too," she says.
"Why?"

Her eyes meet mine, and I nod. "Whitlock was a client of Max Acrile. Anderson had photos and was killed because of it."

"Photos? Are you sure? Have you seen them?"

She doesn't answer right away but finally says, "Yes."

"How does that put me in danger?"

Cara takes a breath. "You were working with Anderson, and we all know you were his favorite. Whitlock might think you know something."

Canton is silent for a moment. "Okay. If I'm in danger, I need to leave my place. Any ideas where I can go?"

"I have a cabin. I'll text you the address."

"Harding, thank you. But if you know about these photos, you're in danger, too. You should come to the cabin as well."

The man's words show concern, but there's something off in his tone.

"Of course. I need to take care of a few things, but I'll be there in a couple of hours," she says.

"Thanks for calling. I'll see you then." Canton ends the call.

I cross my arms. "Something was off about him."

Cara pockets her phone. "Yeah, he was lying most of the time."

"Are you sure?"

She nods. "He never takes sick days. I overheard him talking to another agent about how they make you appear weak. Either he's in the office, or he knows something is up."

I take another drink of my water. "He's suspicious. Why was he asking you for a safe place to go? Shouldn't he have his own?"

Cara nods. "He should, but he did just transfer here not long ago."

I don't care if he was transferred here last week; he would have a contingency plan. Nodding to the laptop. "I'll make a copy of these files in case someone finds this." I walk into the kitchen and find a USB stick in a drawer.

"We should go to the cabin and stake it out," Cara says.

I return to the laptop and begin to copy the files over. "You don't think Canton will come alone?"

She stares out the front window. "I'm not certain."

"In that case, I'll call the guys and see if anyone can give us backup."

Pulling on her coat, she nods to me. "You can make that call on the way. As soon as those files are copied, we need to head out. If Canton's in Seattle, we'll get to the cabin first if we leave soon."

Once the files finish copying, I grab the USB stick and put it into my pocket. I hide the laptop in the attic.

I toss my keys to Cara. Once we hit the road, I text the guys asking for help.

Fox: *Send the address. I'm on my way.*

Trax: *Me too.*

CHAPTER THIRTY-FIVE

Cara

IT IS TAKING ALL my self-control not to speed right now, but the last thing I need is to get pulled over and delay getting to the cabin.

Grayson is typing away on his phone, hoping one of the guys can come help back us up.

We're halfway there when he asks, "What's the address to the cabin?"

That's when I realize that I never texted Canton the address. I pull over and check my phone. "I never gave Canton the address. And he hasn't texted me asking for it."

"Maybe he hasn't left yet," Grayson offers.

I nod. Maybe. But something tells me he knows where it's at. After sending the address to Grayson so he can just forward it on, I get back on the road.

Before we reach the cabin, I park the car at another property that appears to be vacant. We hike through the woods past two other houses until my dad's comes into view. No cars are in the driveway, and it appears no one is there.

"Did he ask for the address yet?" Grayson asks.

I check my phone. "Nope."

"If he shows up, we need to wait here until we have backup. Fox and Trax are driving up."

I lean against a tree and replay the night Max was killed in my head. Why would they untie Max's hands when there was a weapon—the razor—in full view? No agent would do that. Even a rookie would know better. And neither of them were rookies.

A car pulls up, and we duck even though it's unlikely anyone can see us in the darkened woods.

Canton gets out and walks to the house but doesn't try to go in.

"He doesn't have the passcode," I say.

Canton walks the perimeter of the property and comes closer to us than I care for. Then he gets down on the ground and backs into some bushes until he's hidden.

"Shit, he plans to ambush me."

"Looks that way."

Did Whitlock ask Canton to take me out? There's only one way for me to find out. I've never texted Whitlock before. All of our communication has been in the Seattle office, but I do have his number.

Me: *Anderson is dead. I'm worried I'm in danger. I'm going into hiding until you can confirm all is clear.*

I send the message, and he responds right away.

Whitlock: *Harding, glad to hear you're safe. Can you confirm your location?*

Me: *Sent Canton to my cabin. I was going to join him but decided it's best if we stay separate. I'm going to a warehouse outside of Fisher Springs. It's safe.*

I show the exchange to Gray, and he nods. Whitlock doesn't respond, but five minutes later, Canton crawls out of the bush he's in and wipes himself off. He gets into his car and leaves.

"Well, now you know who's calling the shots," Gray says as he pulls out his phone. "I'm going to call Fox and let them know we don't need them after all."

While he's doing that, I stare at the cabin. I still don't understand why I was sent on an assignment to watch Max if

Whitlock was working with him. Whitlock could have sent Canton down to kill the man and claimed it was self-defense.

"Okay, I let them know what was going on," Gray says. "Do you think Whitlock will go to the warehouse?"

I shake my head. "No."

He holds up the USB stick. "We should get this to the FBI now. I have a contact."

"So do I."

We both say "Carter" at the same time.

* * *

WE DRIVE BACK to Seattle and make it to the FBI office before it closes. Fortunately, Carter is willing to see us. Gray gives him the USB. After he reviews the files, Carter leans back in his chair.

"We've had Max Acrile under surveillance for a while. Our agency was working with the CIA on this. But I did find it odd that despite sending agents in, the CIA never could find one shred of evidence against this man. Thank you for bringing this to me."

I nod. "Will you arrest Whitlock? He and Agent Canton are trying to kill me."

Carter leans forward. "We need to go through the proper channels, but yes, we will be pursuing charges against these men. And we will also look into both of them for the bombing of Anderson's car."

Gray leans forward. "Going through proper channels? That will take some time, won't it?"

Carter clasps his hands together. "It will. In the meantime, I recommend you leave town and go somewhere he can't find you."

My mind is racing. Where should I go? I can't go back to my apartment, so I don't have clothes. Whitlock is likely tracking my credit cards. And Gray's.

"Thank you, Carter. Please keep us updated on the progress," Gray says as he writes down his cell phone number and hands it to the man.

"I will. Stay safe. Both of you."

We stand, and I'm trying to put together a plan when Gray steps in front of me.

"CT will get us cash. He knows I'm good for it. Then we'll drive somewhere in the middle of nowhere."

"No," I say.

Carter and Grayson stare at me wide-eyed.

"Cara, you're in danger. Please let me protect you."

I turn to Gray's pleading eyes. "But the best way to lure Whitlock and Canton anywhere is by using me.

Carter leans back. "We don't need you. We know where Canton is, and as soon as I give the go-ahead, we'll arrest him. But that will take some time because I need to get the paperwork first. So please, listen to Peaches and go somewhere unexpected."

I sigh. "Fine. But I want to know the moment he's in custody. Deal?"

Carter nods. "Deal."

As we ride down the elevator, Gray is typing away on his phone. He stops me from going outside.

"We're going to wait. I called for a car. It will be here in a couple of minutes." He takes my hand in his. "I know it is hard for you to sit this out. But we'll have fun, I promise."

A car pulls up in front of the building, and he leads me to it. Once he confirms the destination with the driver, he turns to me. "I think you'll like where we're going."

I nod. "Thank you for doing all this."

He shrugs. "I didn't really do anything. It's CT. I'll tell you about it when we get there."

I close my eyes and try to relax for the ride. Two hours later, we arrive at a development in the woods. There's snow on the ground, but the road has been plowed.

"Here you are," the driver says.

"Thank you."

As I step out of the car, I stare at the house. Well, house isn't accurate. It's more like a shack. Clearly, the place has been abandoned, and there is plywood up where there should be windows.

"We're staying here?" I ask.

Gray waves to the driver. "No, but we want the driver to think so."

He takes my hand and leads me toward the front door. By the time we get there, the driver has backed out and is gone.

"Okay, let's go to the real cabin." He winks.

There are those flutters again. This man can make me smile even in the midst of running for my life.

We stay on the plowed road as he leads me to the other end of it. Finally, we turn and walk down a driveway. The cabin comes into view. Thankfully, it's nothing like the last place.

He finds a keypad on the side of the house and punches some numbers. The garage door opens. We go through it and into the main building. It screams ski cabin. There are paintings on the wall of snow-topped trees and mountains and several stuffed bears wearing various winter sweaters. I stop as I take it all in.

"I can assure you these bears do not have cameras. The cabin belongs to CT's parents."

He opens the backdoor and steps out. He returns with grocery bags.

"CT had food delivered before we got here. He asked they be left at the back door."

I follow him into the kitchen. "You guys thought of everything."

After he sets the bags on the counter, he takes my hands in his. "Don't think of this as hiding out. Think of it as an extended date."

"An extended date? I can do that." I step closer and move my hands to his chest. "And what are we doing on this date?" I push up onto my toes and kiss his neck.

He growls. "That depends on whether you keep doing that or not."

I move my lips up his neck to just below his ear. "I don't plan to stop."

In one quick move, he bends down, puts his arm under

my knees, and then sweeps me up. He walks down the hall and enters the first room—a bathroom.

"Have you been here before?"

"No, but I'm pretty sure there must be a bed around here somewhere." He walks past another door, not liking what he sees, to the final door. "Found it."

He sets me down on the mattress and climbs over me. When he kisses me, all the stress, frustration, and fear I've been feeling bubbles up, and I can't get close to him fast enough.

I pull at his T-shirt, and while he's taking it off, I unzip his jeans. He begins to unbutton my blouse, and I take over for him, yanking it over my head. Before I make it back to his jeans, his lips collide with mine as his hand finds my breast.

"You are so fucking beautiful," he says between kisses.

I wrap my legs around him, and he grinds into me. Despite still wearing jeans, having him between my legs feels so good. My hand moves down his back, feeling his muscles contract as he pushes against me.

"I need more," I say.

He sits up.

"Take off your pants," I order.

Grinning, he stands, then shucks his pants and underwear.

"No commando today?"

"Not today. I grabbed some new underwear the other day. How about you? I want those pants off."

I unbutton and unzip my jeans, and he helps me pull them off. He loops his fingers into the sides of my underwear and pushes them to my ankles. When he leans down, his hot breath hits my thighs, and I stop him.

"I need you inside me. Now." I grab his arms and pull him up.

He willingly changes positions, and his hands go behind my back, unhooking my bra. I get it off my arms and throw it across the room. He stares into my eyes but doesn't move.

"Something wrong?"

His eyes become glassy as he lowers himself to his

elbows. "Nothing's wrong. It's just that I have fallen completely in love with you."

My chest feels like it's going to crack open. "Gray, I'm so deeply in love with you, too."

He smiles and then kisses me. As he does, I move my hands and give him a nudge so he knows I'm ready. He pushes inside, but instead of the urgency I felt moments before, I want to take this slow and savor every moment with this man.

My hands go to his face as he stares into my eyes. He begins to roll his hip—in and out slowly. With each movement, I swear I can feel his love.

CHAPTER THIRTY-SIX

Grayson

As I stare into Cara's eyes, all I can think is how much I love this woman and I will do anything and everything to protect her. I've never felt this connected to another human being. It's something I don't want to end. And while we started wanting to rip off each other's clothes, it all changed when I told her I love her. Now I want to cherish every inch of her.

"Gray, I'm close."

I move my hand down and find her clit. I pinch it, and she jerks against me and moans. I rub circles the way she likes.

"So responsive. I love that about you." I take her nipple into my mouth and gently bite.

"Oh, yes." She presses her chest up, searching for more pressure.

I suck lightly as I work her with my fingers.

"Yes! Yes! Oh, fuck yes!" she shouts, clenching me as her climax hits.

I watch the pleasure hit her in waves. It's hot, and I can't hold on any longer. I thrust harder, and my orgasm takes over. I push in as far as I can as I grunt out something unintelligible.

Her eyes well up.

"What's wrong?" I ask as I move a few stray hairs from her face.

"I've never felt so much for someone. I'm just a little over-whelmed."

I lean down and kiss her. It's slow and deep as I'm trying to convey all the emotions I'm feeling to her as well. I press my forehead to hers and rub our noses together.

She laughs. "That really is our thing now, isn't it?"

"It is. Whenever we're away from each other, I want you to remember that. And that I will always love you."

A tear escapes her eye, and I wipe it away. Being away from Cara will be hard, but we both knew what we were getting into.

"I'll be right back."

I get up to get a washcloth and help her clean up. We climb into bed, and she lies on my chest. I'll have to thank CT for this cabin. It's exactly what we needed. Despite the chaos of our lives, right here in this bed, it feels like home.

"Make it stop," Cara grumbles.

"What?" I open my eyes, and the room is dark.

We must have fallen asleep. There's a vibrating noise.

"Make the noise stop," she says.

I get up and find the vibrating is my phone in my pants on the tile floor.

Seven missed messages. Shit. How long have we been asleep? I check the time. Only a few hours. I turn on the speakerphone as I listen to the messages.

"Carter here. Both Whitlock and Canton have been detained. You can come back to town."

Cara sits up. "They got him?"

I nod as the next message plays.

"Hey, I hope you found the cabin. Can you let me know you made it?"

"You should probably text CT before he calls again."

I delete the message, and the third one plays.

"Seriously, did you make it?" CT asks.

The fourth message plays. *"Dude, just text me already,"* CT says.

"They're probably having sex. Leave them alone," Rover says in the background. The message ends.

The next message. *"Okay, so it's been a couple of hours. There is no way you could still be having sex, so for fuck's sake, call me."*

The next message is from Rover. *"Hey, why don't you call me and not CT? You know, just to fuck with him."*

The last message I figure is CT, but I'm wrong. *"Peaches, it's Stormy. The guys tell me you're hiding out with Harding. Call me."*

Cara gets up and grabs her clothes off the floor.

"What are you doing?" I ask.

She frowns. "Getting dressed. Aren't we heading back?"

I run my hand through my hair. "It's late, and there isn't much we can do tonight. Let's stay here, and we can head out early in the morning if you want."

She drops her clothes. "Sounds good to me. Let's see what groceries CT got us." She walks past me completely naked. Yeah, I'm one lucky man.

"I'm going to call Stormy, then I'll join you."

After sending CT and Rover a text, I call my boss.

"Peaches, I heard you went out of town. Does this mean you're taking time off?"

I wince. I should have told him what was going on. "No, I'll be back in the morning. We're not far from Seattle. I had to get Cara out of there."

"CT filled me in. I get it. But in the future, I need you to communicate with me."

"Yes, I'm sorry. I'll keep you posted."

He sighs. "Good. I'll see you tomorrow." He ends the call.

I hate leaving Cara's side when we still don't know where Ivan is or if he's a threat. I drop the phone onto the bed and walk out to the kitchen.

Music is playing, and Cara is dancing, naked while making sandwiches. My first thought is who can see her, but all the curtains have been closed on the windows.

"What are you making?"

She jumps and turns to face me. "Sandwiches." She smiles. "But you will have to put on your own condiments since I don't know if you like relish on your sandwich."

I walk to the counter to see what she has laid out because I swear I misheard her. But no, there is a jar of sweet relish open. "You put relish on your sandwich?"

She cocks her head. "Of course, it's my secret ingredient."

Now I'm both concerned and maybe a little disgusted.

She laughs as she touches me between my eyes. "You're clearly upset by this. It's just relish."

"Not a fan of pickles."

She pulls her hand back, and her eyes widen. "All pickles or just sweet pickles?"

"All."

Her eyes close. "I'm sorry to hear that. I really thought we could have been great together."

There's no way she's serious, but nothing about her demeanor indicates she's kidding. I arch a brow, and the corner of her mouth turns up.

"You'd choose pickles over hot sex?"

She bites her lip and thinks a moment. I tickle her side, causing her to scream. I grab the mayo, squeezing it onto the sandwich she made me.

"Thanks for the sandwich."

Now she smiles. "And thank you for the hot sex."

We finish our sandwiches and spend the rest of the evening in the bedroom. One thing I never expected from Cara, she's insatiable. Not that I mind. But as promised, we head out early the next morning.

CT said I could use the car parked in the garage. I'm thankful they happen to keep a spare vehicle here and have someone start it now and again.

I drop Cara off at the federal building. Carter asked her to come in. Apparently, Whitlock insisted on talking only to her. I want to be with her, but she says she needs to do this on her own. Since an interrogation can take hours, I drive to MTS. She agreed to text me when she's done.

Somehow I manage to get in without Cheeto noticing.

That damn bird has it out for Fox, though. It might have something to do with the fact that both Rover and I place a few Cheetos around his car any chance we can.

I'm laughing about it as I walk until Stormy spots me. "Peaches, grab the other guys and come to my office."

"Sure thing," I say. I find the guys in the kitchen watching coffee brew. "Wow, guess it's a slow day," I say.

"Finally," CT says. "We've been waiting for you. Stormy says he has news."

"He asked me to tell you to go to his office," I say.

Rover comes up beside me as I walk down the hall. "Are you late because you were with Cara?"

I stop walking and turn to the guys. "I'm sure you all know I was protecting Cara. And before you ask, yes, we're dating."

"Congratulations! I'm happy for you," Rover says.

"We all are," CT says.

I glance at Fox, who's smiling, too. "Where are Cody, Maverick, and Trax?" I ask.

"Cody and Trax are on a new assignment as of this morning. Maverick took a personal day," Rover says.

"Okay, guess it's just us. Let's find out what Stormy wants," I say.

When we enter his office, Stormy is sitting at the conference table, frowning. After we all join him, he stands and walks to his desk to grab his phone.

"I have news on the cigarette, but it isn't good. Detective McNamara let me know that it won't be possible to get any DNA from it. But she did recognize the brand. Apparently, there's some kid McNamara is familiar with who smokes that brand and has been suspected of breaking into businesses in Pine Valley."

"Has he been questioned?" Fox asks.

Stormy nods. "He claims he was out of town with his family that night. McNamara confirmed it. We're back where we were at a dead end." He sits in a chair and lets out a deep breath.

CT leans forward. "There's no way this was done by a kid.

Someone came in here, found confidential information, and shared it with that so-called news source."

He's right. This likely wasn't done by some kid.

"Do you think this is related to the rotten candy? Wasn't it here that morning?" Fox asks.

"Oh, the maggot candy?" Rover gags. "I had one in my mouth."

Stormy leans forward. "Where did you find it anyway?"

Rover gags a few more times. "It was in the kitchen. I thought you'd put it in there."

Stormy shakes his head. "No, I didn't. Did any of you?" He glances around as we all shake our heads.

"Maybe it has fingerprints on it," Fox says.

"Uh oh," Rover says.

We all turn to him.

"I said something to Stormy about it, and he said to throw it away, so I did."

"It's okay, Rover. We didn't know. But if anything else shows up, confirm someone here brought it in before you eat anything," Stormy warms. "We need to be vigilant. Between the fire earlier this year and then someone stealing confidential information, it's possible someone out there is trying to hurt MTS."

Rover crosses his arms. "I thought we were sure Valerie Gardiner was behind the fire."

Valerie Gardiner is Cody's future mother-in-law, but she also ran several criminal enterprises in Pine Valley after her husband died. We went after her, and she didn't like it. We all figured the fire was set by her.

"There was never any proof that she was behind it," Stormy says. "Until we know more, stay on guard. That's all for now."

I head out of the conference room to my office. There's still a pile of paperwork I need to get through, so I work on that until Cara texts me that she's ready for a ride home.

Home. Anywhere she is feels like home. And now I know what I need to do.

CHAPTER THIRTY-SEVEN

Cara

I TAKE a deep breath and nod. Carter opens the door, and I walk in. The FBI's interrogation room is small. Smaller and drabber than most interrogation rooms I've been in. But that's not important. What's important is the that I get answers from the man now before me.

"Harding, I'm surprised to see you."

"Why? Because you thought Canton killed me? I didn't go to the warehouse."

Before I came in here, Carter informed me that Whitlock sold out Canton the first chance he got, and now, Canton is sitting in some holding room somewhere in this building.

Whitlock laughs. "No, obviously you didn't."

I sit down across from him. He's in a suit, but it appears rumpled, and his hands are cuffed and hooked to a loop in the middle of the table.

"Why did you assign me to follow Max?"

He laughs. "You do get right to the point, don't you? That's something I've always liked about you. It makes you a good agent."

Carter steps into the room and closes the door behind him.

"You hear to keep an eye on me?" Whitlock asks.

Carter shakes his head. "I'm here to remind you that as part of the deal you cut, you must answer Ms. Harding's questions."

Deal? What deal? That wasn't my understanding. I glance at Carter, but he's avoiding my gaze.

Whitlock leans back as best he can with his hands bound to the table. His watery eyes meet mine. "I had to send you on that assignment. Max asked for you. And if I didn't, he threatened to reveal all he had on me. You're one of our best agents, Cara. I'm sorry."

Max asked for me? "Max knew who I was before I went to Chile?"

"No, he asked for the agent who had been tracking Ivan Kralik."

"Why? As far as we were concerned, Ivan was dead."

Whitlock shrugs. "It appears Max was friends with the Kraliks. You confirmed this in your report when you said you saw Max and Ivan together in Brazil."

I lean back and cross my arms. "You sent me down there and sent Max photos of me so he'd find me."

Whitlock glances at Carter, who nods. "Yes."

That's all he has to say? *Yes?*

I stand up and step away. But I turn back. "Max intended to give me to random men. Any of them could have killed me!"

Whitlock stares at the table. "I'm sorry. I didn't know what to do. Max kept threatening to turn those photos over to the FBI."

I lean forward on the table. "Are you fucking kidding me right now? Maybe you could have not had sex with those girls!" I'm shouting, but I don't care. "You're unbelievable. You put agents at risk for your own selfish motives."

I turn to Carter. "What's his deal for? Giving you Canton's whereabouts?"

Carter shakes his head. "No, he gave us Ivan Kralik's location."

That I did not expect. Whitlock avoids my gaze.

"You knew where Ivan was?"

"No. He keeps a place in Denmark, and since he's being hunted, he's likely there."

He knows? He knows! I lunge across the table and grab him by the collar, pulling tight. His face turns red.

"Too tight," he says.

"You knew where he might be? I've been working on tracking Ivan for years and you knew? How long have you known?"

Fortunately for me, Carter hasn't made a move to stop me.

"Only after you told me you saw Ivan alive. I swear!" he says.

I pull a little tighter and am right in his face. "And why was I sent to bring Ivan in if you and Max were out to protect him?"

The man's eyes widen. "No! I was not protecting Ivan. I've wanted to take out the sonofabitch for years. He's sold countless weapons to terrorists."

I release him and step back. "Why did you tell Max I was in Costa Rica?" I'm fishing now, but I want to keep him talking.

He coughs and rubs his neck. "I never told Max that. I don't know why he was there."

He appears to be telling the truth, but at this point, I can't trust anything he says. But I wonder if his deal covers murder.

I glance at Carter and then back to Whitlock. "Why did you have Canton kill Max?"

Whitlock laughs. The man fucking laughs.

"What's so damned funny?" I ask.

He leans back again. "I didn't ask Canton to kill anyone. As for why he did it, you'll have to ask him."

The man smirks. He's lying. Taking out Max solved all his problems.

I turn and leave the room. I can't stand another minute in there with him. Everything about that man disgusts me.

Carter follows me out. "Follow me," he says. He leads me to his office and closes the door.

"What the hell kind of deal did you make with him?"

Carter sits behind his desk. "In exchange for Ivan's whereabouts, Whitlock will serve three years in a minimum-security prison."

I throw my hands into the air. "Three years? That's it? You've got to be kidding me. He got away with murder."

"Canton is sticking with his story that it was self-defense. And since Anderson backed that up in the reports, we aren't pursuing it. As for the deal, I've been in direct contact with Whitlock's superior. He wanted this deal if it means we capture Ivan."

I stand straight up. "And if you don't find Ivan?"

Carter shrugs. "Then no deal."

As much as I don't agree with only a three-year sentence, we do need to get Ivan in custody. He's caused too much damage already.

"Will you let me know if you find him?" I ask.

"I will."

I nod and walk out of his office. I need to get as far away from this building and Whitlock as I can.

With Ivan on the run, I decide to go to my apartment. But once I walk inside, I realize this was a bad idea. The place is a wreck. My coffee table and a lamp are broken. A painting I loved was on the floor, torn when I tried to fight off Max and Dan. There was a time when this apartment felt like home but not anymore. I text Gray and let him know where I'm at. I wait on my couch.

One case has managed to make a shit show of my career. Because of Whitlock, my identity has been compromised. I received a message yesterday that my future is being discussed. *Discussed*. Someone else will decide if, after all my years of serving the agency, I'm simply let go.

There's a knock on my door. It seems too fast for

Grayson. I check to see who it is, and I can't believe who I'm seeing.

I open the door.

"Hello, Cara."

"Dad?"

"Can I come in?"

I step aside, and he walks in.

He takes in the mess. "I can't say I agree with your decorating style." He sits on the couch as if this is a typical visit.

"Why are you here?"

The man has never been to my apartment. Aside from the incident in Panama, I haven't seen him in years.

"Look, I made mistakes when you were growing up. I had no idea what shape your mother was in. And for that, I'm so sorry."

I walk to the kitchen so he doesn't see the tear that falls from my eye. I've waited years for an apology. But why now? He follows me, so I turn to him. "You chose your job over me. You left me with her. I heard your apology, but you can't just erase all that damage." I sniffle. Dammit. I'm crying.

He wraps his arms around me, and I stand there stiff. "I'm so sorry. I had no idea."

I can't hold back any longer, and I let the tears go. "She never wanted me. Do you have any idea what it's like growing up with someone like that?"

"No. I'm sorry."

I step back. "When I was home, she ignored me, never helped me. She went out all the time, leaving me alone. I finally made one good friend, and you know what she did?"

He swallows and shakes his head.

"She moved us away. I know it wasn't for your job because I heard you fighting about it the next time you were home."

He sinks into a chair at the kitchen table. "I never understood why she moved across town. It made no sense."

Thinking about it brings up all my old anger. "It made sense. Because we moved, I had to change schools which meant I never got to see my friend again. That's how she wanted me. Alone. I never knew why."

He closes his eyes, and tears fall down his cheeks. "I didn't know. I was so caught up in my career; I thought your mom was happy. She never told me she wasn't."

"She wasn't unhappy! She lived her life as a single woman. Why didn't you ever ask me?"

He shakes his head. "I don't have an excuse. I'm so sorry. She asked me once to quit. I didn't. Instead, I put my job first and neglected my family. That will always be my biggest regret."

At least he seems remorseful, more than I ever saw from my mother.

"Toward the end, I discovered your mom was taking pills."

I frown. "She was an addict?"

He stands and walks to me. "No, nothing like that. These were for depression. She wouldn't talk to me about it, and I'm not trying to make any excuses, but I think there was something more going on than I—or we—ever knew."

I cross my arms. "It doesn't matter now. As far as I'm concerned, I never want to see that woman again."

He nods. "I understand. But Cara, I really do want to make things right between us."

I take another step back. "I'm not sure."

He stares at the floor. "It's a lot to take in. I'll be stateside for a couple of weeks. If you change your mind, I'd really like to spend some time together." He finds a notepad and pen on the counter. He writes something down and then rips the paper off the pad. "Here's my number."

I stare at it as he leaves. Will I call him? I don't know. I'm still staring at it when Grayson appears in my doorway.

"Was that your dad?"

"Yeah."

He steps in and closes the door behind him. "Do you want to talk about it?"

"No."

I'm not sure I fully understand what just happened. My

father has been closed off all my life, and now he wants to make things right. Do I want that? Tears well in my eyes. Grayson takes me in his arms, and I don't even try to stop crying. I let it all out, and he holds me the entire time.

Finally, I lift my head and wipe my eyes. "Thank you. I needed that."

As I step back, his hands move to my shoulders.

"Anytime, I'm here for you. Got that?"

I nod.

"Now, we should talk about your living situation."

We both take in the mess my apartment currently is.

"I want you to move in with me."

I meet his eyes. Is he serious?

"Now, hear me out. This isn't because you need a place to live or because you could still be in danger due to Ivan. This is because I love you, and I want you with me every chance I get. Both of our jobs take us away at a moment's notice. I want to be with you before you go on an assignment and when you return."

I start crying again. "Wow. I never would have thought Peaches was such a romantic."

He grins. "Get used to it. Now, will you move in with me?"

"Yes. I'd love to." I grab his arms as I step closer, but he winces.

"Oh, sorry. Your injury. How is it?"

He moves my hands behind his neck. "It's much better. I see you are no longer bandaging your hand. That's a good sign."

I hold it up to show him. There will be a scar, but it's healing. "Only band-aids."

"That's good because I know some things you can do with that hand." He kisses me.

I pull back. "Oh yeah? Like what?"

He bends down and tosses me over his shoulder, carrying me down the hallway. He finds my bedroom and tosses me onto the mattress.

"Well, let me show you."

CHAPTER THIRTY-EIGHT

Cara

THE LAST THING I wanted to do was untangle myself from my hot boyfriend and get out of bed to fight all the guys at MTS, but this means a lot to Gray, so here I am wearing three layers of clothing, ready to show these guys who the real paintball champion is.

CT was excited that everyone was back in the office for the day, so he put this together at the last minute. They originally had a championship game planned but had to cancel it since not enough of the guys were around.

I've played with them before, and Trax is the one I need to keep an eye on. He goes deep into the woods behind the MTS building and waits for the guys to take each other out. Then he comes forward, takes on one or two at most, and is declared the winner. Almost every time. But not today.

After a fierce battle this summer, I remained outside while the guys went inside. That's when I found my perfect spot.

"Okay, here are the teams," CT announces. "On the blue team, we have Rover, Connie, Amber, Trax, Maverick, and me. On the red team, we have Peaches, Cara, Cody, Lucy, and Fox."

"Hey, that's not fair," Cody says. "You have one more person."

CT shrugs. "Yeah, but it's Amber so you have nothing to be worried about."

"Hey!" Amber yells. "I want to switch teams because I'm coming after you!"

CT sighs. "Fine. Amber is now on the red team."

Amber grins

I walk up to her. "I'll help you take him out."

"Dream team right here!" she shouts.

CT shakes his head. "Okay, is everyone ready?"

"Yes!"

"Go into the woods, and when you hear the horn, it's on," CT says.

We all run into the woods. As usual, Trax runs back and to the left. I run straight back. I've already lost track of Gray.

The horn blows, and I keep making my way back until I find my tree. I climb it as silently as possible and ready my paint gun.

"Fuck!" CT yells.

Amber laughs, and she loudly runs through the trees. I'm surprised Rover hasn't taught her how to make her way through quieter.

The sound of a paintball hitting something echoes in the air close to me.

"Rover!" Amber yells.

"Don't take out my best friend," Rover yells.

He runs in front of my tree, none the wiser that I'm here. I remain calm and let him go. The other guys will take him out.

Over the next thirty minutes, several of the guys fall. Rover and Cody apparently shot each other at the same time, but Rover tried to argue he shot first and Cody's shot shouldn't count.

Connie giggles before the sound of another paintball blast.

"How the hell did you sneak up on me with that giggle?" Fox asks.

But Connie doesn't respond. I suspect she's got her sites on someone else.

And that is confirmed when Lucy screams. "Ouch! Why Connie? I thought we were friends."

Connie doesn't respond, and I don't hear her running through the woods like Amber. I guess Rover gave her some pointers.

I see Gray slowly making his way around a tree. He spots me, and I nod. He grins, then keeps moving in the direction Trax went. He moves out of sight, and the sound of at least twenty paint gun blasts go off.

"Dammit. I thought I had you," Maverick says.

Gray laughs. "Yeah, I thought I was smart dodging to the left. I didn't see Connie until it was too late."

"Yeah, I was so excited I got you. I didn't see Maverick," she says.

The sound of their footsteps on the back steps of the MTS deck echo in the air.

"Who's left?" Rover asks.

"Just Trax and Cara," Gray says.

And now I wait out Trax.

"Hey, where's CT? He always likes to see the end of this," Fox says.

Rover laughs. "Amber probably insisted he help her clean paint off her clothes or something."

"Why would she do that?" Fox asks.

But my attention turns when I hear a twig snap below me. I smile as Trax comes into my sights. I aim and fire before he can react.

He laughs and glances up at me. "Good one. No one takes me out."

I climb down and pat him on the shoulder. "You got too predictable. You always go back and left."

We walk through the woods back to the building.

"Damn, you're right," he says.

A scream stops me in my tracks. "What the hell was that?"

Trax points up. "Cheeto."

Rover grins. "He's our defense peacock."

I glance at Gray, and he shakes his head, so I take his lead and let it go.

Amber storms out the back door with CT on her heels.

"Why the hell did you ask me to clean that for you if you thought I'd ruin it?" he asks.

Rover grins. "See, I was right."

Amber holds up a blue-stained washcloth. "Everyone knows you don't rub a stain! You blot!" She tosses the wash-cloth onto the railing.

"Well, I don't!" CT yells.

"No kidding!" she yells back.

Cheeto swoops down and grabs the washcloth. He takes it a few feet away.

"Oh no!" Amber says. "The paint might be poisonous. CT, get it back."

CT's eyes widen. "Uh, no. I'm not going anywhere near the beak of death."

Amber's hands go to her hips. "Beak of death? Exaggerate much?"

CT looks at Rover and motions with his hands. "Tell her."

Rover unzips the coveralls he's wearing and slips them off. "One time, CT and I were housesitting for a friend and watching her parakeets while she was out of town."

"Wait," Amber says as she holds up her hands. "You two were parakeet sitting?"

They both nod.

"Which one of you was trying to get into this woman's pants?" Amber asks.

Rover places his coveralls in a garbage bin we have on the deck for dirty paintball gear.

"It doesn't matter," he says.

"Okay, so it was you." Amber grins.

"It doesn't matter," Rover repeats. "Anyway, we're playing with the parakeets."

CT smiles. "They were fun. They'd jump through hoops and fetch."

I frown and glance at Trax, who is shaking his head. The thing about Rover and CT is that they get going on these stories, and you never know whether to believe them because they are so ridiculous. One time, Trax called bullshit on a story they told about llamas blocking the road, causing them to be late to our meeting. Sure enough, they pulled up an article confirming their tale.

"Yeah, it was amazing how far you could throw their little sticks, and they'd still fetch it." Rover smiles while staring up as if reliving it.

"One time, instead of picking up the stick, the parakeet picked up a joint," CT explains.

"Yeah, turns out this woman smoked a lot of pot, but we didn't know it at the time. Anyway, the parakeet comes flying at us with a joint in its mouth, and we realize we need to get it away from the bird."

Trax crosses his arms. "Why not just light it and let the bird enjoy it?"

I cough to hide my laugh. Trax clearly isn't buying this story. CT and Rover both frown.

"I don't think that would be safe," Rover says.

"Anyway, Rover gets the bird in his hands, and I go to pry open its beak.

I slip out of my coveralls and toss them into the bin. "Why not just pull on the joint?" I ask.

Rover's eyes widen. "I tried, but it began to shred. And I didn't know what would happen if the bird ingested that shit."

CT laughs. "I remember he was worried about killing her birds."

Rover whacks CT in the stomach. "It wasn't funny."

"So, did you get the beak open?" Maverick asks.

Rover smiles. "No. But I found the bird's stick and threw it. It dropped the joint to pick up the stick. Problem solved."

"What the hell does this have to do with that bird having a towel?" Maverick asks, pointing to the roof where the peacock stares at us with the paint-stained towel in his mouth.

Rover shrugs. "Nothing."

"Oh, for fuck's sake," Maverick mutters as he goes into the building, leaving the rest of us out there to deal with the situation.

Fox walks out of the building and holds up a handful of Cheetos. "Don't worry, I got this."

He drops one on the ground. Then another two feet away. Then another. The damn bird swoops down to the ground, drops the towel, and begins eating the Cheetos.

"Well, I guess you have a pet now," Trax says, shaking his head.

Amber grabs the towel and tosses it into the bin of clothes.

"Thank you, Fox. While these two were yammering away, you solved the problem." Amber hugs Fox.

Fox stands still with his eyes on Rover. Rover has made it clear no one is to touch his little sister, Amber, but that doesn't stop her from driving her brother crazy.

"Thank you for inviting me today," I say. "I needed this. It's been a crazy last few months."

Gray steps over to me and wraps his arms around me. "Yes, it has."

"Oh, it's like our kids are finally blossoming out of the nest," Rover says.

Connie tosses her dirty coveralls at Rover.

"Hey, babe! Why?"

"Let's leave them alone. You've caused enough trouble today." She takes his hand and leads him inside.

The rest of the group puts their coveralls into the bin and congratulates me on winning.

Once everyone's inside, I nod to the bin. "Who takes care of that?"

Gray grins. "This time, it will be CT. We all agreed on it when he was inside with Amber."

I laugh as I snake my arms around his neck.

He leans down and kisses me. "Let's go. I want to celebrate your win back at my place."

I tip my head back to stare into his eyes. "Oh yeah? And what did you have in mind?"

He kisses my neck. "Well, I plan to strip you out of these clothes, make you come on my tongue, and then fuck you until you see stars." He pulls back, scanning my face for my reaction.

I grin. "You do talk dirty."

He grins, too. "Sometimes."

"I love it."

"We're not fans as much, so you two should probably head home." Rover's voice drifts out from an open window.

"Dax! Get away from that window!" Connie yells.

"Never a dull moment with these guys," Gray says. "Let's get out of here."

CHAPTER THIRTY-NINE

Grayson

IT'S BEEN two weeks since Cara's father made his peace offering. She's stared at his phone number countless times but still hasn't called him. I suspect she will in her own time, so I'm not pressuring her. The situation has me thinking about my brother. He and I will never see eye to eye as long as he continues to drink. Maybe even sober, we'd still fight. He changed after that night. I'd never realized how much might have been due to his concussion until I saw how a head injury changed some of my teammates when I was still in the service.

Cara walks out of our bedroom, yes, *our* bedroom. She agreed to move in with me, and I've been the happiest of my life these last two weeks.

"Do you think this is okay?" she asks, referring to her blue sweater and jeans.

I stand up and take her in my arms. "You never worried about what you wore around the guys before. Why now?"

Her hands go to my chest. "Well, now that we're dating, maybe I need to impress these guys."

I laugh. "Babe, just being you impresses these guys."

"Well, aren't you sweet?"

She kisses me, and it turns hot and heavy quickly. Then my phone rings, and I pull back as we listen.

"Is that Rod Stewart singing about a peach?" she asks.

I arch a brow. "Yes, it is. This song is new to my phone. And you know it." My eyes widen as I realize this is the first time I've had a peach song ring outside the office. "Oh no! It's you!" I back up, pointing at her.

She's laughing. "No, it's not."

"It's never had the peach ringtone anywhere but MTS. And you're grinning like a cat that got a mouse."

That makes her laugh harder. "Seriously, it isn't me."

Finally, I pull my phone out of my pocket. It's Carter. I answer it and put it on speakerphone. "Carter, have you found Ivan?"

"We did. He was taken into custody last night."

Cara sits on the couch, and I sit next to her. "Where?" she asks.

"He was tracked to Denmark and was staying at his mother's place. It's a sprawling farm with several outbuildings. The agents found an arsenal of guns, all meant for the US Army."

Cara smiles. "It sounds like he might actually do some time."

"Between this and what was found on his boat, yes, he's going away for a long time. Oh, just a second." Muffled sounds come through the phone. "I have to go. I wanted to make sure you were updated."

"Thank you, Carter. We appreciate that," I say.

He ends the call.

"Wow. I never thought this day would finally come that both Kraliks are in custody." She climbs onto my lap. "We should celebrate."

I know exactly what she's thinking about by her smoldering eyes. "We can't miss CT's party."

CT invited everyone over, and I'm excited to bring Cara as my girlfriend.

She unbuttons my shirt. "We won't miss it. We just won't be on time." She knows I can't say no to her.

* * *

WE'RE ALMOST out the door when Cara gets a call.

"It's the agency; I need to take this." She steps away, so I check my messages. When she returns, she's smiling.

"I hope that means good news."

"It does. It was decided my cover has not been blown, and I return to work Monday."

Cara has been on leave pending an internal investigation to determine if Whitlock's sharing her identity with Max meant she could no longer perform her job. We both thought it was bullshit since everyone involved had been detained or killed. But they had to go through their hoops.

I pick her up and spin her around. "I'm happy for you."

"Me too. But we better get going; we're already late."

I laugh. "I blame you for that."

"Yeah, but you loved it."

I bend down and rub her nose with mine. "Yes, I did."

We arrive late to CT's party and try to slip in unnoticed, but unfortunately, CT sees us.

He whistles to get everyone's attention. "Peaches and Cara finally arrived!" he shouts.

All eyes turn to us, and Cara squeezes my hand tighter.

"Are you two official now?" Maverick asks.

"We are," I say.

He smiles. "Congratulations. I'm happy for you both."

We say thank you as he turns away, and we continue to make our way toward the kitchen.

"If Maverick is here, Sarina must be, too. I'd like to chat with her," Cara says, glancing around.

"She's with Amber in one of the bedrooms. I think they're plotting something," Rover says as he leans against the kitchen counter.

"I'll go check it out," Cara says.

I grab a beer from the fridge and join Rover. "Are all the guys coming?"

He shakes his head. "Fox and Cody are on assignment. I haven't heard back from Trax, so I'm not sure about him."

CT wanders in.

"Hey, you didn't need to announce our arrival," I say to him.

He shrugs. "We all knew why you were late. It's cool."

I cross my arms. "And why were we late?"

CT looks at Rover and grins.

"What?"

"Well, let's see," Rover says as he pushes off the counter. "The back of your hair is a mess, and your buttons aren't aligned."

I glance down at my shirt. Shit. He's right.

"Both signs of someone who was getting busy but then tried to get ready to leave in a hurry," CT says.

"Yes, I'd have to agree. It reminds me of a story I heard about this wrestler," Rover says.

I hold up my hand. "Stop. No. I know how you two get with your stories, and I'm not falling for any of your BS."

They both laugh. "Well, I guess getting sex regularly hasn't loosened you up," CT says.

I unbutton my shirt.

"Woah there. That wasn't an offer," CT says.

I glance up at his smug grin and shake my head. "I'm fixing my damn shirt."

"Really, you should focus on your hair first." Rover grins as he takes a sip from his beer.

"You two are exhausting. You know that?"

In unison, they both say, "Yes."

"Can I get your attention, please?" Maverick calls from the living room.

We walk in there and see him and Sarina holding hands and smiling.

"We have some news," he says. He holds up Sarina's left hand. "She said yes."

Cheers and congratulations are shared all around. Then

Rover's sister, Amber, clinks a spoon to a glass to get everyone's attention again.

"Congratulations to the couple. And as the first couple at MTS to get engaged, we are going to start a new tradition!"

Uh oh. I suspect this is what the women were talking about in the bedroom.

Amber holds up a bouquet of fake flowers. "Sarina will toss the bouquet, and whoever catches it, you're next to get engaged!"

The men grumble.

"Okay, get ready," Amber says as she hands the bouquet to Sarina with a wink.

Yeah, something's up.

Amber counts down. "Three, two, one!"

Sarina tosses the bouquet right at CT, who catches it. All the other guys cheer. "Congratulations, CT! I'm so happy for you," Rover says.

CT's eyes cut to Amber, and he arches a brow. Amber shrugs. This is what the women were planning? I have to admit, I'm disappointed. I hoped it would be something bigger.

I make my way to Cara and lean down. "That was what Amber and Sarina were discussing?"

She smiles. "The bouquet toss?"

"Yeah."

"That was something they discussed. Yes."

She turns away but not before I see the corners of her mouth turn up.

"What are you—"

Before I can finish asking, Rover flies through the house, screaming at the top of his lungs.

"Get it off me! Get it off!" He races out the front door, and we follow and watch him. Somehow he's managed to find a hose and turn it on.

"You should put your hoses away for the winter," Maverick says to CT as he tips his beer bottle back.

"They were packed away. But Amber said she needed one."

Rover douses himself with water from the hose as we watch. When he finally drops the hose and makes his way back to the door, Amber is standing there with a towel.

"Oh no," CT says. "You can't come in here dripping wet."

Rover rolls his eyes. "Amber, come here and help me dry off." Rover stomps to the walkway, and Amber follows.

Before she knows what's happening, Rover picks up the hose—that he never turned off—and sprays Amber.

She drops the towel and screams. She tries to get back into the house, but CT has closed and locked the door. Maverick opens a window so we can hear them. Finally, Rover is laughing too hard to continue, so he stops.

Amber turns toward him, and even from here in the living room, you can feel the anger coming off her. Rover is laughing so hard that he falls over.

"What is so funny?" she asks.

"CT overheard you plotting this with Sarina."

She grabs the now-wet towel and wraps it around herself. "And that performance you put on running from the kitchen?"

Rover sits up and grins. "Pretty good, huh? I should take up acting."

CT comes running from the hallway, carrying several towels. He opens the door and hands one to Amber, then moves to Rover to hand one to him.

As his back is turned, Amber pulls the hose until she has the nozzle in her hands, and she sprays CT's back.

"Oh shit!" he yells as he freezes up.

She drops it and rushes into the house. He chases after her, apparently no longer caring about the floors getting wet. She sprints down the hall into a bedroom, and he chases after her. All we hear is screaming and giggling.

Rover walks in, drying his hair. "Well, that was refreshing."

Amber giggles again.

Rover takes off in their direction. "You hold her CT, and I'll tickle her."

Cara is laughing with Sarina.

I walk over to them. "What did you do to Rover in the kitchen?"

Sarina holds up a fake bat. "This jumped out of the cupboard at him."

Rover, CT, and Amber rejoin the group, still toweling themselves off. CT flips a switch and turns on his gas fireplace.

"Rover, if you thought a bat was coming at you, why did you go outside and use the hose?"

Rover grins. "To get any germs off me. CT overheard their plot, but he never said the bat was fake. Those things are nasty."

"Your call sign should have been something to do with bats. You should have seen this guy one time we had to go into a cave. All badass until a bat flew by." CT rolls his eyes.

"I kept my cool, and you know it. But there I had on all sorts of protective gear."

The door opens, and Connie walks in with Lucy behind her. "I'm so sorry I'm late." Her eyes catch on Rover, who is clearly still drenched. Her brows lift. "What did I miss?"

Connie is Rover's girlfriend, and I can't imagine that seeing him like this could be that surprising to her. Lucy is Cody's girlfriend but was best friends with Connie first. I'm happy to see her hanging out here even though Cody isn't in town.

"Amber tried to pull a prank," he says.

Connie's eyes shift to Amber. "I see it backfired."

I spit out the sip of beer I had just taken. Connie says it like it is and she's funny as hell.

"Yeah, well, this guy," Amber points her thumb at CT, "blew my plan."

CT smiles.

Connie nods. "Okay, where's the wine?"

"I'll show you," Sarina says and loops her arms through Connie's and Lucy's."

"Are you a prankster?" Cara asks.

I shrug. "I can be, but only when it's called for."

She smiles. "And when exactly is it called for?"

I lean in and kiss her. "I'll let you know."

"Should I be worried?"

I shake my head. "Maybe a little."

"How about we work together instead?"

"I like the sound of that. Once I find out who is behind the whole ringtone situation, I'll need a master planner."

She wraps her arms around my neck and gives me a quick kiss. "I'll always be your master planner or whatever you need."

"Hmm." I wrap my arms around her waist. "Whatever I need? That could be fun."

She laughs. "I love you."

"I love you, too." Then I kiss her deeper.

"Get a room!" Rover yells.

Cara and I both flip him the bird as we continue our kiss. Yep, she's perfect.

EPILOGUE

Paxton "Lightning"

"PAXTON, I'm sorry, but I can't do this anymore," Alicia says through her tears.

There's no way I'm hearing her correctly. Things between us have been going great. Perfect even.

"What exactly can't you do?" I ask.

Her back is turned to me. Since I arrived, she hasn't made eye contact once. Something's not right.

"I can't date you. I'm sorry."

Her words cut deep. I'm truly falling for this woman, and she's just going to end it out of the blue?

"Why?"

She still doesn't turn around. "Because I want kids."

I stumble backward. We'd talked about this. As soon as things were getting serious, I was upfront with her about my inability to have children. She said she didn't want them. That's why I opened my heart to her.

She turns, and pain emanates from her eyes. It's true. This is what she wants. I can't breathe as it all hits me. I need to get out of here, away from her.

I turn to go.

"Paxton, I'm so sorry."

I don't stop as I storm out of her house and get into my car. I punch the steering wheel several times. My buzzing phone gets my attention. I yank it from my pocket.

Thunder: *You free tonight?*

Am I free? Shit. Apparently, I'm really free now.

Fuck. This is why anytime I really like a woman, I make sure they know. That's usually when the woman ends it. But not Alicia. She was all in. Or so I thought.

Me: *Yeah, I'm free. Alicia just ended things.*

His response is fast.

Thunder: *Shit, I'm sorry. Come over. You can ride out the storm here.*

I'd heard there might be snow tonight, but it wasn't something I paid much attention to because we had plans to stay at Alicia's this weekend.

Me: *I'll head over. Thanks.*

I glance back at Alicia's house. She's staring out the window, watching me. I tear down the street, needing to get her eyes out of my head.

Instead of going straight to Thunder's place, I take the long way to give myself a chance to clear my head a bit. I replay the last time I saw Alicia. She gave no indication of anything being wrong.

What happened in the last few days?

The more I think about it, the more pissed I am. She had to have known I was falling for her. If this was even a possibility, why the hell did she lead me on?

The road winds down a hill, and I take a turn fast. I pump the brakes to slow down, but nothing happens. I press them harder. Nothing. I stomp down on them. Nothing.

What the fuck is going on? I just had this car serviced, and everything was working great.

I'm picking up speed as I continue downhill. Fortunately, the road straightens out. There's a turn coming up that I'm not going to make. No vehicles are coming toward me, and no one is behind me, so I pull up on the emergency brake which causes me to spin. I try to steer into the spin, but the car is moving across the oncoming lane. I turn the other way, hoping for some sort of control, but I hit something on the side of the road and the car careens off the road.

It feels like slow motion as I become airborne, but then my vehicle hits the ground and continues to move forward until it hits something hard and comes to a sudden stop. The dash pushes in on me, and the airbag deploys.

I don't move as I try to assess my situation. At least the automobile is still upright; that's a good sign. Turning to my left, I can only see the hillside and not the road. To my right, trees.

My left leg aches. I try to move it and discover it's wedged under the new dashboard location. I pull, but pain shoots through my entire leg. Shit, I'll need to be pried out.

I reach for my phone, but it's not in the console cubby next to me. It's dark, but my eyes catch on a light on the passenger floorboard. My phone. Someone is calling. I reach for it but don't even come close. Dammit. I need to get my leg unpinned.

My hands feel around for anything I can reach, and it isn't much. Nothing that will help me get my phone. My hand grasps something behind my seat. A bottle of water.

It's left over from walking in Central Park with Alicia earlier this week. I guess that's one plus from not cleaning my car.

Snow begins to fall on the windshield. Shit, the storm. Fuck, I should have gone straight to Thunder's place. When I don't turn up, he has no reason to check this road. It's not on the way.

But why did my brakes give out? I lease a new vehicle every two years to avoid dealing with broken shit.

A horn honks not far away. At least there's traffic on this road. Someone will have to see me. I glance back up at the street. Fuck! I'm too far down this hill to see the road.

Which means anyone driving by won't see me. I have to get out of here. I try to pull my leg out again but pain sears through me. Nope. Don't do that.

Okay, I can't reach my phone. My leg is trapped. But on

the good side, Thunder is expecting me, so he'll know something is wrong when I don't show up. I have a bottle of water. And I reach into my jacket and smile. I have a protein bar. I glance out the windshield, but now it's completely covered in white.

The storm. The engine is still on, so I turn on the radio. It doesn't take long to hear a weather report.

"The storm is now hitting most of the city. I hope you're inside because if the models are correct, this is a big one. We're expecting three feet in the next twenty-four hours."

Three feet? Fuck.

"And with the temperatures this coming week, it's going to stick around."

I shut off the radio. At least, maybe I can stay warm in here. The engine sputters and stalls out. I turn the key, but nothing happens.

I zip up my coat and hope, like hell, that it will keep me warm enough because it looks like I might be here for a while.

WANT to know what happens to Paxton? Click here for Lightning.

CAST OF CHARACTERS

Morgan Thompson Security
Owners
Josh "Cowboy" Morgan (Shaw Seymour)
Poseidon "Stormy" Thompson

Employees
Cody "PP" Anthony (Lucy Gardiner)
Donny "Maverick" Reis (Sarina McIntyre)
Dax "Rover" Adams (Connie Stevens)
Grayson "Peaches" Walsh (Cara Harding)
Ford "CT" Mora
Reed "Fox" Davenport
Lance "Trax" McClure
Aaron "Trip" Anderson

Reed Hawthorne Security Employees
Lars "Thunder" Guthrie (Madison Wilkes)
Paxton "Lightning" Beck

CIA
Cara Harding – Special Agent
Canton – Special Agent

Pat Anderson – Cara's boss
Whitlock – Deputy Director

FBI

Carter – Special Agent in Charge of Seattle's Field Office

BOOKS BY DANIELLE PAYS

Morgan Thompson Security Team
Defending Sarina
Shielding Connie
Rescuing Cara

* * *

Dare to Surrender
Chasing Her Trust
Taking Her Chase
Saving Her Target
Trusting Her Hero

* * *

Dare to Risk
Deceived
Pursued
Played
Consumed

* * *

Reed Hawthorne Security Team
Thunder
Lightning

Other Works
Steamy - A Steamy Romance Anthology (Paperback only)
Conceal - A Salvation Society Novel

Love is Coming to Town - A Christmas Anthology

To learn more about her books, please visit her website at
https://daniellepays.com

ACKNOWLEDGMENTS

I want to thank Susan Stoker for allowing me to write in her Operation Alpha world. I love all of her characters but am particularly drawn to the SEAL of Protection: Legacy series. In this story, you will find Rocco, Gumby, Bubba, and Phantom. I also want to thank everyone at Aces Press.

I want to give a huge thank you for my readers. I really appreciate your support!

To my betas readers Kerry, Melissa, and Tesh, thank you.

Thank you to Furious Fotog/Golden Czermak for the fantastic cover photography. And to Maria @ Steamy Designs for the cover design. Thank you to Wallflower Edits for all your editing and to ReGina Raham for proofreading.

ABOUT THE AUTHOR

Danielle Pays writes steamy romantic suspense with twists you won't see coming. She enjoys romance as well as mystery and suspense and blends them both using her beloved Pacific Northwest for inspiration with its mix of small towns and cities.

When not trying to write her characters into some kind of trouble, she can be found guzzling coffee while trying to convince her dog to learn the command drop.

Want to Connect with Danielle?
Sign up for her newsletter and get a free short story. https://BookHip.com/FBZMJRL

Facebook Reader Group: https://www.facebook.com/groups/DaniellePaysReaderGroup
Website: https://www.daniellepays.com
Facebook: https://www.facebook.com/daniellepays/
Instagram: https://www.instagram.com/daniellepays/
Bookbub: https://www.bookbub.com/authors/danielle-pays
Goodreads: https://www.goodreads.com/author/show/19241197.Danielle_Pays
Twitter: https://twitter.com/DaniellePays

There are many more books in this fan fiction world than listed here, for an up-to-date list go to www.AcesPress.com

You can also visit our Amazon page at:
http://www.amazon.com/author/operationalpha

Special Forces: Operation Alpha World

Christie Adams: Charity's Heart
Linzi Baxter: Dangerous Rescue
Misha Blake: Flash
Anna Blakely: Rescuing Gracelynn
Julia Bright: Saving Lorelei
Cara Carnes: Protecting Mari
Kendra Mei Chailyn: Beast
Melissa Kay Clarke: Rescuing Annabeth
Samantha A. Cole: Handling Haven
Lorelei Confer: Protecting Sara
KaLyn Cooper: Spring Unveiled
Janie Crouch: Storm
Jordan Dane: Redemption for Avery
Tarina Deaton: Found in the Lost
Riley Edwards: Protecting Olivia
Dorothy Ewels: Knight's Queen
Lila Ferrari: Protecting Joy
Nicole Flockton: Protecting Maria
Hope Ford: Rescuing Karina
Amy Gamet: Guarded by the SEAL
Michele Gwynn: Rescuing Emma
Desiree Holt: Protecting Maddie
Jesse Jacobson: Protecting Honor
Rayne Lewis: Justice for Mary
Kristin Lynn: Worth the Risk
Callie Love & Ann Omasta: Hawaii Hottie
JM Madden: Rescuing Olivia
A.M. Mahler: Griffin
Ellie Masters: Sybil's Protector
Trish McCallan: Hero Under Fire

Rachel McNeely: The SEAL's Surprise Baby
KD Michaels: Saving Laura
Olivia Michaels: Protecting Harper
Annie Miller: Securing Willow
Keira Montclair: Wolf and the Wild Scots
MJ Nightingale: Protecting Beauty
Melinda Owens: Betraying Katie
Victoria Paige: Reclaiming Izabel
Danielle Pays: Defending Sarina
Lainey Reese: Protecting New York
KeKe Renée: Protecting Bria
TL Reeve and Michele Ryan: Extracting Mateo
Deanna L. Rowley: Saving Veronica
Angela Rush: Charlotte
Rose Smith: Saving Satin
Tyler Anne Snell: Cowboy Heat
Lynne St. James: SEAL's Spitfire
Sarah Stone: Shielding Grace
Jen Talty: Burning Desire
Reina Torres, Rescuing Hi'ilani
LJ Vickery: Circus Comes to Town
R. C. Wynne: Shadows Renewed

Delta Team Three Series
Lori Ryan: Nori's Delta
Becca Jameson: Destiny's Delta
Lynne St James, Gwen's Delta
Elle James: Ivy's Delta
Riley Edwards: Hope's Delta

Police and Fire: Operation Alpha World
Freya Barker: Burning for Autumn
B.P. Beth: Scott
Jane Blythe: Salvaging Marigold
Julia Bright, Justice for Amber
Hadley Finn: Exton
Emily Gray: Shelter for Allegra
Alexa Gregory: Backdraft

Deanndra Hall: Shelter for Sharla
Jenna Harte: Dead But Not Forgotten
India Kells: Shadow Killer
Amber Kuhlman: Protecting Paisley
Reina Torres: Justice for Sloane
Aubree Valentine, Justice for Danielle
Maddie Wade: Finding English
Laine Vess: Justice for Lauren

Tarpley VFD Series
Silver James, Fighting for Elena
Deanndra Hall, Fighting for Carly
Haven Rose, Fighting for Calliope
MJ Nightingale, Fighting for Jemma
TL Reeve, Fighting for Brittney
Nicole Flockton, Fighting for Nadia

As you know, this book included at least one character from Susan Stoker's books. To check out more, see below.

SEAL Team Hawaii Series
Finding Elodie
Finding Lexie
Finding Kenna
Finding Monica
Finding Carly
Finding Ashlyn (Feb 2023)
Finding Jodelle (July 2023)

Eagle Point Search & Rescue
Searching for Lilly
Searching for Elsie
Searching for Bristol
Searching for Caryn (April 2023)
Searching for Finley (Sept 2023)
Searching for Heather (TBA)
Searching for Khloe (TBA)

The Refuge Series
Deserving Alaska
Deserving Henley (Jan 2023)
Deserving Reese (May 2023)
Deserving Cora (TBA)
Deserving Lara (TBA)
Deserving Maisy (TBA)
Deserving Ryleigh (TBA)

Delta Team Two Series
Shielding Gillian
Shielding Kinley
Shielding Aspen
Shielding Jayme (novella)
Shielding Riley
Shielding Devyn

Shielding Ember
Shielding Sierra

SEAL of Protection: Legacy Series
Securing Caite (FREE!)
Securing Brenae (novella)
Securing Sidney
Securing Piper
Securing Zoey
Securing Avery
Securing Kalee
Securing Jane

Delta Force Heroes Series
Rescuing Rayne (FREE!)
Rescuing Aimee (novella)
Rescuing Emily
Rescuing Harley
Marrying Emily (novella)
Rescuing Kassie
Rescuing Bryn
Rescuing Casey
Rescuing Sadie (novella)
Rescuing Wendy
Rescuing Mary
Rescuing Macie (novella)
Rescuing Annie

Badge of Honor: Texas Heroes Series
Justice for Mackenzie (FREE!)
Justice for Mickie
Justice for Corrie
Justice for Laine (novella)
Shelter for Elizabeth
Justice for Boone
Shelter for Adeline
Shelter for Sophie
Justice for Erin

Justice for Milena
Shelter for Blythe
Justice for Hope
Shelter for Quinn
Shelter for Koren
Shelter for Penelope

SEAL of Protection Series
Protecting Caroline (FREE!)
Protecting Alabama
Protecting Fiona
Marrying Caroline (novella)
Protecting Summer
Protecting Cheyenne
Protecting Jessyka
Protecting Julie (novella)
Protecting Melody
Protecting the Future
Protecting Kiera (novella)
Protecting Alabama's Kids (novella)
Protecting Dakota

New York Times, USA Today and *Wall Street Journal* Bestselling
Author Susan Stoker has a heart as big as the state of
Tennessee where she lives, but this all American girl has also
spent the last fourteen years living in Missouri, California,
Colorado, Indiana, and Texas. She's married to a retired
Army man who now gets to follow *her* around the country.

www.stokeraces.com
www.AcesPress.com
susan@stokeraces.com

Made in the USA
Coppell, TX
25 November 2022

87049811R10187